Lost Hours

Alex Walters has worked in the oil industry, broadcasting and banking and provided consultancy for the criminal justice sector. He is the author of thirteen previous novels including the DI Alec McKay series set around the Black Isle in the Scottish Highlands where Alex lives and runs the Solus Or Writing Retreat with his wife, occasional sons and frequent cats.

Also by Alex Walters

Detective Annie Delamere

Small Mercies
Lost Hours

Alex
WALTERS
LOST
HOURS

First published in the United Kingdom in 2020 by Canelo

Canelo Digital Publishing Limited
31 Helen Road
Oxford OX2 0DF
United Kingdom

A CIP catalogue record for this book is available from the British Library.

Print ISBN 978 1 80032 043 7
Ebook ISBN 978 1 78863 953 8

Look for more great books at www.canelo.co

Printed and bound in Great Britain by Clays Ltd, Elcograf S.p.A.

Chapter One

'Be a dear. Fetch me another drink. Plenty of wine.' Michelle Wentworth waved her empty glass in the air.

'What did your last slave die of?'

'Disobedience. Just get me the sodding drink. It's not like you've anything else to do.'

'I'm revising,' Justin said.

Wentworth was wearing her wraparound sunglasses so she knew Justin couldn't see she was watching him. He thought she was half asleep, lying out here in the scorching sunshine. The little toerag ought to know by now that she was never half asleep. 'You're not revising. Your books are all up in your bedroom. You're just sunbathing, and playing some game on your bloody phone. So get off your fat backside and get me that drink.'

Justin sighed. 'Your wish is my command, Mother.'

She watched as he grumpily slid his way off the sunlounger, picked up her empty glass from the terrace and stomped his way back into the house. Ungrateful little prick, she thought. The only reason he was able to enjoy all this was because of the efforts she'd put in over the years. He was happy to take advantage of the benefits while looking down his nose at her. But then he wasn't the only one.

For a moment, she closed her eyes, enjoying the sensation of the sun on her exposed skin. It wasn't often she took time off, even over the weekend, not even using the time to examine the books or double-check contracts that had already been reviewed by her lawyers. The managers who worked for her hated the way she read through everything, was on top of every detail. They felt she didn't trust them, and the truth was they were right. She'd spent a lot of time trying to develop new talent in the business, identifying the ones with potential that over time she might mould in her own image. She'd had a few successes, but more failures. Even now, with only a handful of exceptions, she didn't really trust any of her management team. Not as much as she trusted herself, at least.

So she mostly spent the weekends reviewing the actions and decisions taken the previous week. She almost always spotted something – a miscalculation, an unacceptable risk, a questionable clause in a contract. Her instinct for spotting problems and her eye for detail infuriated her subordinates, but those attributes had made her a wealthy woman.

Over the past couple of months, she'd finally finished negotiating the first of a series of contracts that she hoped would take the business to a whole new level. She'd even taken the team out for a celebratory piss-up on Friday evening, which wasn't something she did often. Not that they'd seemed particularly grateful.

So today she'd decided to treat herself to a day off. It was glorious weather, following the best summer she could remember in years. As she'd driven back from the office every night this week, she'd seen the moorlands basking in the heat, every slope and undulation thrown into relief by the late evening sun. The landscape felt endless, the hills lost in a warm haze. She passed through villages where pub gardens were thronged with cheerful drinkers, cafes and restaurants taking a rare opportunity to offer *al fresco* dining to the hordes of tourists.

This kind of weather could make her wonder what it was all about. She'd found herself increasingly struck by that question in recent months. She'd built up a decent income over the years, and was on the verge of becoming even wealthier. She could enjoy living in a very impressive house in the middle of this glorious countryside, with every luxury she might desire.

But she had almost no other life. She had no close friends or family, other than the snotty, lumpen Justin. She had money to spend, but little to spend it on. She'd tried a few pastimes – golf, grouse-shooting – but hadn't enjoyed them. Why bother when she could spend that time growing her business?

She didn't waste time feeling sorry for herself. This was the life she'd chosen. She enjoyed work. She got a kick out of signing a new contract, and an even greater kick out of delivering the results that filled her bank account. She loved getting one over on her competitors, whether by fair means or foul. That really was the main thing, she thought. She loved winning.

But now and again, over recent months she'd found herself wondering about the point of it. Why accumulate yet more wealth if there was nothing to spend it on? What sense was there in working all these hours if you had no time to relax at the end of it?

This thought would surface in her mind for a while, and then be submerged under more immediate concerns. But she was conscious it was bobbing up with increasing frequency. Perhaps it was time to start thinking differently about her life.

After all, if there was anything in what Peter was claiming, she was on the way to becoming a genuinely wealthy woman, with no practical reason for amassing more or for continuing working. She could retire, head off to somewhere in the sun and enjoy herself. Or at least she could begin to pare it back, do a little less, allow herself some leisure time.

It was a thought, and today had been her first attempt to see what it might actually feel like. She'd told herself just to stop. To look at no documents. To refrain from booting up her laptop. To make and receive no phone calls. Just lie in the sun, maybe read some kind of trashy novel, and have a few drinks.

She'd more or less managed it. She'd felt twitchy in the morning, knowing all she wanted to do was turn on the laptop, send a few emails, review some documents. But she'd forced herself to lie in the sun, reading some thriller she'd picked up at the airport on the way back from a business trip. She'd intended it for the flight, but had instead spent the time catching up on her emails. Today she'd forced herself to read it, and was finding it at least mildly diverting.

She'd prepared a light lunch for herself – knowing Justin would have been happily pigging himself on anything he could find in the fridge – and sat outside to eat it with a glass of chilled white wine. She'd felt better after that, sipping a second glass of wine diluted with sparkling water. She didn't mind feeling relaxed, but she'd no desire to allow herself to become pissed in Justin's presence.

Which reminded her. Where was Justin? It seemed like ages since she'd sent the young oaf to top up her drink. But Justin did everything at his own pace. He'd appeared out here in the late morning, having finally dragged himself out of bed. Instead of doing anything useful, he'd immediately removed his shirt and thrown himself down on one of the sunloungers around the edge of the pool.

She wouldn't have minded if he actually used the pool occasionally, but he never did. She increasingly felt the money she'd spent on building and maintaining the pool were wasted. She'd had plans to take at least one daily swim herself but she managed that only sporadically. She'd hoped that Justin would take to it, perhaps with some of his school or university friends. But he rarely brought anyone back here, and the most he did himself was to lie beside it, playing endless games on his phone.

She looked around the garden. It was glorious in the early autumn sunshine, she thought, the epitome of what an English garden should look like. She couldn't claim any credit for that herself. She didn't know the first thing about horticulture. But she paid a local man to tend to the place, happy to leave him to decide what to plant and where. He knew what he was doing, and she was happy with the results. The house was well-positioned, so that, although the garden was surrounded by tall stone walls, the area close to the house was sufficiently raised to provide a clear view of the moors and the hills beyond.

Where the hell was Justin? He'd probably been distracted by something, and was sitting in his room playing yet another computer game. He really was a waste of space. He was back here for the summer, having completed his first year at university. She'd told him she wanted him to get off his backside and earn himself a bit of money. That way, at least he wouldn't be sponging off her.

He didn't even have to go and find himself a job. She'd have handed him one on a plate, doing admin or something in one of the offices. The only danger was that he'd make an arse of himself and embarrass her, but she couldn't mollycoddle him for ever. 'Just let me take a few days off first and then I'll get straight into it,' he'd said. That had been weeks ago. She'd give him another day or two, she told herself, then start getting tough.

The truth was that she'd never really loved Justin. Not in the unconditional way that mothers are supposed to. He'd arrived in her life just at the wrong time, when she was first beginning to make a success of the business, and she'd always seen him as a burden. She'd felt bad about that and had compensated over the years by spoiling him in ways that had no doubt just made it all worse.

As it was, he couldn't even manage to bring her a drink without screwing up. She swivelled on the lounger and sat up, her desire for another glass of wine finally overcoming her inertia. Irritated now, she pulled her robe on over her bikini and made her way back into the house.

The architect had done a decent job. He'd retained the shell of the original farm buildings, some of which supposedly dated back to the seventeenth century, but the interior had been refigured as an airy, largely open-plan space. It had been cleverly done, with the skylights that admitted most of the light largely invisible from the exterior, enabling the original facade to be undisturbed. The combination of the thick stone walls and the modern insulation meant that the house felt warm in winter, while offering a cool sanctuary on a day like this.

'Justin! Where the hell's my wine?'

He might well have just gone back to bed, she thought. It wouldn't surprise her. Not much about Justin could surprise her. He was his father's son, she supposed. A bit brighter than Ronnie – but that wasn't difficult, and Justin presumably got that from her. But his dad was an idle waste of breath, too.

She looked around the kitchen. Her wine glass was sitting on the large farmhouse table, still empty. Justin clearly hadn't even got around to pouring her drink. So where the hell was he?

The living room was separated from the kitchen by a stone archway created from what had once been the wall between the former stables, now occupied by the kitchen, and the adjoining farmhouse. The sitting room was deserted, though the television had been left on, silently playing some daytime property show. Justin had no doubt switched it on and then buggered off to amuse himself elsewhere.

'Justin!'

There was no response. But there rarely was. He was most likely sitting in his room, headphones on, far away in some digital fantasy land. She strode down the hallway and climbed the oak stairs to the upper floor. All the bedrooms up here were positioned to provide views of the open moorland. On a day like this, the haze of Manchester was visible to the north.

Justin's bedroom was at the far end of the landing. She hammered on the door. 'Justin. Get out here!'

Normally, this was enough to rouse even Justin from his reveries, but this time she could hear nothing from inside. She slammed down the handle and pushed open the door. 'Justin, I've been shouting—'

The room was empty. It was, as always, a tip, with Justin's clothes strewn all over the floor. The desk was covered with the usual array of plates, mugs and glasses, along with his laptop, which appeared to be turned off.

So where the hell was he?

Justin's life here was essentially oriented around no more than three or four locations – his bedroom, the living room, the kitchen and the occasional limited venture out into the garden to laze outside.

She made her way back downstairs. It was only now that she noticed a faint breeze blowing through the house. Justin must have opened a window somewhere. She stopped at the bottom of the stairs, wondering where to look next.

She was almost tempted not to bother. Just pour herself another glass of wine and head back outside into the sunshine. Justin would reveal himself before too long.

But something was nagging at her. A sense of unease she couldn't explain.

The breeze was blowing down the hall, meaning that the open window must be somewhere at the front of the house. She wasn't keen on that, either. She was a bit of a public figure – at times a controversial one – in these parts, and there were plenty of people who were envious of her wealth. She'd had a couple of attempted burglaries, though fortunately neither had succeeded in penetrating the tight security, and she'd become increasingly cautious.

As she walked further down the hall she realised that the current of air was coming, not from an open window, but from the front door. The large oak door was set in an alcove off the main hallway and had been invisible from the foot of the stairs. But now she could see it was standing slightly ajar.

Was Justin out there?

She'd never known him use the front garden. He generally went out that way only if he was heading to the car she'd bought him for his eighteenth birthday, an act she now regretted. He'd finally passed his test on the third attempt, but was still an utterly inept driver, too prone to showing off and easily distracted by nothing much. The only consolation was that he wasn't the type to go out drinking with his mates. Or even, she added to herself, the type to have that kind of mates.

She peered out. Justin's car was in its usual place, next to her own compact four-by-four. The front garden, largely given over to lawn and shrubbery except for the long gravel drive that wound down towards the large wrought-iron gates, was deserted.

'Justin! Are you out here?'

She had taken another couple of steps forward before she saw it. Something lying on the ground between the two cars, a white shape, part of something otherwise concealed behind Justin's car.

A trainer.

Baffled, she walked towards the cars.

Justin was lying between the two vehicles, face down on the gravel.

She hurried over, still calling his name. She couldn't begin to imagine what might have happened. Had he collapsed or had some kind of accident? And what had brought him out here in the first place?

She crouched beside him, taking his hand in hers. She had no idea what to do. She had no idea about first aid or what you were supposed to do in a situation like this. But already she was aware that it didn't matter. There was some warmth in Justin's hand, but she had little doubt that he was already dead.

It was only then that she noticed the small pool of blood gradually encroaching across the gravel from beneath Justin's skull. He must have fallen and struck his head, she thought.

But then she shifted her position so she could see the far side of his head, and realised the truth. Whatever had caused that wound, it was more than just a fall on to the gravel.

She felt a chill despite the heat of the day, crouched here in only her bikini and dressing gown. Even her mobile phone was back in the house.

She pulled herself to her feet, clinging to Justin's car for support, trying to force herself to think clearly. She needed to go back into the house. She needed to find her phone. She needed to call 999 and get an ambulance out here, even though she already knew it was too late.

And she'd have to call the police. There was no way of avoiding that. Even if she didn't do it herself, the paramedics would as soon as they saw that head wound.

But before she did any of that, she thought, she had first to make one other call.

Chapter Two

'Lovely part of the world,' DS Zoe Everett said. 'Especially on a day like this.'

'Makes you wish we could just skive off and get a pub lunch in Bakewell,' DI Annie Delamere said. 'Though I don't think Jennings would approve.'

'He's such a killjoy.'

'He's always like that with murder,' Annie said. 'Takes it seriously.' She could only imagine what her boss would say if he learned his detectives had delayed their investigation to grab a bite to eat. Annie looked across at Zoe, who was focused on her driving. There'd been a period, after their last major case, when she'd seriously wondered whether Zoe would be up to returning to work. She hadn't even fully known what Zoe's problem was. The case had been traumatic enough for both of them, but Zoe had had some kind of panic attack at a key moment and had seemed knocked sideways by it in a way Annie hadn't really understood.

At the time, most of Annie's attention had been taken up by the impact of the case on her own partner, Sheena Pearson. Sheena had narrowly escaped with her life and for a period had been shattered by the experience. It was only in the last couple of months that she'd been able to resume her full workload as an MP.

Annie had felt bad that she hadn't been able to devote more time to supporting Zoe, though Zoe had been well supported by her husband Gary at home and by their senior officer, DCI Stuart Jennings, at work. Jennings wasn't exactly a people person, but he was a half-decent manager who recognised that the force owed Zoe a duty of care and he'd pulled the necessary strings to ensure she got it.

Zoe turned off the A6 towards Ashford-in-the-Water following the satnav's directions. It was a glorious day, unusually hot for this late in the year. But then most of the summer had been like that, one long languid day after another. Annie had expected the weather to break as they headed towards autumn, but so far the warm weather had continued. There'd been the usual talk of drought and threatened hosepipe bans, although the reservoirs had remained reasonably full after the previous wet winter.

Today offered the Peak District at its best. They were in the heart of the National Park, surrounded by low rolling hills, fields and moorland, the landscape seeming almost to glow in the afternoon heat. Some of the leaves were beginning to turn, a scattering of crimson among the greenery.

'So what do we know?' Zoe asked. 'I only picked up the tail end of the briefing.'

'Stuart seemed quite exercised by it. It could be a high-profile one. This Michelle Wentworth is a bit of a controversial figure.'

'Saw some TV piece about her a few months back. Made a small fortune taking over outsourcing contracts or something?'

'That's the one. She doesn't have a good reputation, though. I looked her up briefly before we came out. Her approach seems to be to undercut the competition to win the contracts, then to squeeze all the profit she can out of it. Lots of talk about the benefits of digitisation and streamlining the back office and other stuff I didn't really understand, but as far as I could see most of it really amounted to getting rid of as many employees as possible and sticking the rest on zero-hours contracts.'

'Has she ever had any criminal charges?'

'No, but she seems to pull every legal trick in the book to achieve what she wants.'

'Lovely.'

'I suppose she's not the only one who's behaved like that. She probably just gets disproportionate coverage because she's a successful woman. And the sort of woman that the tabloids can happily feature on their front pages, if you get my drift.'

Zoe had slowed now, the satnav indicating that they were approaching their destination. 'She seems to have picked the right place to live, too. This is pretty spectacular.'

They'd turned off the main road on to a single-track lane that led gradually uphill, with the land falling away to open fields and then moorland to their left. Annie could see the River Wye sparkling in the afternoon sun before the land began to rise again to the darker hills beyond. The right-hand side of the road was bounded by a large stone wall, which Annie guessed marked the edge of Michelle Wentworth's land.

Sure enough, after another hundred metres or so, they rounded a turn in the road and Annie spotted a large pair of wrought-iron gates set in a stone archway. 'I'm guessing that's the place. Even the entrance is ostentatious.'

A brass plaque on the archway confirmed that this was indeed the address they'd been given. The gates were standing open, and Zoe signalled and turned in.

The area beyond was largely given over to lawn, with a gravel drive winding down to the house in front of them. It was an impressive space with a line of trees and the stone wall marking the boundary to their right and the garden backing on to moorland beyond the house.

The house itself was almost a disappointment in the midst of this impressive setting. Annie had half-expected a Victorian or Edwardian manor house – there were a few scattered about the region, typically built by self-made business types in the nineteenth century. But this wasn't one of those. Annie guessed that these had once been farm cottages, a row of smaller residences now transformed into one substantial building. It was clear that a lot of money had been spent on the reconstruction. The most striking aspect was a large vaulted roof that soared above the ridge height of the surrounding building, creating a dramatic contrast to the gently rolling moors and hills beyond. The old stone walls of the house were lined with Virginia creeper, just beginning to redden.

Beside her, Zoe gave a low whistle. 'Nice place.'

'You can see she's not short of a bob or two.'

In front of the house, the gravel driveway opened into a parking area, now occupied by two marked cars, the CSIs' vans and three other vehicles, presumably belonging to Wentworth and her family. A crime-scene tent had been erected close to the house between the cars that Annie guessed were Michelle Wentworth's and her son's. From the short briefing she'd received, Annie understood that the body had been found there.

'The victim's her son?' Zoe said as they made their way along the drive.

'That's what I was told. All seems a bit odd. Wentworth was out at the back sunbathing. Son went to get her a drink, apparently. He didn't come back so she went to look for him, and found him on the ground out here. Looked as if he'd been struck a hefty blow on the head with some kind of blunt instrument, probably more than once.'

'And this was just out of the blue?'

'That's what she reckons,' Annie confirmed.

'Sounds a bit odd. In a place like this in broad daylight. Not exactly the place for a mugging.'

'Quite. And it sounds like more than a mugging. If he was hit more than once, that suggests whoever did it wanted to finish the job.' Annie shrugged. 'No point in speculating. Let's go and find out.'

Zoe pulled up behind the marked cars and they climbed out into the sunshine. After the car's air conditioning, the heat was almost stifling, though there was a light breeze blowing in from the moors. There was a faint scent of woodsmoke in the air, perhaps from a distant barbecue or bonfire.

The area beyond the cars had been marked off with police tape and, as they climbed out of the car, a uniformed officer hurried over to greet them. Annie recognised him as Paul Burbage, a fairly young, enthusiastic officer who she knew to be both capable and sensitive in his dealings with the public. 'Afternoon, Paul,' she said. 'Decent afternoon for it, at least.'

'I can think of things I'd rather be doing on a day like this,' Burbage said.

'What's the story?'

Burbage gestured behind him. 'Body was found over there. Mother came out looking for him and found him lying between the two cars. Really nasty head wound, apparently. Looks as if he'd been struck several times.'

Annie exchanged a look with Zoe. 'Sounds like someone wanted to do a thorough job.'

'Sounds that way, doesn't it?' Burbage agreed. 'Horrible business, anyway. The mother had already seen the wound so she knew it wasn't an accident, so we were called along with the ambulance.'

Looking beyond Burbage, Annie saw that Danny Eccles, one of the senior CSIs, had emerged from the tent, still clad in his white suit. He waved to her and made his way over, removing his helmet as he did so. 'Afternoon, Annie. Zoe. You've drawn the short straw then?'

'Looks like it. Seems a strange one.'

'Strange to happen in a place like this, certainly.' Eccles was a rotund man with a mop of curly hair, capable of maintaining a cheery demeanour in the face of almost any kind of crime scene. 'Looks like it was targeted.'

'Targeted?'

'In the sense that it doesn't look just like some kind of opportunistic killing. If he'd – I don't know – got into a fight with someone or interrupted a potential intruder, they might have struck the first blow, but I can't see why they'd have stuck around to deliver three or four more.' He took a breath. 'He was clubbed to death. Somebody really wanted to make sure the job was done.'

'Jesus.' Annie looked around her. The bucolic scene suddenly felt much less cosy, and she felt a chill despite the heat of the day.

'Quite.'

'Anything else so far?' Annie asked. 'What about a murder weapon?'

'There's nothing immediately to hand,' Eccles said. 'It would have to have been something pretty solid and heavy, but not too large. A hammer or something of that kind. There may be traces left in the wound, but there's nothing obvious. Not much else yet.'

'How old was he?' Zoe asked.

'Just nineteen, apparently,' Eccles said. 'A student. He was back here for the summer.'

'Poor kid,' Annie said. 'And his poor mum.' She paused. 'Assuming she wasn't responsible for this, of course.'

'You think she might be?' Zoe asked.

'I guess we can't discount it. Always look at family first. We've known stranger things.' She turned to Eccles. 'You think a woman could have done this?'

'It's possible. The murder weapon would have had to be something pretty solid, but I don't think that precludes the possibility of it being wielded by a female. His own mother, though...'

'Like I say, we've known stranger things. She's got to be on the list till we prove otherwise. Is she inside?'

Burbage nodded. 'She is. She's got some man with her.'

'Some man?'

'Yes, he was here when we arrived. A friend of hers. She said she'd called him for moral support after she'd called us.'

'I can see you wouldn't want to be here on your own after this,' Annie said. 'Good that she had somebody close at hand, I suppose.'

'I hear that slightly sceptical note in your voice,' Zoe said.

'You know me too well, Zo. Just seems convenient she had someone she could call on so quickly. We're sure he only came after she found the body?'

'Pretty sure, actually,' Burbage said. 'He must have arrived just before us. When we were coming up the drive he was just parking his car. It's the dark green Jag at the end there.'

'Well spotted, Paul,' Annie said with a smile. 'So at least we're fairly sure he wasn't here all along.' She looked up, her eyes scanning the facade of the building. 'Is there any CCTV?'

'There's a security camera there,' Burbage said. 'Don't know if it's operational. If it is, there'll presumably be others around the place.'

'Something for us to check out, anyway. You think Mrs Wentworth's up to talking to us?'

'She seemed pretty calm,' Burbage said. 'Upset but not hysterical. She gave us a pretty clear explanation of what had happened when we arrived.'

Annie turned back to Zoe. 'Okay, let's go and see what we can find out. We'll leave you to get on with it, Danny.'

'You do that,' Eccles said. 'I only came out for a breath of air. Trust me, this is not the day to be stuck inside a tent with a dead body.'

'You know what,' Annie said, 'on that subject, I'm only too happy to take your word for it.'

Chapter Three

'You were a witness to this, Ms Pearson?'

Sheena sighed. She could tell the police officer was feeling out of his depth and keen to extricate himself from the situation he'd been landed in. For her own part, she was reluctant to become involved in what was in danger of becoming a controversial incident. As it was, she'd probably be criticised by some of her fellow MPs even for showing her face here. Many of them remained unwilling to be too visible in their support for this kind of cause, worrying that it would be perceived as 'anti-business'. Sheena's view was that it was fine to be pro-business, as long as business behaved ethically towards the employees it relied upon. Too often, as here, the well-being of the employees seemed to be secondary to the drive for profits. Even so, she couldn't defend what had clearly been a criminal act.

Roger Pallance had made good on his threat to call the police, and a car had duly arrived half an hour later bearing two officers. Sheena guessed they'd probably been told to come out because of the profile of the strike, rather than because they were taking Pallance's complaint particularly seriously.

That wasn't really the point, she acknowledged. Pallance, the site manager, was an arrogant so-and-so looking for an excuse to cause trouble, but the reality was he'd been given one. Someone had thrown a potentially dangerous object, and the damage could easily have been more serious.

The picket line had already been in place when he'd arrived in his sleek grey BMW. She'd been told he'd made a similarly staged entrance every day since the strike had been called, sounding his horn as he cruised past the assembled group to park in his designated space near the entrance to the building.

He was in his late thirties or early forties, a tall, good-looking man with close-cropped fair hair. He was dressed semi-formally, with no jacket and an open-necked business shirt. His relaxed demeanour had suggested he felt no unease at braving the picket line.

He'd reached back into the car and pulled out a laptop bag, which he slung over his shoulder. Then he'd strode towards them, nodding and smiling at the assembled group, apparently oblivious to the comments directed back at him.

'Morning,' he'd said to Keith Chalmers, the trade union representative. 'All still here then?'

'Aye,' Chalmers had said. 'And we'll be here for a good while yet, if you lot don't start talking to us.'

'We'll talk to you as soon as you stop this nonsense. We're not going to be held to ransom.' He'd turned to Sheena and smiled. 'Ms Pearson. Good to see you here, though I'm surprised you've decided to lend your reputation to this dubious cause.'

Sheena hadn't known whether he really had recognised her or whether he'd been briefed about her presence here today. Quite possibly the latter. She'd spoken to various local journalists about her intention of visiting the picket line, in the hope that it would receive some coverage in the local media later in the day. She and Chalmers had given a short interview to a TV crew earlier, which would presumably be on the local news at lunchtime.

'I won't regret supporting my constituents in seeking fair treatment, Mr Pallance.'

'If we remove these jobs from your constituency, you may find you're not so popular. I believe your majority is wafer-thin, even now.'

That wasn't quite true. Her majority had reduced at the previous General Election, although less than the national swing against the party. She couldn't afford to be complacent, but she knew she was building a good reputation as a constituency MP. 'My primary concern is to stand up for what I believe in. And one of those is the basic principle of a fair day's pay for a fair day's work.'

'Which we provide, I think you'll find.'

'As things stand, you pay the minimum wage. You want to move your staff to contracts that offer no guaranteed hours. Which means that in practice even fewer of them will be able to live on what you pay them.'

'Many people enjoy the freedom offered by flexible contracts,' Pallance had said.

'In that case, they can volunteer for them,' Sheena had countered. 'You're offering people no choice.'

'With respect, Ms Pearson, I'm not sure you really understand the realities of business.'

She'd been about to respond to what she saw as patronising nonsense when Pallance had suddenly stumbled forward, almost falling on to her. 'Shit! What the hell…?'

At first, Sheena had been unclear what had happened. Her own thoughts had fled back to the incident the previous year when she'd been the victim of an apparently random shooting in the midst of a very different kind of protest. That had been the start of a series of events that had left her seriously traumatised and, for a period, unable to perform her constituency duties. After extensive counselling, she'd thought she'd finally put the trauma behind her, but in the previous moment she'd immediately found herself back there.

What had happened here was less serious than that, though it was troubling enough. Looking behind Pallance, she'd seen a scattered pile of broken brown glass on the tarmac. Someone at the back of the crowd had thrown an empty bottle at Pallance's head.

Keith Chalmers had been understandably furious, and had berated the group at some length, pointing out that whoever had done this had played right into the company's hands. 'This is going to be all over the media tonight and all over the tabloids tomorrow. It makes us look like irresponsible thugs. We've just risked throwing away all the goodwill we've built up over the last few weeks. Just for one moment of idiocy!'

Most had appeared to agree with him, and, in response to his demand, no one had been prepared to step forward and admit to being responsible. Some of the younger men at the rear of the group looked uncomfortable, but when Chalmers had challenged them they'd denied all knowledge.

'Someone must have seen who did it,' Chalmers said. 'But to be honest I don't much care. I just want you to know that if anything like this happens again, I won't be prepared to stand up for you.'

Sheena had heard one of the young men at the rear of the group mutter a derogatory comment about the union not being much cop anyway, but whoever it was had been immediately silenced by those around him. Chalmers had glared at him and then turned back to the rest of the picket line. 'The point is,' he said, 'we can win this. But we can only do it by being disciplined, by making the best of the resources we have. And by not handing this kind of gift to the other side.'

When the police had turned up, after entering the building to speak to Roger Pallance, they'd eventually emerged and gone through a similar routine. They'd clearly realised straight away that there would be little mileage in trying to identify the culprit if no one was prepared to admit to having witnessed the action. After a few moments, they'd taken Sheena and Keith Chalmers aside to talk to them privately.

'I saw the outcome,' Sheena said, in response to the police officer's opening question. 'But my attention was on Mr Pallance. I didn't even know what had happened at first. Not until I saw the broken bottle on the ground.'

'Neither of you have any idea who was responsible?'

'I'm afraid not,' Chalmers said. 'As Ms Pearson says, our attention was elsewhere until it happened. It just came from the back of the group somewhere. But feel free to interview every one of them as far as I'm concerned. I'm as keen to identify the bloody idiot as you are.'

The police officer glanced at the group behind them, clearly not attracted to the idea. 'I guess feelings were running high,' he said, finally.

'If you want my impression,' Sheena said, 'I think the picket's generally been very good-natured. That was certainly the way it seemed until Mr Pallance arrived.'

'It's no excuse,' Chalmers said. 'But I do think that Mr Pallance's arrival and interaction with the group here was intended to be provocative. It's happened every day.'

'He's entitled to attend his place of work, sir,' the officer said.

'I appreciate that. But we are trying our best to conduct this in a peaceful and civilised manner. It would help if all parties were willing to cooperate with that.'

Sheena could see that Chalmers, no doubt with the best of intentions, was beginning to dig himself into a hole. 'Can I ask if Mr Pallance is badly hurt?'

'It appears not, thankfully,' the officer said. 'Although we've suggested he perhaps gets himself checked out at A&E if he's concerned. This could have been much more serious.'

'I think we all appreciate that,' Chalmers said. 'And, believe me, I'm not taking this lightly.'

'You have a legitimate right to take this action,' the officer said, 'just as Mr Pallance has a right to attend work. We're not looking to take any sides in an industrial dispute, but we have a duty to maintain order. If there's a risk of your people committing a public order offence then we'd have no option but to step in.'

Chalmers nodded wearily. 'I'll do everything in my power to make sure this isn't repeated. Most of the people here are just decent ordinary citizens trying to protect their jobs and livelihood. One or two of the younger ones can be a bit hot-headed, but we'll try to keep them under control. I'm hoping they've all learned a lesson from what's happened today.'

'I hope so, too, sir.' The officer looked around him, clearly wanting now to bring this to an end. He nodded to Sheena. 'I imagine this must be a bit of an embarrassment to you, Ms Pearson?'

'I'm never embarrassed to be supporting people with a legitimate grievance,' she said, 'and I think these people have one. But I don't condone violence on any side.' She could imagine that she was going to have to repeat these words to the local and perhaps national media later. She also wondered if the remark indicated that the officer knew DI Annie Delamere was Sheena's partner.

The police officer nodded. 'I'm prepared to let this go for the moment. I don't think it'll do anyone any good for us to start getting involved in any formal action. But I'm warning you, if there's any repetition of this kind of behaviour, we'll have no option but to take it very seriously indeed.'

'Thank you,' Chalmers said. 'I'll read this lot the riot act.'

The police officer took one last look at the group of pickets, his expression clearly intended to suggest that he might easily reconsider his decision. Then he walked back to the car to rejoin his colleague.

As they drove away, someone from the back of the group – perhaps the same man who had spoken before – gave an ironic cheer. Chalmers swivelled round. 'We've had a bloody narrow escape there.' His voice was measured but his fury was unmistakeable. 'And we're on our final warning. If you want us to win, then show a bit of sense. All of you.'

His words were addressed to the group as a whole, but it was clear to Sheena that he had the support of most of those gathered in front of him. Even the younger contingent seemed to have been largely chastened by his words, at least for the moment.

'I'd better get on, Keith,' Sheena said. 'Got a whole pile of constituents' cases waiting for me back in the office. Good luck with it.'

Chalmers walked with her back to her car, ostensibly just to see her off, but she could tell he had something more to say to her. 'What is it, Keith?' she said, as she fumbled in her coat pocket for her keys.

'I just wanted to say that I'm grateful for you coming along. It's good for them to know there are people like you on their side.'

'I'm not sure what I can really do other than provide some moral support and a bit of extra media coverage.'

'It's all appreciated, believe me.' He paused. 'I've an uneasy feeling about this one.'

'In what way?'

'Partly, it's just that it feels like an unequal fight and I don't like getting into those if I can help it. In this case, I don't think we had much choice but I prefer it when I can pick the time and the place of the battle. We'll give it everything we've got, but I'm not optimistic. I think they've got the resources to ride this out if they choose to. But we'll see.'

'You said it's "partly" that. What else is it?'

'That's the thing. You saw what just happened.'

'With the bottle? You always get a few hot-headed numpties.'

'Maybe so.' Chalmers appeared to hesitate. 'But I've just got a feeling we're being set up.'

'Set up? By who?'

'I'm not sure. Maybe by the company. I honestly wouldn't put it past them. They've tried every trick in the book to discredit what we're doing. It wouldn't entirely surprise me if they'd organised one or two ringers in our ranks.'

'Have you got any other evidence for this? Apart from some idiot throwing a bottle?'

'There've been other things. Some bits of disruption and sabotage in the workplace. Not the sort of stuff we'd condone. One or two of the younger ones worry me.' He gestured towards a young man at the end of the picket line. 'Mind you, there are some decent ones too. That guy there, for instance. Sammy Nolan. Bright and enthusiastic. He's a good example of the kind of potential they're wasting here. But he's fighting back in the right way. Already got himself on the local union committee.'

'That's good to hear,' Sheena said. 'As for the other stuff, feelings are running high. People do stupid things.'

'I know. But there's still something about it all that doesn't feel quite right to me.' He shrugged. 'I'm probably just being paranoid. But that's what my gut's telling me.'

Sheena smiled. 'Your gut's got a good few years of experience behind it, so I wouldn't ignore it. But don't get paranoid either. Maybe that's what they really want. Just to keep you on the back foot.'

'That thought had occurred to me. Still, as you say, I've a few years under my belt. I'm not going to give up without a bloody good fight.'

'That's the spirit, Keith. Good luck with it. Let me know if there's anything you need from me.'

'Thanks, Sheena. Appreciated.' He looked back at the cluster of people gathered outside the building, most of them chatting amiably in the afternoon sunshine. 'They're decent, hardworking people, most of them. I'll do whatever I can to stop them getting shafted.'

She watched him as he walked slowly back towards the building. Just in those moments, Sheena thought, he no longer looked like the Keith Chalmers she thought she knew. They hadn't always seen eye to eye on political matters, but she'd always thought of him as smart, solid and reliable. He was an old-fashioned trade unionist, and from their past dealings she'd concluded he was broadly one of the good guys. His heart seemed to be in the right place, and he was a smarter tactician than some of his peers. That sometimes made people think he was a soft touch. But he reckoned he'd delivered more for his members than many of those who simply shouted loudly about their principles. She always seen him as someone who'd take whatever life threw at him, and come through smiling and undaunted. He'd seemed that way when she'd first arrived here, the same old Keith. Now, he looked different. He looked as if he wasn't up to it any longer.

He looked anxious and defeated even before the battle had really begun.

Chapter Four

'Bloody hell.' Zoe Everett stared around her.

'Quite a place, isn't it?' Annie watched Zoe's expression with amusement. Zoe herself lived, apparently contentedly, in a box-like detached house in an estate on the outskirts of Derby. She seemed mildly awestruck by the vast open-plan space in which they were now sitting, its ancient stone walls contrasting pleasingly with the glass and oak features – the large windows and skylights, the beamed ceiling and vaulted roof, the open staircase leading to the upper floor – that largely dominated the room. The afternoon sun was shining in through one of the skylights high above them, filling the room with golden light.

For her own part, Annie was struggling to work out how so much space had apparently been created within a row of converted farm cottages. Whatever architectural magic had been worked, the effect was oddly satisfying. It was a room that felt both vast and cosy at the same time.

They'd been greeted at the front door of the house by a man who'd introduced himself as Peter Hardy. 'Friend of Michelle's,' he'd said as he ushered them in. He was a tall man, probably in his early forties. He was dressed formally in a suit, though without a tie. He was a good-looking individual, Annie thought, and he knew it. The expensively trimmed hair, slightly greying at the temples, along with the designer suit and smart shoes, suggested a man all too aware of his appearance. 'Just here to provide a bit of moral support. Awful, awful business.' He'd led them through into this room, inviting them to take a seat. 'Michelle's having a bit of a lie-down. It's been a dreadful shock, as you can imagine.'

'Is she up to talking to us, do you think?' Annie had asked. 'We'll obviously need to get a formal statement from her as soon we're able, but for the moment we'd just like to ask a few questions so we can get things moving. Make sure we've got straight what happened.'

'That's what none of us knows, though,' Hardy responded. 'What did happen? Who'd do that to a young boy like Justin? It beggars belief. I'm sure she'll want to talk to you. I'll go and check with her.'

While they waited for him to return, Annie took the opportunity to take stock of the room. As Zoe's response had indicated, it was impressive, but it seemed somehow impersonal, with no obvious indication of the owner's personality. It felt as if the original house had simply been hollowed out and filled with expensive-looking designer furniture. There were no photographs, no books. The pictures on the walls were of local landscapes and, though attractive enough, looked as if they'd been bought by the metre.

After a few moments, Hardy returned, Michelle Wentworth following close behind him. She was wearing a dressing gown and Annie guessed she hadn't changed her clothing since she'd come inside in search of her son. According to the initial report they'd received, Wentworth had been sunbathing immediately before discovering the body.

Wentworth sat on one of the two sofas that filled the centre of the room, facing Annie and Zoe. Hardy said, 'I'll go and make us all some coffee.'

'I hope you don't mind us asking you a few questions, Mrs Wentworth. If you feel up to it, that is.'

She looked white-faced and drained, though there was no sign of emotion in her expression. She was silent for a moment, as if deciding how to respond. 'Yes, of course. I want to find the bastard who did this.' Her voice was strong, the tone resolute. She seemed unexpectedly composed. Annie's experience was that bereavement affected people in very different ways, but Wentworth's calmness was sufficient at least to raise questions about her relationship with Justin.

'Your son was out in the garden with you?' Annie asked. 'Beforehand, I mean.'

'He came out to sunbathe,' Wentworth said. 'I was lying out there reading and he was playing some game on his phone. He only came in because I asked him to top up my drink...' She trailed off and Annie wondered whether she was blaming herself for what had happened.

'He didn't indicate he was going anywhere else?'

'Why would he be going anywhere else? He's spent most of his time in the house since he came back from university.' There was an edge of bitterness in her tone, Annie thought. She wondered what the relationship between mother and son had been like. Not an area to explore in detail now, but worth checking out in due course. Annie's brief online search had revealed that Wentworth was divorced, but she'd found no reference to Justin's father.

'Is there any reason he might have gone out to the front?' Zoe asked.

'Not that I'm aware of. He didn't spend much time out there. I suppose it's possible he went to get something from his car, but I can't think what. He doesn't use the car much—' She stopped, clearly realising what she'd said. 'He didn't use it much, I mean. I suppose the other possibility is that someone came to the door. I might not have heard the doorbell out by the pool.'

Annie nodded. 'I noticed you have some CCTV at the front. Is that operational?'

'It's all operational. The security's pretty tight here. The main gates are electric too, although stupidly I've tended to leave them open during the day when I'm at home. But if you're a wealthy woman living by yourself in the back of beyond you don't take too many chances. I'll let you have access to the footage. I thought about checking them myself but I decided all that was best left to you.'

'Thank you,' Annie said. 'Did Justin seem preoccupied at all? Or just his usual self?'

'If you're asking whether Justin had got himself into some kind of trouble, I can't see it. Justin wasn't that sort. I don't mean because he was some kind of goody-goody. But he kept to himself. He was quiet, didn't have many mates. Spent most of his time playing games on his laptop or his phone—' She stopped again. 'I used to tell him to get out more. I wanted to put a rocket up his backside at times. But he didn't have much of a social life.'

'You can't think of anyone who might have had a reason to harm Justin?'

Wentworth paused, perhaps longer than Annie might have expected. 'Nobody. It just doesn't make sense.'

Annie hesitated, trying to decide how best to frame her next question. 'I don't want to seem insensitive,' she said, finally, 'but I do need to ask this. My understanding is that your business reputation has been a little controversial. Are there people who might wish to harm you?'

Wentworth stared at her for a moment, then nodded. 'I suppose it's possible. I've made enemies over the years. It goes with the territory. But I can't believe anyone would do something like this. Not just to get back at me.'

'We can't discount the possibility,' Annie said. 'Is there anyone in particular who might have had a reason to do this?'

'I don't know. I mean, there are people whose noses have been put out of joint because we've beaten them to win contracts, and we take a pretty hard-nosed approach to dealing with our suppliers. But that's just business. I'm not a soft touch, but I play by the rules. None of that would be a reason to do something like this. I suppose there are individuals who've suffered as a result of our business deals. People who've lost their jobs or had their pay cut. Some of those might think they had a grievance against me. But I'm not running a charity. My job's to make it pay. It doesn't give anyone a reason to do this.'

Annie was less sure. She'd known murders committed, particularly in anger, for much more trivial reasons. 'Do you have anyone in mind?'

'There must have been dozens of people we've let go since we started. It's partly what we do. Streamlining, reducing costs and overheads. We do it by the book, but we have to make some tough decisions.'

'Have you received any previous threats?' Zoe asked.

'Once or twice. I never took them very seriously. Green ink stuff from the odd disgruntled ex-employee and the like.'

'You didn't report them?'

'If I had, what would you have done? I don't imagine there'd have been any way of tracking down the sender. In most cases, they were just venting their spleen.'

'Have you received anything of that kind recently?' Annie asked.

'Not for a couple of years at least. Job insecurity's part of the landscape now, isn't it? People recognise it's just the way it is. You don't expect a job for life any more.'

'It would be helpful if you could give us a list of anyone you think might have reason to harm you. Competitors, suppliers, former employees. Someone out there must have thought they had a reason to do this.'

'If you think it's worth it, but it just seems insane.'

'There are other possibilities, obviously. It may have been a totally random killing. Maybe Justin was just unlucky enough to open the door to the wrong person. We'll be exploring all that. At this stage, we have to keep every possibility on the table.'

At the tail end of this exchange, Peter Hardy had re-entered the room with a tray laden with a steaming cafetière and mugs. He placed the tray down on the coffee table between them, and sat down on the sofa beside Michelle Wentworth. He'd clearly overheard at least part of what had been said. 'Does keeping every possibility on the table include treating Michelle as a suspect?'

'Peter—'

'I'm just being realistic, Michelle.' He leaned forward and began to pour the coffees. 'We all know that in this kind of case the police look at the family first. That's right, isn't it?' he asked Annie.

'It's usually a line of enquiry, certainly,' Annie said non-committally. There was no question that Wentworth was a suspect. At this stage, though, Annie was keen to encourage Wentworth to talk freely and didn't want her to feel she was under immediate suspicion.

Annie was wondering again about Hardy's role here. Was he Wentworth's partner? He'd called himself a friend. Was he some kind of business associate? 'We'll need to take a formal statement from Mrs Wentworth in due course.' She took the coffee that Hardy had held out to her. 'Thank you. I understand you arrived here just before our officers, Mr Hardy, so presumably you weren't in time to witness anything.'

'Literally just a few seconds before. I was just parking up as they arrived. Michelle called me after she'd called you.' He glanced across at her. 'Just for support. I hope that's not a problem?'

'Of course not. It's good that Mrs Wentworth has someone with her at a time like this.'

'But, no, I was too late to witness anything. I'm sorry. We want to do everything we can to help you find whoever did this.'

Annie noticed the 'we'. She had also noticed that, since he'd re-entered the room, Hardy had very much dominated it. There was something proprietorial about his relationship with Michelle Wentworth. That was surprising; Annie imagined that, in other circumstances, Wentworth could be a pretty dominant presence in her own right. Even now, she seemed more composed than Annie might have expected. Annie made a mental note to check up on Peter Hardy.

'Is it possible for us to have a quick look at Justin's room?' she asked.

Wentworth exchanged a look with Hardy that Annie couldn't read. 'I'll take you up there, if you like,' Hardy said. 'I'm not sure Michelle's really up to that at present.'

'Of course. If you prefer, we can leave it for the moment, but obviously the quicker we can start making progress the better.'

'We fully understand,' Hardy said. Again, the 'we' was noted by Annie. He rose and led them towards the large oak staircase at the far side of the room. 'The bedrooms are up here. Michelle had the roof-space opened up over the living room so the second floor is now just on this side of the house.' He had the air of an estate agent offering a guided tour. Annie found herself intrigued by his knowledge of the house.

Hardy led them to the door at the far end of the landing, giving a rueful laugh as he pushed it open. 'I nearly knocked then. Justin used to get furious if anyone burst in without asking.'

The room looked like Annie's idea of a typical teenage or student bedroom. There were discarded clothes strewn across the floor, an array of glasses and plates on a desk beside an open laptop, posters showing images of bands and characters presumably from computer games, neither of which meant much to Annie. The air in the room offered a rich scent of sweat and aftershave.

'Sorry it's a mess,' Hardy said. 'Typical teenager, I guess. Feel free to look around.'

There didn't seem a lot to see. There was a small en suite shower room, which, from a quick glance, seemed as messy and disreputable as the bedroom. There were a number of books on the desk and bedside table, most of them apparently either classic or contemporary novels. 'What was Justin studying at university?'

'English literature,' Hardy said. 'Much to Michelle's disapproval. She wanted him to do something useful like business studies. But Justin was a bit of a law unto himself. I sometimes think he inherited Michelle's stubbornness.'

'Did they have a good relationship, generally?' Annie asked.

Hardy shrugged. 'Like I say, he was a typical teenager. Could be surly and uncommunicative at times, and that led to some tensions. But I dare say he'd have grown out of it.' He shook his head. 'It's just so tragic.'

Annie noted that he hadn't really answered her question, but decided not to push it further for the moment.

Zoe had wandered further into the room, apparently looking round aimlessly. She leaned over and casually tried one of the drawers on the bedside cabinet. 'Locked.'

'I'm afraid I've no idea where Justin might have kept the keys,' Hardy said. 'Do you need to look in there?'

'Not at the moment,' Annie said. 'But it would be useful if one of our officers could check out the room in detail, including looking at the laptop if possible. If Justin was targeted for some reason, that may give us some leads.'

'I'm sure Michelle won't have any problem with that,' Hardy said.

'You don't know any reason why someone might want to harm Justin?'

Hardy shrugged. 'Not a clue. I caught the end of you asking Michelle about whether she might have been the target. That feels more possible. Success always breeds resentment, doesn't it?'

Especially when it's success built on the exploitation of others, Annie thought. 'Do you have anyone in mind?'

'I'm sure Michelle will give you a good list of contenders,' Hardy said. 'Though it's hard to imagine any of them would do anything like this.' He paused, as if unsure whether to say more. 'There are one or two might be worth a look at, though. Michelle's trodden on a few toes in her time. She's bumped up against a few of the wrong sort of people, sometimes without realising at first.'

'The wrong sort of people?'

'Look, Michelle's a respectable businesswoman. A ruthless one at times, but she plays by the rules. My impression is that some of the people she competes with, maybe even some of the people she deals with herself, are a bit less scrupulous and have some more questionable connections.'

'And can you give us the names of these people?'

Hardy held up his hands. 'Don't get me wrong. I've got no firm evidence for any of this. It's just an impression I've formed. But I'm sure Michelle can pull together some names for you.'

'What's the nature of Mrs Wentworth's business dealings with these people?'

'I'm thinking of competitors mainly. People she's taken work from. Michelle has a habit of winning contracts that the opposition thought they'd got sewn up. She can be ruthless. But she's also bloody good.'

'What about Justin's father? Can you tell us anything about him?'

'Not really. Can't see him being involved. They split up a long time ago. Guy called Ronnie Donahue. They were married, but Wentworth is Michelle's maiden name.'

'Did he have contact with Justin?'

'No. There was a history of domestic violence. I reckon Michelle was the first one who gave him as good as she got. From what I understand, he never wanted access. According to Michelle, he's just a lazy, self-pitying bugger who's never done a proper day's work in his life.'

Annie took a last look around the room, again wondering how Peter Hardy came to know such intimate details about Michelle. Zoe was flicking, apparently aimlessly, through the clothes hanging up in the wardrobe. Annie assumed Zoe was quietly checking, as Annie herself would have done, that there was nothing concealed in the back of it.

'We'll leave you and Mrs Wentworth in peace for the moment, Mr Hardy. I'll have a word with Mrs Wentworth before we leave, but we'll allocate a Family Liaison Officer to be the primary point of contact with her during our investigation. We'll need to take a formal statement from her, as I said, so I'll set the wheels in motion on all that.'

'I wasn't joking downstairs. About you treating Michelle as a suspect. Is that what your Family Liaison Officer is for? To keep an eye on her?'

'The FLO is just what I say, Mr Hardy. Yes, they're part of the investigative team, and their primary role is to help gather evidence from the victim's family that might contribute to the investigation. But their role is also to ensure that the family is kept informed of any developments in the case and to provide a supportive presence.'

Hardy nodded, his expression sceptical. 'I just don't want Michelle to be taken advantage of, that's all.'

'That's not the way we work, Mr Hardy.'

'Michelle seems a tough cookie, and in many ways she is. But she's only human and she's going to be in a very vulnerable place. I just want to make sure she's treated fairly.'

'We've no intention of doing otherwise. Our job is simply to bring to justice whoever was responsible for this.'

Hardy stared at her for a moment, then nodded. 'Fine. I've said what I had to say.'

He turned and made his way downstairs, leaving them to follow. Annie looked over at Zoe and shrugged.

'I don't know what that was all about,' Zoe said. 'Interesting, though. It just made me wonder what it is they've got to hide.'

Chapter Five

'We need to get moving on this one,' Stuart Jennings said. 'I've a bad feeling about it. I've already had the Chief on the phone.'

Annie sighed inwardly. When Jennings said he had a bad feeling about a case, that meant he thought his seniors would be breathing down his neck. He was no doubt right. Annie had carried out more background research since meeting Michelle Wentworth. It was clear that Wentworth had never been shy about expressing her brash and uncompromising views, and she provided an alternative profile to the usual middle-aged male captain of industry. That, combined with the fact that her business dealings had sometimes between controversial, meant she'd become a familiar face on the local TV news and in the local papers.

The tragic death of her son and the additional lure of a spectacular Peak District backdrop were guaranteed to pull in the reporters. Annie had now read enough about Wentworth to guess she wouldn't be averse to pulling whatever strings she could to put pressure on the police if it suited her. She was clearly skilled at using the media to her own advantage, whether boosting her own profile or subtly denigrating her competition. It seemed unlikely that she'd have been in touch with the Chief Constable already, and she hadn't been hostile at the house, but

Annie imagined she wouldn't have any hesitation in doing so. The fact that the Chief had already contacted Jennings suggested she wasn't the only one to think so. 'We're pushing ahead as quickly as we can. The team's in place. Any further resources you can drum up will be more than welcome, but we're generally good to go.'

'So what do you make of it?' Jennings said.

When Jennings had first transferred over to lead the team, Annie had found his manner disconcerting and more than a little irritating. He often gave the impression that his mind was elsewhere, as if he'd already mentally moved on from whatever you were discussing with him to something more important. He could often be abrupt, seemingly forgetting basic human courtesies such as remembering to say hello, goodbye or thank you.

At first, she'd thought this was a deliberate management tactic to wrong-foot his subordinates. But she'd soon concluded that it was just how Jennings was. He was a bright enough bloke but he had a short attention span. It had taken her a little longer to realise Jennings was as wary of her as she was of him. It was partly her family history. Her mother had been a former Assistant Chief in the force, who had retired in mildly controversial circumstances and who was now enjoying an unexpectedly successful post-retirement life as an outspoken pundit on anything relating to policing. It was partly that Jennings had joined a well-established team and was struggling slightly to define his own position. And it was partly, Annie suspected, simply because Jennings wasn't entirely comfortable managing women.

But over time she'd slowly warmed towards him. He'd been helpful and supportive when Zoe had been working through her personal issues, even if at times he'd sounded as if he was reading from the HR manual. He did his best to ensure that, in the face of continuing pressures on funding, they had the resources they needed to do their jobs. Above all, he'd worked hard to shield them from the usual crap that tended to rain down from the senior ranks in the face of political and media pressure. Unlike many bosses she'd had, Jennings saw part of his role as taking the flak so the team didn't have to. That was a rare quality in Annie's experience, and it more than compensated for any deficiencies Jennings might display in other areas.

They were having a short debrief following the kick-off meeting with the team, with Jennings providing his usual upbeat introduction to her own more detailed briefing. The meeting had gone well, with thoughtful questions from the team and some useful suggestions on potential lines of enquiry.

'I'm not sure what to make of this one,' she said. 'Young man beaten to death in broad daylight in the well-secluded garden of his own home. It doesn't really compute.'

'So what are the options? An argument that got out of hand? Some kind of grudge killing? Or just something opportunist? An intruder?'

'The last one seems unlikely. It wouldn't be surprising if Wentworth's place were to attract potential burglars — she's well known for having a bob or two — but why come in the middle of the day when there were two cars parked outside? And why attack Justin Wentworth, even if he'd challenged them? Wouldn't you just come up with some excuse and make yourself scarce?'

'I wouldn't know,' Jennings said. 'I've never really gone in for housebreaking. But people panic. Wouldn't be the first time.'

'I'm just struggling to come up with the scenario that would end up with Wentworth being bashed repeatedly about the head with a blunt instrument. I haven't seen the pictures yet, but from what Danny Eccles has said, it sounds like a savage attack. Not just a one-off blow in a moment of panic.'

'So what about the other options?'

'They seem more likely. Some kind of grudge killing directed either at Justin himself or at his mother. On the face of it, the latter seems most feasible.'

'I imagine she's made more than her share of enemies over the years. She doesn't seem to go out of her way to be popular.'

'That's my impression. Whether that would translate into this kind of murder, who knows?'

'What about the son? Anything suspicious there?'

'You mean any reason why someone might want to kill him? There's nothing obvious. According to his mum, he was a pretty quiet kid. Not exactly a chip off the old block, if so. But we'll get all that checked out.'

'Still waters and all that.'

'Mother seems a more realistic target, though,' Jennings agreed.

'This guy Hardy certainly seemed keen to give us the names of business competitors who might potentially be in the frame.'

'Just being helpful?'

'Maybe.' Annie tilted her hand back and forth to show her uncertainty. 'But it felt slightly odd to me. A bit over-the-top. He was also keen to let us know he realised we'd be treating Wentworth as a potential suspect. Had a feel of trying to warn us off.'

'Who is Hardy anyway?'

'That's the other interesting thing. He obviously had a good knowledge of both Wentworth and her business dealings. I looked him up when I got back. Didn't take me long as he's a non-executive director of Wentworth's business. He's also apparently a lawyer.'

'Not a criminal lawyer, presumably.'

'No, or at least not in the sense you mean.' Annie smiled. 'It looks like he specialises in contractual law, which I guess makes sense given the nature of Wentworth's business. I assume he was mainly there to give moral support. I couldn't work out whether he and Wentworth were an item. I had a sense they were more than just friends.'

'We seem to have a lot of hunches but not much concrete,' Jennings said. 'I'd like to have something substantial I can report upstairs. You think the presence of this Hardy character was significant?'

'There's nothing odd about Wentworth wanting someone with her. But his behaviour felt strange. More calculated than I'd have expected. Made us wonder whether they had something to hide.'

'If it turns out that Michelle Wentworth's the killer, the media really will have a field day.'

'Anything's possible,' Annie said. 'Though she's not high on my list at the moment, given the nature of the killing. What would drive a mother to do that to her son? And in practical terms, she's much smaller and slighter than he was.'

'Wouldn't be the first time we'd have something like that, though. And she could have caught him by surprise or had help from this Hardy guy.'

'PC who was there said they saw Hardy arrive just before them, so he couldn't have been involved unless he'd done a round-trip to throw us off the scent. But we'll see if forensics throws up anything.'

Jennings changed the subject. 'How's Zoe doing?'

'Fine, as far as I can tell. But I'm keeping an eye on her.'

'You never found out what the issue was?'

'I've not pushed her on it. I think it's her business unless it starts to affect her work again.'

Jennings looked unconvinced. 'Okay, your call. But I want to know if there's any sign of a problem. Keep me posted and tell me if there's anything you need from me.'

'I will. And let the Chief know we've got it all in hand.'

Jennings was already scanning the papers for his next meeting. 'I already have, Annie. Don't make me a liar.'

Chapter Six

'Of course I'm upset. He may have been a useless lump but he was my son, for Christ's sake.'

'That's not what I meant, Mickey. You know that.'

Michelle Wentworth swallowed the rest of her glass of wine and glared at him. 'It's what you said, Peter.'

Hardy sighed. 'I understand how you're feeling—'

'You can't possibly understand how I'm feeling.'

'No, of course not, but it must be awful. To have found him like that—'

'Yes, thank you, Peter. I don't need you to remind me.'

'I just meant that we've got to be careful. Obviously you're upset—'

'Good of you to permit it.'

'Obviously you're upset, but we have to be alert. Someone did this—'

'Is that right? I'm surprised the police haven't drafted you on to their team, Sherlock.'

'Someone did this,' Hardy continued patiently, 'and we don't know who or why. If it's not connected to Justin—'

'Who'd care enough about Justin?'

'Which means this was almost certainly targeted at you.'

'Thanks, Peter. You're a real comfort in times of trouble, you know that?'

'I'm just trying to be practical, Mickey. That's what you pay me for.'

'I don't pay you for your bedroom skills, that's for sure.' She took a breath and stopped. 'Sorry, Peter. I'm in a state. It's not like me. I've never faced anything quite like this before. I'm being a bitch.' She finally gave him a smile. 'Though I suppose that's not exactly unprecedented.'

'You're probably still in shock,' Hardy said, calmly. 'It was a hell of a thing to find. That's why I'm trying to help you. I'll top you up,' he went on, gesturing towards her glass. They were sitting by the swimming pool. It was mid-evening, the sun hanging low above the horizon in an otherwise empty sky.

'Okay, but I don't want to get pissed. I don't think that would be good at the moment.'

Hardy picked up the two glasses and headed back into the kitchen. Exactly as Justin had done, Wentworth thought uneasily to herself. For the first time since she'd moved here, she felt vulnerable. Peter was right. Someone had done this for a reason.

Her security here was as good as it could be. She'd insisted on that when they'd been converting the place. But it was designed to deter opportunistic burglars, not someone who was determined to harm her. For the first time in many years, she was beginning to feel she wasn't entirely in control of events.

Hardy returned and placed a full glass of white wine on the table beside her. 'Do you want something to eat?'

'Maybe later.' Though she knew she was unlikely to feel hungry any time tonight.

He sat himself down on the other side of the table, staring out across the landscape. 'I still can't believe this has happened.'

'Tell me about it. What did you mean about being careful?'

'Just that if this was targeted at you, you've made a pretty bad enemy somewhere.'

'I've made enemies,' Wentworth said. 'Some of them utter bastards. But I still can't believe any of them would do something like this.'

'And yet someone did.'

'It just seems unbelievable. This isn't business.'

'Maybe it's someone who's not even on our radar yet. Getting their retaliation in first.' Earlier in the evening, at Hardy's instigation, they'd finished compiling a list of individuals who might have reason to harm her. It hadn't been a long list, but even so she'd felt it was overstated. Most were little more than competitors. In some cases, the individuals in question were undeniably ruthless individuals, but she still couldn't see them as murderers. But Hardy had apparently promised the police that they'd produce a list of possible suspects, and she'd been happy to go along with the idea.

'What do you mean, someone not on our radar?' Wentworth asked.

'I don't know. But if you're right about our current competition, maybe we've provoked someone we don't even know about yet.'

'With these new contracts, you mean? That's your baby, Peter. You tell me.'

'I don't know. But these are big opportunities and they're bound to take us into unknown territory.'

'But you've done all the due diligence? We're not going into this blind.'

'You know we've done everything we can.'

'I'm putting a lot of faith in you on this one, Peter. It's your idea, your area of expertise.'

'We know who the competition is, and we've done all the research possible on them. But it's impossible to be sure that we've identified all the interests that might be involved.'

'What are you suggesting?'

'We always knew there was a risk in stepping outside our comfort zone. We just need to be careful.'

'Look, Peter, it takes a lot to make me throw in the towel, but there are some risks that aren't worth taking.'

He held up his hands. 'Let's not be hasty. I'm just saying it's something worth bearing in mind. I might be talking utter bollocks.'

'So who else killed Justin?' She looked at Peter defiantly, challenging him to give an answer.

'It could be anyone. Maybe some disgruntled nutter who lost his job as a result of one of our contracts. Who knows?' He paused, then continued speaking in a quieter voice. 'Anyway, it's not just that you need to worry about.'

Wentworth took a sip of her wine. 'It never is. What else?'

'Whoever was responsible for Justin's death, it means we'll have the police sniffing round us for some time to come. Which, frankly, is not something I'm keen on at the best of times. And this is far from the best of times. We've got to make sure we appear squeaky clean.'

'You think they'll start probing into the business?' Michelle was alert now. 'Christ, Peter, if they really start digging around in there they could uncover stuff that would destroy me.'

'Mickey, if they don't get a result quickly, they'll be looking into everything. I've had dealings with them before. Not on anything like this, but even so they can be like a dog with a bone. Just won't let go until they've extracted every ounce of meat. If we get to that point, we need to make sure we're a step ahead of them.'

'That was why I called you today. You're supposed to look after this stuff.'

'I know, and it was the right decision. I'll do some checking in the morning. Make sure there's nothing that can trip us up. We're careful with everything, but, yes, there's stuff buried in there we wouldn't want the authorities to know about.' He paused. 'There's one other thing.'

'Go on.'

'This Family Liaison Officer they're attaching to you. They'll tell you it's all for your benefit. That it's just a mechanism to make sure you have appropriate access to the investigative team. To make sure you're kept in the loop. All that kind of stuff.'

'That's more or less what they said, yes.'

'I'm sure it's all true. But the FLO is also a member of the investigation team. They want to gather evidence from you to help find Justin's killer. They'll try to build up a trusting relationship with you.'

'That doesn't worry me,' Wentworth said. 'For Christ's sake, Peter, I didn't kill him. They can think what they like.'

'That's not the point,' Hardy said. 'The point is that they'll be looking for you to make a slip. That was one reason I kept harping on them treating you as a suspect earlier, and why I wanted to give them the list of competitors. I'd prefer they were looking in that direction rather than paying too much attention to our business dealings. Sorry if that sounds a bit cold-hearted, but it's your interests I'm thinking of.'

'I know that, Peter. That's what I value in you. Your level-headedness, even at a time like this.' She was conscious her words sounded sarcastic. But maybe that was for the best. She'd always found his judgement invaluable, but there were moments, increasingly so in recent months, when he was in danger of getting too big for his boots. That was one reason she'd given him his head on the new contracts. To see if he could really deliver.

His expression suggested he'd registered the implied rebuke. 'All I'm saying is, watch what you say to them. It's all too easy to get suckered into letting your guard down if you start to trust someone.'

She gazed at him for a moment before responding. 'Trust me, Peter. I know that only too well.'

Chapter Seven

'I had a little run-in with one of your colleagues today.' Sheena was sitting on the patio outside the open kitchen door, supping a gin and tonic and enjoying the last of the day's hot sunshine, while Annie was inside cooking. At this time of the year, as summer slowly slipped into autumn, their west-facing garden acted as a suntrap in the evenings, having gathered the heat in the course of the afternoon.

'That right? What was that all about?'

Their evenings had no set routine, not least because when parliament was sitting Sheena spent much of the week in London. For her part, Annie worked late when Sheena was away and usually satisfied herself with not much more than an instant meal from the freezer. But when both of them were around, they tried to make something more of the evening, sharing the cooking and enjoying a glass of wine or two. At present, parliament was in recess for the autumn party conference season, so Sheena was spending some rare extended time in the constituency.

Annie was preparing pork, aromatic with herbs from their own garden, which she was intending to serve with roast potatoes and a fennel salad. She slid the pork back into the oven, poured herself a glass of red wine and stepped back outside into the sunshine.

'It was this Payne's affair,' Sheena said, in response to Annie's question.

'Payne's affair?' Annie seated herself beside Sheena at the garden table. The sun was low now, shining through the trees, dappling the garden around them. After what had happened earlier in the year, she'd wondered whether they would stay here. The place had felt too exposed. The question was still supposedly up in the air – they'd initially postponed a decision until Sheena had fully recovered – but with each week that went by, their presence here felt increasingly re-established. On an evening like this, it was difficult to imagine wanting to be anywhere else. 'Sorry. Missed that one.'

'Manufacturing company, over near Matlock. They've got half their staff on strike. I went to do my bit to support the picket line.'

'Are you still allowed to do that? Thought you were supposed to be all moderate and sensible again these days?'

'You know me. I've never been moderate and sensible in my life. Luckily, nobody's likely to want me in their shadow cabinet, whichever wing of the party they come from. I prefer just being a maverick. Anyway, this one strikes me as a good cause.'

'I've not seen much about it on the news.'

'That was one of the reasons I thought it was worth going over there. It's been under the radar a bit, which is probably how the company prefers it. Thought my presence might help raise the profile.'

'Especially if you got yourself arrested.'

Sheena grinned. 'I didn't get myself arrested. Try to avoid that kind of thing these days. No, some numpty threw a bottle at one of the managers.'

'Not helpful,' Annie said with a wry expression.

'It was the usual story. Fault on both sides. The manager in question was being an arsehole. Deliberately provocative. Doesn't justify what happened, but not smart when feelings are running high. Then of course he made a meal of it. Called the police. Even wanted to call an ambulance, though it was only a scratch.'

'What happened?'

'Your lads were very good. Must have calmed the so-called victim down. Came out and dealt well with the crowd, such as it was. None of us had seen who'd actually thrown the bottle – or at least no one was prepared to admit it – and the police obviously realised there was no mileage in pursuing it. But they made it clear it wasn't acceptable and warned they'd take action if there was further trouble. Just what was needed.'

'They're usually good at handling that kind of stuff, other than a few trigger-happy smartarses. What's the strike about?'

Sheena took another sip of her drink before contin-uing. 'It's a long story, but basically the company's outsourced its support processes. They promised the employees' terms and conditions wouldn't be affected. But the outsourcing firm who took on the contract have played all kinds of tricks, and in the end staff were offered the choice either of redundancy on minimum terms or retention on what amount almost to zero-hours contracts. Most of the employees have only short service, so it's not much of a choice.'

'Can they get away with this?'

'It's the usual story. They shouldn't be able to. But the contract company have got the whole thing down to a fine art. They've got the best legal advice to make sure they don't get caught out. Even the strike seems to have been deliberately provoked. They knew there'd be protests so they've done their best to make sure it happened on their terms. The union have done well in combatting the various shenanigans so far, but I suspect they're on a hiding to nothing.'

'It seems to be the way of the world now,' Annie said. 'I must be in one of the few lines of business that still offers a career and a job for life.'

'Too right. It's short-term contracts and precarious conditions everywhere you look these days. Even academia. If I get ousted from this job – which must be on the cards eventually – I wouldn't want to go back.' Sheena had been a lecturer in politics prior to her election as an MP. 'And it's going to get worse. Even the legal protections that are still there are gradually being whittled away.'

'And presumably someone's getting rich out of this?'

'It's the usual story,' Sheena said. 'The rich get richer and the poor get screwed. In the Payne's case, the original company have been able to boost their balance sheet and profits by hiving off a load of overheads. The result is that people like Michelle Wentworth get to build a new swimming pool.'

Annie had been sitting with her head tilted back to soak up the sunrays, but she snapped to attention now. 'Michelle Wentworth? Where does she fit into this?'

Sheena looked surprised. 'Wentworth? She owns the contract company. You must have seen her on the news and stuff?'

Annie and Sheena tended not to discuss the detail of their work with each other, other than elements already well in the public domain, each recognising that the other's work involved a high level of confidentiality and discretion. 'I've not just seen her on the news. I was interviewing her today. Look, Shee, this hasn't been released officially yet, but we're investigating the murder of Wentworth's son.'

'Jesus. I'd no idea. When did this happen?'

'Earlier today. Brutal killing, too. At Wentworth's home. At the moment at least, seemingly motiveless.'

'I didn't even know she was married. She seems the kind who'd put her career first, last and everywhere.'

'I suspect she's exactly that kind. She's divorced. Lives alone, apparently, with the son away at university. He was back on summer vacation.'

'I've no time at all for Michelle Wentworth,' Sheena said. 'But that's an awful thing to happen to anyone. Unless...'

'Unless she was responsible? It's possible. In any killing, we look at family members first, but I'm not convinced in this case, particularly given the nature of the killing.' Though Annie was still wondering if they'd been too quick to assume the murderer was an outsider. Something was definitely off with Michelle Wentworth and her lawyer friend.

'She always struck me as the kind who'd do anything to get her way,' mused Sheena. 'Ruthless as they come. But I don't know if that would extend to killing her own son.'

'On the other hand,' Annie said, 'there does seems to be plenty of bad blood among her competitors and some of the people she's screwed over. I imagine she wouldn't exactly be on the Christmas card lists of most of the people on your picket line today, for example.'

'Too right,' Sheena said. 'Hers was the name that kept coming up, much more than the managers they actually had to deal with. There was some real venom in what people were saying.'

'Any of them likely to be suspects, you reckon?'

Sheena shook her head. 'I've no idea. I only really spent time with a handful of them. They seemed remarkably upbeat and good-natured in the circumstances, but there were clearly one or two who were angrier. It's not exactly the basis for murder, though if people are feeling desperate who knows what they might do?'

'You'd be surprised.' Annie rose from the table. 'Right. Pork should be about ready. I'll get it out to rest while I get the salad sorted. Want some wine?' She nodded to Sheena's now empty gin and tonic glass.

Sheena squinted at the almost-setting sun. 'Think so. I've got a bit of paperwork to get out of the way, but a glass of wine normally helps with that.'

Annie nodded. 'I've got some admin to see to, too. And, yes, the wheels could definitely do with oiling.'

Chapter Eight

Roger Pallance stared at his own reflection in the tinted mirrors that lined the interior of the lift. God, he looked tired. He wasn't used to this kind of play-acting. He just wanted to do his job. He didn't mind working hard. He didn't mind working long hours. He didn't even mind putting up with all the pressures and crap that he had to in this job. That went with the territory, and it was why they paid him what they did.

What he didn't want was all the theatricals.

That was the stuff he found so wearying. Having to go through all that charade with those poor buggers out in the car park. The thing was, at a personal level, he really did feel sorry for them. They'd been well and truly shafted. There was no question about that. But that was business. He'd been shafted himself more than once, and he'd done the same to others. It wasn't nice, but it's a ruthless world and you're either the predator or the prey. Pallance knew which he preferred to be.

That part of it was fine. What he didn't like was having to rub their noses in it. But that was Michelle's style, and no one argued with Michelle. Not if you wanted to have any future in the business, and at the moment Pallance hoped his own prospects were looking bright. He knew he was one of Michelle's rising stars, and he owed her a lot. When he'd first joined the firm more than ten years before, she'd quickly identified him as someone with potential. He had been rewarded with a series of rapid promotions. Michelle liked to do that if she took a shine to you – 'growing our own', as she called it, a way of creating a business that she hoped might outlive her. But Pallance was smart enough to recognise that Michelle's affections could be fickle, and that not all of her protégés made the grade. If she suddenly decided he wasn't up to it, even after all these years, he wouldn't be given a second chance.

So Pallance was content to do what he was told, however pointless some of it might seem. They didn't really even need to be coming into this building any more. The majority of the staff – those who weren't out on the picket line – had already been transferred to other locations. That was part of the strategy – to reconfigure the work and the locations of the staff, supposedly to create a new centralised structure with the aim of improving efficiency or some such bollocks. The real aim was to change the work sufficiently that staff lost the right to transfer under their existing conditions. They either took redundancy or they accepted the new, much less attractive contracts.

Michelle had simply wanted them out, and this contract had been typical of her approach. She'd refused to talk to the union, made it clear that the company had no intention of recognising it, and had behaved with her typical ruthlessness towards the workforce.

She'd used every legal means at her disposal to block the union. The union's own legal team had, as far as Pallance could judge, been smart in countering her and had finally succeeded in calling the strike. That was what Michelle had wanted all along. She wanted to wear the union down, deplete its resources, and then allow the strike to happen at her preferred time and location. The strikers were picketing this site as their existing place of work, but the bulk of the operation had already moved elsewhere.

The lift reached the ground floor and he stepped outside into the reception area. The clock over the desk told him it was nearly 7:30 p.m. The main doors of the building were locked and the picket line had dispersed for the night. As usual, Pallance was the last to be leaving the building. He found his keys, unlocked one of the doors and stepped outside into the warm evening air, turning to lock the door behind him.

After the relative gloom indoors, the early-evening sun was dazzling. It was only just above the surrounding hills, filling the valley with dappled golden light. Pallance reached into his pocket for his sunglasses and slipped them on to his nose. He took a few steps towards his parked car, then stopped. 'Shit.'

It took him a moment to process what he was seeing. First, he registered the flat tyres. The two on the near side of the car had been slit, and the angle of the car suggested that the two on the far side had been subject to the same treatment.

That was only the beginning of the damage. The near side of the car had been decorated with a variety of abusive graffiti, the most prominent of which was the word 'SCAB' painted in white spray-paint. As Pallance drew closer he saw that this was not the end of the damage. The car windows had been shattered, and the possessions that Pallance had left on the seats – some CDs, an umbrella, a bottle of water – thrown out on to the car park.

It was a company car, so the loss would be to the company rather than to Pallance himself. Michelle couldn't complain too much given that she was the one who'd forced him to stay here.

Even so, he was furious. Apart from anything else, he was an hour's drive from home with no immediate means of getting there. His wife wasn't going to be keen on driving all the way over here with two kids who'd be well past their bedtime. He was also reluctant to leave the car here in this condition, though there was little chance of getting it transported anywhere else before the morning.

He walked round the car, still cursing under his breath. He needed to call the police, too, he realised. This was major criminal damage. He'd felt slightly embarrassed in retrospect about his decision to call the police earlier. He'd done it in it the heat of the moment, still angry that those cheeky young bastards had had the nerve to throw a bottle at him. It had hurt his pride – much more than it had hurt his head – and he'd wanted revenge.

But it had been evident from the moment the two police officers had arrived in his office that they were simply humouring him. They were polite enough, and they'd gone through the motions of noting down all the details. But he'd known they weren't going to take any action beyond having a quiet word with the union guy downstairs. They'd probably only turned up in the first place because the dispute had received some coverage in the local media and they'd got wind of the fact that that self-righteous MP was here too.

His first thought was to dial Michelle's number and let her know about the vandalism, but he prided himself on being able to handle anything. That was one of the qualities that Michelle most valued in him. She could throw him into a situation and let him get on with it. Some of his colleagues, even some of the more experienced ones, were wary about taking decisions without consulting Michelle. She found that infuriating. 'If I wanted a performing monkey,' she said, 'I'd pay you fucking peanuts. For what I pay you, I expect you to make a fucking decision. And I expect you to make the right one.'

Roger knew he had to deal with the car. Do what Michelle would want him to do, then bring her up to speed later. He took another deep breath and forced himself to think. His initial shock was subsiding, and he was able to think more rationally. Inconvenient as this was, it played in Michelle's favour. It was a more extreme outcome than they'd expected or intended, but the whole point was to discredit the union, and get public opinion on their side. They could milk this incident for all it was worth. It was probably worth whatever extortionate sum the car repairs would cost.

Okay, he thought, you buggers wanted a fight. Now you're going to get one. He'd worry later about how he was going to get home. For the moment, he had a couple of calls to make. First, to the police, to report this incident of appalling criminal damage, even more unnerving following so soon after the morning's physical assault.

After that, a second call, this time to a mate who worked as a freelance journalist. The guy did sports stuff mainly these days, but he had the contacts Pallance needed.

He smiled as he thought of the headline on the front-page story in tomorrow's *Evening Telegraph*.

Chapter Nine

'Not exactly what I expected,' Zoe Everett said.

'What were you expecting?' DC Martin Yardley was a relatively new member of the team, who'd joined after a couple of years as a beat copper in Derby. He was a graduate, clearly bright, who treated every day as a school day. That was a positive trait, Zoe supposed, though there were times when his eager curiosity could become wearing. She could imagine him as the overenthusiastic student in the front row waving his hand around to ask a question even before the lecture had concluded.

'I was just stereotyping, I guess. From the way he was described to us I was expecting – I don't know, some run-down tower block flat, I suppose.'

'This isn't that,' Yardley said unnecessarily.

It certainly wasn't. It was a small, well maintained cottage in a picturesque Peak District village. The cottage itself was tiny, but Zoe guessed that its location and condition would add a tidy sum to its value. Which raised the interesting question of how Ronnie Donahue could afford the place.

In fairness, her only guide to Donahue's character and circumstances was the assessment provided by Peter Hardy. What was the description he'd given to Annie? A lazy, self-pitying bugger who's never done a proper day's work in his life. Something like that. But she guessed that Hardy wasn't exactly an impartial witness.

The cottage was just off the main road and there was nowhere to park outside. Yardley continued past it and turned into the village's small public car park. It was still relatively early on a weekday, but the fine weather had already brought out the first of the tourists and day trippers and the car park was rapidly filling up. Yardley found one of the last available spaces and pulled in. 'Busy place.'

'Peak District, innit?' Zoe said. 'One hot day and you can't move for tourists.'

They made their way back to Ronnie Donahue's cottage. It was one of several near-identical stone-built homes on a narrow street leading off the main road through the village. Zoe was no expert, but they looked to pre-date the bulk of the surrounding buildings by a century or so. She could envisage them standing initially by themselves at this junction, gradually becoming encircled by other residences as the decades had passed.

There was a small garden at the front of each of the cottages, all immaculately maintained, each replete with stone pots of blooming flowers as if part of some organised display. A middle-aged man was standing outside Donahue's address watering the plants.

'Mr Donahue?'

The man looked up, squinting in the sunlight. 'Who's asking?'

'Police, Mr Donahue. Do you mind if we have a word?'

'Do I have a choice?'

'We just want to talk to you. I'm afraid we have some bad news.'

Donahue stared at her for a moment, then said, 'You'd better come in, then.'

They followed him through the front door, Yardley having to duck his slightly gangling body to pass under the lintel. The interior was dark and cool after the morning sun. There was a faint scent of rosemary in the air, mixed with the smell of freshly baked bread. None of this was what Zoe would have expected.

The cottage itself was as small as its exterior suggested. The front door opened directly on to the living room, a kitchen area visible through an archway at the rear. A flight of stairs led up from the left-hand side of the living room, presumably to bedrooms and a bathroom upstairs. Zoe could see double glass doors at the rear of the kitchen leading out to a back garden. Donahue said, 'I'll make us a brew. I'm parched.' He had a strong local accent.

Zoe seated herself gingerly on the edge of the bulky-looking sofa, and Yardley took a seat beside her. The living room was as tidy as the front garden, its white-washed stone walls and sturdy oak furniture creating a cosy environment. There was a small television, with a games console beneath it, a bookshelf containing a scattering of paperbacks, and a couple of pictures depicting local landscapes on the walls.

After a few minutes, Donahue re-emerged from the kitchen bearing a tray containing three steaming mugs. Zoe briefly introduced herself and Yardley as Donahue passed round the drinks and took a seat. 'So what's this all about? What's this bad news?' He spoke the last two words as though the concept was unknown in his life.

'I'm afraid it's about your son.'

'My son?' He shrugged. 'I'd almost forgotten I had one, to be honest. What's the little bugger done? Got sent down from Oxford? I assume that's where he ended up, given all the money his mother spent on his education.'

'I'm afraid he's dead.'

Donahue looked up at Zoe, his expression suggesting that he was interested but not particularly concerned. 'That right? Poor bastard. What happened to him?'

'We believe he was murdered, Mr Donahue,' Zoe said. 'I'm sorry.'

'Don't waste your sympathy on me. I haven't seen him for the best part of eighteen years. Still, I wouldn't wish murder on anyone. What happened?'

'We can't reveal any detailed information while the investigation's still proceeding. But he was the victim of a violent attack and as yet we aren't clear about the motive.'

'I'm guessing the motive will be his mother.'

Zoe tried not to overreact, but her interest was piqued. 'Why do you say that, Mr Donahue?'

'Because she's universally detested.'

'That's a rather extreme statement.'

'It's true, though. Or as good as true. She's a ruthless bitch. She doesn't care who she treads on, who she hurts, as long as she gets what she wants. I always thought that one day it would come back to bite her. Although it's typical that she walks away scot-free and some other poor sod takes the rap.' He stopped, as if suddenly conscious how vituperative his words had sounded.

'I take it your divorce from Mrs Wentworth wasn't an amicable one,' Zoe said.

Donahue laughed. 'I can see you're a detective. Well spotted. Yup, far from amicable. She accused me of unreasonable behaviour, claimed I'd been violent towards her.'

'And that wasn't true?'

Donahue took a large swallow of his tea. 'I'm no angel. I've been known to lose my temper. In those days, I drank too much. But I'm not a violent man. That was just an

67

image she was keen to establish for her own ends. I should have realised what was happening earlier. Whenever we had any kind of big argument, she'd end up calling the police. Claiming I'd attacked her.'

'And you hadn't?'

Donahue was silent for a moment. 'Once or twice I might have pushed her a bit. Just in the heat of the moment. But I never did anything to hurt her. Nothing like she claimed I'd done.'

Zoe had heard enough of these kinds of stories over the years to take this one with a shovelful of salt. Violent men often seemed incapable of acknowledging – sometimes even of recognising – their own violence. 'So what happened?'

'First couple of times it came to nothing. Police turned up, but it was clear nobody had been hurt and they just gave me a warning. Third time, I was pissed and made the mistake of getting a bit stroppy. They took me in. I was bound over, given a caution and all that, though thank Christ it didn't go any further. But I learned my lesson. I got out before things got worse. I'm convinced that if I'd stayed, she'd have had me set up on some serious charge. At the time, I thought it was because she was a vindictive cow, but I realised later she was setting everything up for the divorce she wanted. She made sure I was the one who walked out on her, and she came up with some cock and bull story about me leaving for another woman.'

'You hadn't?' Zoe asked.

'If anyone was playing away, it was her. I had my suspicions. But she twisted the truth, the way she always did. And she could point to my supposed history of domestic violence. I was denied access to my boy. I was ousted from the business I'd helped her to build, and she lied about my contribution to that. I walked away from the split with a few bob, which is how I was able to buy this place. But basically she ripped me off good and proper.' He stopped, as if aware how far the conversation had drifted. 'Sorry. You can see how much she still winds me up, even now. But she's a nasty conniving bitch, so there'll be plenty of people out there with good reason to wish her ill.'

'Including you,' Zoe pointed out. 'From what you've just been saying.'

Donahue blinked, clearly registering the implications of Zoe's words. 'I've plenty of reasons to wish her ill, sure. I've no reason to wish harm on my own son.'

'You said you hadn't seen him for eighteen years.'

'That's right. I'd no relationship with him. Occasionally, I heard things about him through friends of friends, but I made a point of not enquiring further. There was no reason to. Michelle would never have allowed me back into his life, so there was nothing to gain from thinking about it.' He said nothing more for a moment. 'But, like I say, I'd no reason to have any ill-will towards him.'

'When did you last see Mrs Wentworth?'

Donahue's demeanour changed as he realised the reason for sending a detective to notify him of the death. 'What is this? An interrogation? I thought you just came here to break the tragic news that my son had been murdered. Now you're treating me like a bloody suspect.'

'We're just trying to obtain as full an understanding of the background as we can, Mr Donahue.'

'Of course I'm a suspect. Why the hell wouldn't I be? This'll be her doing, won't it? Her son isn't even cold before she starts trying to shift the blame in my direction. Mark my words, Justin's death will somehow be linked to whatever she's up to. It'll be some dodgy deal gone wrong, some nasty bastard she's got on the wrong side of. But she won't want you poking around in her grubby business dealings so she's going to deflect your attention by pushing you in my direction. After all, I've a history of violence, haven't I? She's putting me in the frame in the hope that nobody looks too closely into her affairs.'

'Nobody's putting you in the frame, Mr Donahue. We just wanted to be clear about the nature of your relationship with Mrs Wentworth and with Justin.'

'Well, I hope I've made it very clear.'

'I think you have, Mr Donahue. Thank you for that.' Zoe allowed Donahue a moment to calm down. 'You say you think this is linked to Mrs Wentworth's business dealings. Do you have any particular reason to believe that?'

She thought she detected a momentary hesitation before Donahue said, 'Only my own experience of dealing with her. And my experience of trying to run a company alongside her.'

'You ran the business together initially?'

'It was my firm. I started it. In those days, we were doing delivery stuff. I started as a man and a van, but we gradually built it up and started doing local deliveries for various small businesses. By the time Michelle and I split up we had half a dozen vehicles and were making a tidy profit. That gave her the foundation for what she's built since. I mean, credit to her, she's turbocharged it all. But that's Michelle. Thinks big and doesn't care who or what gets in her way. She got rid of me partly because I didn't share her ambitions. My guess is that she's come up against someone as ruthless as she is. From what I hear, she's fishing in some pretty big waters these days, so who knows what kind of sharks might be lurking in the depths.'

'You keep tabs on what she's up to, then, Mr Donahue?' Zoe asked.

For a moment, Donahue looked uncomfortable, as if he'd been caught out in some misdemeanour. 'I hear stuff on the grapevine, you know. I wouldn't say we've exactly got mutual friends these days – she's left all of my crowd well behind – but I know people who know people, let's put it that way. Stuff gets back to me.'

Zoe glanced over at Martin Yardley, who'd been dutifully scribbling down notes of the discussion. 'I think we're about done, then. Do you have any last questions, Martin?'

She'd asked mainly because she was conscious she hadn't given Yardley any chance to participate in the interview. He was inexperienced, but she should have set him up with a couple of questions in advance. Give him a chance to learn the ropes. She wanted at least to show she hadn't excluded him.

Yardley thought for a moment, then said, 'I just wondered how it felt for you, Mr Donahue. Losing contact with your own son, I mean.'

The question seemed innocuous enough, simply the first that occurred to Yardley on the spur of the moment. But Zoe noted that the question had disconcerted Donahue. There was something in his expression she couldn't interpret.

'Like I say,' Donahue said, 'I didn't really have any kind of relationship with him. I didn't even really think of him as my son. It was all a long time ago. I've put all that behind me. That's all.'

He stopped, and for a few moments Zoe allowed the silence to continue, intrigued by Donahue's evident discomfort. Finally, she said, 'Even so, our commiserations on your loss, Mr Donahue. The news must have been a shock to you. We won't take up any more of your time at the moment. Thank you for talking to us.'

Donahue stared at her as if he hadn't followed what she'd said. 'Oh, aye. No worries. I'll be here if you need to speak to me again. I usually am.' He allowed the ghost of an ironic smile to cross his face. 'It's not like I've anywhere much else to go these days.'

Chapter Ten

'You're sure you want to do this, Zo?'

'I don't see why not. I worked as a Family Liaison Officer for a good while until I was promoted to DS. It's been a while but it was something I – well, I'm not sure enjoyed is the word, but something I found rewarding.'

'I'd almost forgotten you'd worked as an FLO until you brought it up at the meeting.'

At the briefing session earlier in the day, Annie had been discussing the need to designate a Family Liaison Officer to support Michelle Wentworth. This would have been standard procedure in any case of this nature. It wasn't normally a role that Annie would expect a Detective Sergeant to undertake; but here the circumstances might justify it.

Annie had been keen to identify someone who might encourage Wentworth to be more open with them. She knew Zoe was skilled at building relationships with others, but she also had a detective's nose for what might be important. She knew how to retain her objectivity, and she was sharp and perceptive, astute at spotting the verbal cues that could provide an insight into what someone might be thinking. It wasn't that Annie wanted Zoe to be a spy in the camp, but she felt they needed a better understanding of Michelle Wentworth, her business life and her relationship with Justin.

'So what am I looking for, do you think?' Zoe asked. 'Do we really think there's a possibility Wentworth's responsible for her son's death?' They'd touched on this possibility the previous day but aside from Michelle's derogatory comments about her son's laidback attitude there wasn't much to go on.

'I can't see it, personally,' Annie said. 'What would be the motive, for a start? And I don't see Wentworth as the sort who'd commit a frenzied killing just because she loses her rag. It's not impossible, obviously, but she's not high on my list of suspects at the moment. But I do think there's something. Maybe nothing directly to do with our investigation, but something she's holding back from us.'

'Be interesting to see what state of mind she's in today. Must be an awful shock for her, however resilient she might be.'

'That's my feeling. I wonder if she realises how much of a shock she's had. She strikes me as the type who'd think she can work through it until the reality suddenly hits home. But we'll see.'

They emerged from the car into the scorching sunshine. The weather had remained unchanged, the sky still empty of clouds, the temperature unseasonably high. They were having problems with wildfires on the moors as they had off and on all summer, and there would be more yet if the weather didn't break soon. Out here, the day seemed eerily silent, without even the faintest trace of a breeze.

While they waited at the front door, Annie looked back across the huge front garden. It was largely lawn, but there was enough in the way of bushes and shrubbery to provide cover for anyone wanting to approach undetected. If their killer had driven up to the house, it would have been impossible for them to avoid being caught on one of the cameras, either in front of the house or out by the gate. That suggested the killer had parked somewhere outside the gardens, avoiding the cameras at the main front gate, and had then made their way to the house on foot. Wentworth had said that, prior to the killing, she'd been in the habit of leaving the main gates open in the daytime to admit mail and other deliveries.

Annie had had a couple of members of the team check out the gardens' perimeter. Most of it was securely fenced, but there were several points where it wouldn't have been difficult for a determined intruder to gain access. They'd also identified a number of places where it would have been possible to leave a car unobtrusively. They were in the process of checking out potential witnesses or camera sightings on the surrounding roads. It was laborious work, but so often that was what provided the key breakthroughs.

It was a few minutes before there was any response to the doorbell, though Annie had contacted Michelle Wentworth earlier in the day to set up the meeting. Annie suspected that might be indicative of the kind of woman Wentworth was – keep people waiting, ensure the meeting's taking place on your terms. Wentworth struck her as someone who liked to be in control, even in circumstances like these.

When she finally opened the door, Annie thought Wentworth looked a different woman from the one who had greeted them the previous day. It was partly the simple fact that then she'd been wearing a dressing gown, whereas today she was rigged out in her full business attire. And very imposing she looked, Annie thought, in her expensive-looking suit. Annie wondered whether

Wentworth was heading out to a meeting or two later, or whether she always dressed like this when working at home.

'We won't keep you long, Mrs Wentworth,' said Annie after a brief hello. 'We just wanted to confirm that my colleague, DS Zoe Everett, will be acting as your Family Liaison Officer. You met Zoe yesterday, of course, but we thought it might be helpful for her to explain the role.'

Wentworth gazed at Zoe for a moment, and then led them through the house into the garden. The large table by the pool was spread with files and papers. 'Forgive the mess,' Wentworth said. 'I couldn't face working inside on a day like this. I was planning to go into the office, but everybody told me it was an insane idea.'

'Probably a good idea to have a break,' Annie said. 'In the circumstances.'

'I'm not sure that being stuck alone in here is any better. And I'm not one for taking breaks even after something like this. If I try to do nothing, I get stir-crazy. So I'm working as usual. I can't afford to take any real time off.'

'Are you particularly busy at the moment?' Annie enquired.

Wentworth hesitated for a second. 'Not really. No more than usual. But I generally have to work my arse off to keep us on track. I've got some good people working for me, and I've invested a lot in developing talent in the business. But in the end it's the same old story. If you want to make sure a job's done properly, you have to do it yourself.' She shook her head. 'I just don't want to end up taking my eye off the ball because of what's happened. But it's difficult to keep focused.'

'I'm sorry,' Annie said. 'I can't begin to imagine what you're going through.'

'I'll get through it, I don't doubt. You have to, don't you? Let me get you some coffee.'

'We don't want to put you to any trouble,' Annie said.

'It's no trouble. I'm gasping for one myself so you'll be doing me a favour.'

They took seats at the table while Wentworth headed back into the house. Zoe was looking round, taking in the pool, the large garden, and the spectacular countryside beyond. They had only glimpsed this rear garden during their previous visit, though since then a team of officers had painstakingly searched it and the surrounding countryside in the hope of finding the murder weapon or other potential evidence.

'What do you think?' Annie asked Zoe while they were alone.

'There's something odd about her, isn't there? I know grief hits people in different ways, but something doesn't quite gel. She didn't seem comfortable talking about what they're working on at present.'

'That's what I thought. I'll do some more digging into the business when I get back to the ranch.' She was about to say more when she heard the sound of Wentworth's raised voice from inside the house. Annie placed a finger to her lips and gestured for Zoe to listen.

At first, it was difficult to make out more than the occasional phrase. '...the hell do you think you were doing... me first... I hope you do...' There was an extended silence while Wentworth presumably listened to whatever was being said at the other end of the phone. When she responded, her voice was a little louder. 'I hear all that, Roger. But I don't like it when people go off-piste without consulting me. Even you. Next time tell me before you go off on some frolic of your own. I'm not comfortable with this. Somebody's setting up somebody, that's for sure, but it all just sounds a bit too convenient. Before you go any further, make sure you speak to our PR people. Peter Hardy's got all the details. I just want to make sure it's all properly coordinated, and I haven't got time to think about it at the moment. No, that's fine. You weren't to know. Thanks, Roger. That's much appreciated.' They heard her end the call, and a few moments later she reappeared carrying a tray of coffee mugs. 'Sorry I was so long. Got waylaid by a call from one of my managers. Poor bugger hadn't heard about Justin, so I gave him a bit of an earful to begin with.' She placed the tray on the table, before sitting down opposite them. 'It all comes at once, doesn't it?'

'Problems?' Annie asked.

'Something and nothing, probably. We've got some industrial action taking place at one of our sites. Usual story, but this one seems to be turning a bit nasty.'

Annie thought back to her conversation with Sheena the previous evening. 'Nasty in what way?'

'Some trouble on the picket line yesterday. Then last night the manager's car was vandalised. Your lot have been informed. Could just do without the publicity at the moment. Along with what's happened here, it starts to make us look as if we're not on top of things.'

It was an interesting perspective, Annie supposed. Worrying that your son's brutal murder might reflect negatively on your company's profile. 'It sounds as if you've a lot on your plate.'

'You can say that again. And I feel guilty even thinking about the work stuff after what happened to Justin. But it wouldn't help me to be sitting here brooding. I'm built to work, and throwing myself back into that's probably the surest way of getting me through this.' She sounded as if she was trying to persuade herself. 'Anyway, that's not why you're here.'

'We just wanted to explain Zoe's role,' Annie said. 'The idea is that she'll be your main day-to-day contact with ourselves. If we need anything more from you, we'll organise that through Zoe.'

'And I'll make sure that you're kept fully up to speed with all developments in the investigation, Mrs Wentworth,' Zoe added. 'If you have any questions at any point, then just ask and I'll get the answers for you. Similarly, if you've any concerns about the way the investigation is being handled, please raise them with me in the first instance and I'll ensure the issue's resolved.'

'And no doubt you'll be keeping an eye on me in the meantime?' Wentworth's tone was light-hearted, but it sounded as if she was letting Zoe know exactly where she stood.

'That's not the purpose of the role,' Zoe said calmly. 'If we do need to gather further information from you, then I'll be involved in that. But the primary aim is simply to ensure that you have a single, approachable point of contact with the investigation.'

'If you say so,' Wentworth said.

'It's standard practice in all major inquiries,' Annie said.

'I'm sure it is.' Wentworth was smiling but there was no humour evident in her expression. 'It doesn't really matter. I've nothing to hide. All of my failings are fully out in plain sight.'

There was little point in arguing, Annie thought. In any case, Wentworth wasn't entirely wrong. Zoe wasn't expected to act as a spy, but Annie did want her to build a rapport with Michelle Wentworth and, if possible, to penetrate at least a little below her public image. If there were things Wentworth wasn't saying to them, that might in part be because she didn't trust the police to act in her interests. If they could build up some trust, she might be prepared to be at least a little more forthcoming about her business affairs. Whether that would assist their inquiry remained to be seen, but they were still at the stage where any information could potentially be valuable. 'We won't take up any more of your time, then, Mrs Wentworth. You're obviously very busy.'

'I'll be in touch in due course, Mrs Wentworth,' Zoe said. 'What I'd like to do is set up a regular session with you, either by phone or face-to-face as you prefer, to catch up on any developments. But if you've any questions for us, or if you think of anything that you feel might be pertinent to the inquiry, please don't hesitate to contact me at any time.' She slid a business card across the table. 'My contact details are all on there.'

Michelle Wentworth picked up the card and gazed at it for a moment, as if assessing the value of its contents. Then she dropped it on to her pile of papers, in a manner that suggested she'd rather be dropping it in the bin. 'Thank you,' she said. 'I very much look forward to speaking to you, DS Everett, as soon as you've something worthwhile to tell me.'

Chapter Eleven

Stuart Jennings was pacing up and down the incident room when Annie and Zoe arrived back.

'Where the hell have you been?' Jennings said. 'I've been trying to phone you.'

'And a good afternoon to you, Stuart. We've been up to see Michelle Wentworth. Couldn't get a signal up there, so didn't pick up your message till we were on our way back. Tried to phone you a couple of times but you were engaged.' Annie forced herself to remain calm. Jennings was clearly rattled about something but she wasn't going to let him bully her.

'That was because I've had the Chief and the Assistant Chief on the phone almost constantly for the last hour,' he said.

'Did rather prevent me from calling you back, though,' Annie pointed out. 'What's the problem?'

'This is the problem.' Jennings was holding a copy of the *Evening Telegraph*, which he thrust in her direction.

It was today's early edition. Jennings held it up and jabbed his finger at the front-page headline. *Union Thugs Trash Car.* Below the headline was a picture of a badly damaged BMW with the word 'SCAB' painted along its bodywork.

'Nasty,' she said. 'I take it this is one of Michelle Wentworth's places? She was just saying something about it. Didn't go into any detail, though.'

'Too right it is. Look at the state of that bloody car.'

Annie assumed Jennings' irritation was based on something other than a hitherto unknown love for BMWs. 'I don't understand. What's the concern?'

'It's the Comms team who were concerned in the first instance. They were intending to do the media release about Justin Wentworth's killing this afternoon to catch the early-evening news bulletins.'

'That's what we agreed,' Annie said. 'We thought that would prompt some calls, maybe even help identify some potential witnesses. We've got the call handlers primed. I still don't see what the problem is.'

Jennings slumped down on to one of the chairs, as if he'd suddenly run out of energy. 'You know what Comms are like. They want everything completely under control. Everything just the way they've planned it.'

'Life doesn't always work out that way. We're police officers, for goodness sake. Shit happens. What do they expect? In any case, how does this cause them a problem?'

'They think, maybe rightly, that the media are going to put two and two together and make five. That they'll link the story of the car being trashed with Justin's death, and conclude the murder was politically motivated.'

'That's ridiculous,' Annie said. 'What are they envisaging? A trade union hit squad?'

'You know that most of the press jump at any opportunity to bad-mouth the trade unions. This is right up their street.'

'Even for them, the idea of a trade union taking someone out's a bit far-fetched, surely?'

'It won't be that, though, will it? They'll claim that it was some hothead, high on his own rhetoric. The unions will get the blame for leading him astray, filling his head with dangerous socialist nonsense.'

'But there's nothing to link the two cases. And, just to be pedantic, it would be a bit odd for an activist to progress from murder to vandalism. It would suggest they'd peaked too early.' Before Jennings could intervene, she held up her hands. 'That was a joke, Stuart.'

'Not the best time for your jokes, Annie. That won't stop them making the link. And that will make the whole thing messier and even higher-profile than before. That's why I've had endless calls from whatever the collective noun is for Chief Officers.'

'A murder?' Annie suggested.

Jennings glared at her. 'Very clever. But, yes, that's what they're worried about.' He paused. 'Apart from anything else, I understand your partner was there yesterday.'

Annie felt a sinking feeling in her stomach. Sheena was a relatively uncontroversial figure as Labour MPs went, largely because she avoided shooting her mouth off to the national press about anything and everything. She preferred to get on with working for her constituents. Even so, she was undeniably on the left of the party and the media were generally only too glad to find an excuse to stick their boots in. They'd no doubt be delighted at the opportunity to paint her as an associate of the thuggish tendency. 'She paid a brief visit to the picket line, yes. Just to show solidarity.'

'And there was an incident while she was there?' Jennings asked.

'A minor one. Some idiot throwing a bottle at the manager.'

'The same manager whose car has now been comprehensively trashed.'

'It's a big stretch to link that to Justin Wentworth's murder.'

'I don't imagine they'll say it explicitly. It'll all be innuendo. But they'll leave their readers in no doubt what these thuggish trade unions are capable of. And maybe by extension, these thuggish Labour MPs.'

'That's ridiculous, Stuart. Even they wouldn't suggest that. Apart from anything else, it's in bloody bad taste given Sheena was nearly killed herself in the middle of a far-right protest.'

'I don't think anyone's ever accused the media of good taste. But again, they won't say it in so many words. It'll all just be nudges and suggestions. You can just imagine it. Digging out some out-of-context quote that mentions killing or murder, so they can say "Is this the kind of rhetoric that led to the murder of this innocent young man?" They'll probably even be able to persuade your mother to lead the condemnations.'

'You're getting carried away, Stuart. That's just absurd.'

'I'm just trying to plan ahead. As soon as we release the media statement about Wentworth, the shit's going to hit the fan. This whole thing will be thrust into the spotlight. I just want to make sure we're got our backsides fully covered before it happens.' He hesitated. 'I was even wondering if I should take you off the case, Annie.'

She'd been aware from the moment he'd first mentioned Sheena that the conversation was circling round to this point. 'Why would you take me off the case?'

'In case there's a perceived conflict of interest.'

'There's no conflict of interest. Why would there be?'

'Apart from anything else, because your partner has publicly criticised Michelle Wentworth's company. Do I need to spell it out to you?'

'I think you probably do, Stuart. What are you suggesting? That I might not do my job properly because Sheena disapproves of Michelle Wentworth's business practices?'

'I know you'll do a professional job. You're one of my best officers. But we've got to be realistic. If we aren't seen to be making rapid progress on this one, your relationship with Sheena could become a stick to beat us with. The media are already well aware of your relationship from the previous attempts on her life.'

'You know as well as I do that if we don't make progress, they'll find any stick to beat us with. If it's not Sheena, it'll be something else. We can't let that dictate who handles the case, surely?'

She could see Jennings was close to losing his temper, and she wondered whether she'd pushed him too far in his current state of mind. Unlike some bosses she'd worked for, he wasn't prone to getting angry without good reason, but she'd seen him lose his cool once or twice, especially when under pressure.

'The only person who decides who handles the case is me,' he said. 'I know you're more than capable and for the moment I'm happy for you to continue. But this is a warning, Annie. If we don't resolve this one quickly or if the media start playing silly buggers, I might have to reconsider. We can't afford for this to go pear-shaped, or even to give the press any excuse for claiming it has.'

Annie nodded, knowing there was no point in pushing this any further. If Jennings felt he was being pushed into a corner, he'd feel obliged to show her who was boss. 'I understand that, Stuart. I'm not trying to be difficult. I just don't like to have my professionalism questioned.'

'I'm just watching your back, that's all, as well as my own. If the press start baying for blood, I don't want it to be ours. So get on with the job and prove how good you are.'

Before she could respond, he'd already turned and walked out of the room. He'd clearly recognised a good exit line. Annie shook her head and walked over to Zoe, who'd been watching the exchange from the far end of the room. Annie knew she and Jennings had kept their voices low enough to prevent the substance of their discussion from being overheard. She also knew that she'd be quizzed by her colleague as soon as Jennings had left the room.

'What was all that about?' Zoe asked.

'That incident Michelle Wentworth was talking about. The damage to the car. Stuart's fear is that the press will link it to Justin Wentworth's killing and start implying some political motive.'

'I didn't get the sense that Michelle Wentworth saw any link between the two,' Zoe said. 'She just seemed irritated by the vandalism thing. If she'd thought it might be linked to Justin's death, she'd have said so, surely.'

'If she was any normal person, I'd have thought so,' Annie said. 'I get the feeling that Michelle Wentworth's priorities are a little different from most people's. But, yes, if she'd thought there was a link, I imagine she'd have been only too keen to tell us. I had the sense that she wanted to play it down.'

'For someone who strikes me as a dedicated self-publicist,' Zoe said, 'she seems very keen to keep out of the limelight on this.'

'This is a bit different from banging the drum about her business, I suppose. But you're right. She and that guy Hardy seem very keen for us to look anywhere but at them. Maybe it's just because they're dodgy business types and they don't want us to start looking too closely into what they're doing. In which case, it's not really a priority for us, and we can just pass on anything we might stumble across to our friends in Fraud or the Revenue or whatever.'

'I suspect I'm going to have an uphill struggle trying to gain her trust and confidence,' Zoe said, 'but I've managed to do it before even in very unpromising circumstances. If I can get her onside, she might be prepared to open up a bit more.'

'Especially if you can manage to spend time in her company when Hardy's not around. It's interesting that her first thought after calling the emergency services was to call on the company's legal advisor. He seemed to be playing a chaperone role with her, trying to make sure she didn't say anything out of turn. She seemed more open when he wasn't around.'

'She likes the sound of her own voice,' Zoe said. 'Maybe she knows she's got a tendency to let her mouth run away with her. Calling Hardy might have been a precaution.'

'It's all speculation,' Annie said. 'But if you can start to build up a bit of a rapport with her, we might get a chance to see if there's anything in it.'

'That's a big if,' Zoe said. 'I suspect this is not going to be the easiest assignment I've ever been involved in. But you never know. If she does like to talk, I'm a good listener.'

'Okay,' Annie said. 'Stuart's right about one thing, though. We do need to start making some real progress before the media start filling the vacuum. We've all got plenty to do, so we'd better get on with it.'

Chapter Twelve

'DS Everett?'

Zoe looked up at the man who was standing in front of her. He was probably in late middle age, maybe late fifties, and had the air of a long-out-of-shape athlete. His stomach was straining at his shirt, and his garish braces indicated that the belt on his trousers was no longer up to the job. His twisted nose suggested a background in rugby or boxing, whereas the broken veins around it implied heavy drinking. He seemed genial enough, with a broad grin revealing his yellow-stained teeth.

'Mr Rentoul?'

'That's me, love. Do you want to come through?'

She followed him past the reception desk and into the interior of the building. Rentoul's name had been given to them by Wentworth as one of the competitors who might conceivably have a grudge against her. They'd already interviewed a number of the individuals on the list without learning much new, but Rentoul had looked one of the more promising names, which was why Zoe had been allocated the interview. He had a police record for violent crime in his teens, although there was no evidence he'd been involved in any criminal activity in the intervening years. As a businessman, Rentoul apparently had something of a dodgy reputation but it seemed he'd always managed to stay on the right side of the law.

She'd had a quick glance at the company's entry on the Companies House website before she'd set off, looking to obtain some basic information about Rentoul. Zoe was no expert, but as far as she could judge from the published accounts the company was a sound business, if relatively small by comparison with Wentworth's operation. She'd been impressed by the size of the office building when she'd pulled up outside, but when she'd entered the reception she'd realised it was a serviced unit, accommodating a dozen or more different businesses.

Rentoul's office was a mess. There was a desk piled high with papers, and a meeting table laden with used coffee mugs. Various items of discarded computer equipment littered the corners of the room. Three filing cabinets were piled high with ring binders and other paperwork.

'Sorry,' Rentoul said, as he followed her gaze around the room. 'Bit chaotic, I'm afraid. I'd like to say that it's not always like this, but that'd be a lie. I'm just Mr Disorganised. Or at least that's the way it looks, but I can lay my hands on any document without even thinking about it. I've had various assistants and secretaries try to get me into order over the years, but it always ends in tears.' He had the air of an avuncular end-of-the-pier comedian, Zoe thought. A bit of a character, but perhaps one you should be careful not to underestimate. 'Now, love,' he went on, 'what can I do you for?' He pulled out one of the chairs for her to sit at the table, then swept all the empty mugs aside before sitting down himself.

'Do you know Michelle Wentworth?' Zoe had decided that the direct approach was likely to be the simplest. Rentoul didn't seem the type who would respond well to flannel.

'Michelle?' He seemed surprised at the question. 'Depends what you mean by know. She's a mystery to everyone, to be honest.'

'But you've had dealings with her?'

'We've run up against each other a few times, let's put it that way. What's this all about, anyway? She in some kind of trouble?'

Zoe had agreed with Annie that, although Justin Wentworth's death hadn't yet been formally announced to the media, they could afford to be open with Rentoul. By the time he'd be able to spread the news on the grapevine, the media statement should have been released. 'Her son's been found dead. We believe it was an unlawful killing.'

Rentoul stared at her. 'Jesus, that's awful. I'm not Michelle's biggest fan but I wouldn't wish that on anyone.' Zoe could see him considering the implications of her presence here. 'What's this to do with me, anyway?'

Zoe didn't have a fully convincing answer to this. 'At this stage, we're just exploring the background. We thought it might be useful to talk to some of Mrs Wentworth's business associates.'

Rentoul narrowed his eyes. 'I wouldn't call myself one of Michelle's associates. On the contrary, really. Like I say, we've run up against each other a few times. Usually to my detriment, if I'm honest. She's pretty much screwed me over a couple of times. A couple more times than I should have allowed.' He smiled. 'And before you ask, knowing the way your police minds work, no, that wouldn't give me a motive for harming her son. I was pissed off with her, but I'm not a murderer.'

'No one's suggesting you are, Mr Rentoul.'

'That right? So why are you here? I'd have thought there were plenty of *associates* of Michelle's you could talk to before you got to me.' His words were laden with irony but he didn't seem agitated or concerned to be speaking to the police.

'As you'd imagine, Mr Rentoul, we're speaking to a lot of people. We're just trying to get as full a picture as possible.'

'I don't imagine you'll need to speak to many people before you begin to get a good idea of her business practices.'

'Meaning?'

'Don't get me wrong. It's hard not to admire her. She's a shrewd operator. But she's also ruthless. And she's not averse to – well, let's say to bending the rules when it suits her. I'm going to be very careful what I say here because I can't prove any of this, but there've been a lot of occasions when Michelle seems to have won contracts against all the odds. It's partly because they do it on the cheap – a bit too cheap, I reckon. They talk a lot of bollocks about streamlining the services and improving efficiencies, but all it amounts to is cutting the service back to the bone and paying people as little as they can get away with. But that doesn't entirely explain some of their successes. There've been a lot of rumours.'

'What are you suggesting? Corruption?'

'Not for me to say. If there's been dodgy practice, that's for you lot to find out. But I know what I've heard. Even about some of the big public sector contracts she's got. All I know is, we've lost a few bids against her that we should have won. She had an inside track. Someone in her pocket.'

'And this has happened a lot?'

'Again, not for me to say. To be honest, Michelle's outgrown us now. We used to come up against her on couriering and transport jobs. But that's only a small part of her business now. She's operating in the big league. I wonder if she's bitten off more than she can chew?'

For all his initial suspicion, Rentoul seemed only too happy to shoot his mouth off about Michelle Wentworth, with just the occasional prompt from Zoe. Maybe he was finding it cathartic to vent his spleen against Wentworth after all these years. 'How do you mean?'

'She's got her fingers in a lot of pies these days, from what I hear. Outsourcing contracts. Back office work. Security work. It wouldn't surprise me if she's managed to tread on some toes. Not everyone's as easy-going as I am.'

'Are you prepared to name any names?' Zoe asked, knowing the answer even before she asked the question.

'I wouldn't even if I could. But this is just grapevine stuff. Michelle's never worried about making enemies. Maybe she's made one too many.' Rentoul leaned back in his office chair, which creaked alarmingly under his weight. 'I'm still intrigued as to why you're here, though. I mean, why here in particular. I hear all the guff about exploring the background, but I still reckon I'd be low on the list of Michelle's contacts. Somebody finger me, did they?'

Zoe offered no response. She had no intention of lying directly to Rentoul, but she was happy for him to think whatever he wanted. It hadn't escaped her attention that Rentoul was echoing the words Ronnie Donahue had spoken about his ex-wife's ethics.

'That's the thing about Michelle,' Rentoul continued. 'She's ruthless. Maybe I've got on the wrong side of her once too often. Even though we haven't had any real contact for a good while, she's probably quite happy to throw me under the bus. The question you have to ask yourself is why is she doing that. Maybe because while you're sitting here talking to me, you're not poking your nose into her business affairs.'

'When was the last time you had any dealings with her?'

'Must be at least a couple of years ago, when we were both pitching for some transport work. She won, needless to say. It was at that point that I decided that, if she was pitching for a job, it wasn't worth trying to compete with her. Luckily, since she's largely moved on to bigger and better things, she's left me to operate a bit further down the food chain. That suits me fine.'

'Okay, Mr Rentoul. That's probably all I need for the moment. Many thanks for your time. I'll let you know if we need to talk to you further. I'll leave you with my contact details. If anything else occurs to you that you think might be relevant to our case, let me know.' She'd taken the interview as far as it would go. Her instinct was to believe what Rentoul had told her. Apart from anything else, he did seem to be operating on a much smaller scale than Wentworth, and nothing obviously suggested he had reason to hold a grudge. He seemed to be successful enough, just not as successful as Michelle Wentworth.

As Zoe got up to leave Rentoul offered a final comment. 'There's only one thing I can tell you. Whatever Michelle might have said to you, whatever smokescreen she's tried to create, it's most likely a load of bollocks. It's her you should be looking at. Lady Muck, with her fancy house and swimming pool. Take a close look at her business. That'll be where the answers lie.'

'We're very grateful for your advice, I'm sure, Mr Rentoul,' Zoe said. 'I'll bear it in mind.'

Chapter Thirteen

'Penny for them,' Peter Hardy said.

'I was thinking about Justin,' Michelle Wentworth said. 'Poor little sod.'

'Expressed with your customary compassion.'

'Fuck off, Peter. You might be a completely heartless bastard, but I'm not.'

'Is that right? That's not the impression I've formed over the years.'

'Fuck right off,' she repeated. 'Or at least as far as the kitchen to get us a drink.'

They were sitting outside by the pool, enjoying the last of the evening sun. Wentworth had been working all afternoon, and Hardy had turned up to run through some figures with her. It was a regular pattern in their relationship. They tended to spend two or three nights a week together. Peter would turn up for some legitimate business reason, but always late in the afternoon. She'd invite him to stay for dinner, and that almost invariably also meant staying the night. That was fair enough, she thought. She was happy to keep the relationship simmering away at that level.

Hardy pushed himself to his feet. 'A G&T or do you want to move on to wine?'

'Wine. There's a nicely chilled Sauvignon Blanc in the fridge. If you want red, there's a bottle open on the side.'

'You know what happened last time you sent in someone to get you a drink, don't you?'

'That's in poor taste, Peter. But pretty much what I'd expect from you.'

'I do my best to maintain standards.' He picked up the glasses and headed into the house.

He wasn't entirely joking, she thought. He'd always had a robust sense of humour, and he'd never been averse to some gentle goading. He seemed generally to recognise how far he could push her before the joke wore thin, but he hadn't tempered his behaviour since Justin's death. She suspected it was deliberate. He was testing her, wanting to see how strong she really was. He knew that at some point soon the police would be back here, digging around, probing into the business. If it came to it, they'd probably use some underhand tricks – emotional manipulation or deliberate provocation – to get her to talk more openly. Peter's jibes now were no doubt intended to prepare her for that, to make sure she was able to take it.

She supposed that was sensible. It was certainly typical of Peter, and that was why he'd been so important to her. He stayed calm, thought one step ahead, always making sure they were as well positioned as possible for whatever was coming.

She looked back over her shoulder towards the house. He was taking a long time, she thought, a pang of anxiety gripping her stomach. She'd never seen herself as the nervous type, but events had left her understandably shaken. In a rare moment of sensitivity, Peter had even asked her if she wanted to stay over at his place. She'd been grateful for the offer, but knew that acceptance would have given him the wrong message. In any case, leaving here would be a form of surrender. Whatever might have happened to Justin, she wasn't going to let anyone drive her out of her own house.

She'd always done her best to minimise her vulnerability here. She supposed that, as a wealthy woman living mostly by herself, she might have chosen a more secure environment. But what sort of a place would that have been? Some penthouse in an upmarket tower block? An anonymous house in a gated estate? She couldn't envisage it. She'd been brought up in a mining town, just over the border in Nottinghamshire, in a tiny backstreet house that was little more than a slightly extended two-up two-down with a tiny courtyard garden at the rear. She couldn't exactly say she was brought up in poverty. She and her two siblings had always had enough to eat, and her single mother had had enough to get by. But her mum had struggled to keep things going after their dad had walked out, and it had been a cramped existence, leavened only by the sight of the fields and distant hills between the rows of houses.

Once in a while, usually on a Sunday afternoon if their mum wasn't working, they'd take a trip out into the Peak District. If the weather was fine, they'd go for a walk, usually somewhere up around Bakewell. She could still remember her awe at the sense of space, standing on a hillside watching the shadows of the clouds scudding across the meadows, the sheep clustered on the hillsides. On rainy days, they might end up in Matlock Bath, where on a Sunday afternoon the main street would be full of bikers, their huge motorbikes lined up by the sides of the road. She and her sisters would be allowed to play in the town's amusement arcades, and they'd end the afternoon with takeaway fish and chips that they'd sit and eat by the river, watching the sunlight playing on the water.

That was how she remembered it, anyway. Her mother had died a few years ago, and she'd more or less lost touch with her sisters, who'd both moved away from the area, apart from the usual exchange of Christmas cards. Those memories were really all she had left of her childhood, and she'd always pledged that, when she had some money behind her – and she'd never doubted that that would happen eventually – she'd reclaim those memories by moving out here. This was where she wanted to be, out here among these hills and dales. She had no intention of letting anyone scare her away, if that really was their intention.

She really was becoming nervous about Peter. He'd been gone only a few minutes, but he was taking longer than it would take simply to pour the wine. After what had happened to Justin, she had no inclination to take any chances.

'Peter?' She made her way back into the kitchen. There was no sign of him in there, though two full glasses of wine were sitting on the table ready to be brought out. 'Peter?' The anxiety gripping her stomach increased.

It felt as if she was reliving the experience with Justin, as if the same moments were being replayed. She walked through the kitchen and into the living room.

Peter was standing in there holding the landline phone. He looked up and blinked at her, as if momentarily unsure who she was. 'Mickey.'

'What is it?'

'The phone was ringing when I came in. The landline, I mean. I almost didn't answer it.'

'I never do. It's usually just junk calls. What is it?'

'One of those automated text things. When somebody sends a text to a landline. Like an auto-generated voice.'

'So what? I get all kinds of crap on that line.'

'This wasn't like that. It was just a stream of abuse. I mean, really vicious abuse. Nasty stuff. Aimed at you. Whoever sent it obviously thought you'd answer the call.'

'So we had an abusive phone call. It's not the first time I've had one, and it probably won't be the last. Usually some disaffected ex-employee who's somehow managed to get hold of the number.'

'This didn't feel like that. It felt real. I mean, like a real warning. It mentioned what had happened to Justin. I mean, went into detail about it. Really unpleasant detail about how he was killed. How many times he was struck. I was glad you weren't listening to it.'

'But that's not possible,' she said. 'I had a call from that Family Liaison woman. They've only just issued the media release about Justin's killing and there's no detail included about exactly how he was killed. She read out the proposed text to me to make sure I was comfortable with it.'

'Which just means that whoever sent that message didn't get the information from the police statement.'

'Christ.'

'Exactly.'

'So why did they do it? What did they want?'

'There was nothing specific. The whole thing was clearly just designed to be unsettling. It certainly succeeded in that. But it said this was just the start.'

'Do you think we should take it seriously?'

'It wasn't a joke, Mickey. Whatever else it might have been. Or if it was, it was in bloody bad taste.' He shook his head, as if still trying to absorb what he'd heard. 'I suppose this kind of thing brings out all kinds of crazies. But they knew what was done to Justin. They knew exactly what was done to him.'

'So what do we do?'

'I think the first thing we do is tell the police.'

It occurred to her that she'd never seen Peter respond like this. Only minutes before she'd been reflecting on how much she valued his level-headedness, his calm in the face of adversity. Now, he looked shocked, as if he didn't know how to proceed. 'Are you sure that's wise?'

She could see him forcing himself to think calmly. 'Normally, I'd hesitate,' he said after a moment. 'I'd be worried about giving the police anything that might make them more interested in us and the business. But I'm not sure we have a choice. We don't know where this is going. We can't handle this on our own. The police might be able to trace the call, or at least intercept future calls. They might be able to offer you some protection.'

Without responding, she walked back through into the kitchen and picked up the glasses of wine. Peter Hardy had followed her, and she turned and handed him his wine before taking a large swallow of her own. 'I don't know, Peter. We don't know what they might do or say. Surely we don't want the police sniffing round any more than we can help.'

'Of course we don't. But let's be honest. If whoever's behind this is in a position to reveal anything damaging to the police, they'll probably do it anyway. We've just got to be careful how we position this. We don't know who this is or what they want. We don't know if it's connected to the current stuff or just some arsehole with a grudge. The phone call suggests this is about you, rather than being linked to anything Justin might have been involved in, but that's hardly a surprise.'

'Thanks, Peter. That really does make me feel a whole lot better about what happened to Justin.'

'I'm just being realistic. Justin's not likely to have got on the wrong side of anyone. But there are plenty of people out there who might have had reason to harm you.'

'You're not making it any better, you know. Are you saying I deserved this?'

'Of course not. You know full well what I mean, Mickey. Nothing justifies what was done to Justin. But there are some crazies out there, and this might just be one of them.'

'Okay. So what do we do?'

'We tell the police. We want them on our side, looking out for your interests. Like I say, they might have the technology to follow this up in a way we can't.' He took another mouthful of his wine. 'Call that Family Liaison woman. She said to call her at any time. So give her a call now. Make her work for her money. That's what you're good at.'

'I'm not sure what I'm good at,' Wentworth said. She felt uncharacteristically conflicted, and it wasn't grief. 'I've spent all my life working my socks off so I could live in a place like this. I was just getting to the point where maybe I could begin to think about winding down a little. I don't mean retirement. But just to get the work–life balance thing a bit more sorted. I thought your deals would be enough to take us to the next level. Maybe take a bit more of a back seat. And then this crap happens.'

'But that's business. You know that better than anyone. Some arsehole's being an arsehole.' Hardy sounded now as if he was trying to raise her spirits.

'That arsehole, whoever he is, killed my son.'

'So he's an even bigger arsehole than they usually are. But you've dealt with arseholes before and you'll deal with this one. It's a blip. A tragic blip in this case, but still just that. You're the best, Mickey. You know that. No one handles this stuff like you do.'

'I've never had to handle anything remotely like this before.'

'I know that. But for years you've had to deal with all the crap the business has caused you. You've come through it. And you'll come through this. And when you've come through to the other side, you can finally do the stuff you've been talking about. Get your life back. There's plenty of time.'

'I suppose.' She picked up her wine and walked back outside. The sun had just set behind the hills before her, the clouds above streaked with vivid crimson. It was already beginning to grow darker, and she could feel a stiff breeze rising from over the moors. What had seemed idyllic less than an hour before now suddenly felt bleak and desolate. She found herself shivering, and couldn't tell how much was due to the evening chill.

Peter was right, though. She could handle this stuff. Even this. Even Justin's killing. She could deal with that and come back stronger. She wasn't about to let any vicious little toerag scare her off.

She pulled out her phone and began to dial Zoe Everett's mobile.

Chapter Fourteen

'I still can't believe it,' Keith Chalmers said. 'The stupid little dickhead.'

'You sound as if you knew who it was.' Sheena Pearson took a sip of her beer and looked around the room, conscious someone might be trying to listen in to the conversation. But it was only early evening and the pub was very quiet. Out here there was very little after-work trade and the place tended to fill up later in the evening. That was one reason she'd picked it when Chalmers had suggested meeting. That, and the fact that it was only a ten-minute walk from her home.

She'd never really felt it appropriate to hold a constituency surgery here, even though Trev, the land-lord, had always been keen on the idea. 'This is where ordinary people come,' he'd said. 'Not your libraries and community halls. Hold your surgery here and they'll come flocking in.' But that was Trev. Always keen to find a new way to sell a few more drinks.

Even so, Sheena did sometimes use the place as a bolthole for meetings that she felt would benefit from a less formal setting than her constituency office. Although she had to be careful about confidentiality, she found that people were often more relaxed and willing to talk openly in this kind of environment.

In Chalmers' case, it was a no-brainer. They'd known each other for a while, and he was always more comfortable with a pint in his hand. She had no concern about some chancer taking a picture of them together. Even by the tabloids, Chalmers was generally seen as a respectable face of the trade union movement, though she wondered whether that perception might change as a result of these latest developments.

She still wasn't entirely sure why Chalmers wanted to speak to her. Maybe he was just seeking moral support. Although he'd done his best still to come across as the voice of moderation, a number of the tabloids had taken what had happened as an opportunity to dust off their well-tried rhetoric, inveighing against the supposed trade union thugs and bully-boys, demanding a clampdown on strikes, picket lines and any other expression of dissent they could come up with. As far as Sheena was concerned, it wasn't much more than the usual froth, but Chalmers seemed to have been rattled by it all.

'Sadly, no, I don't know who it was. If I did, I'd be the first one to shop them, trust me.'

'So much for left-wing solidarity, comrade,' Sheena said, in an exaggerated northern accent.

'Criminal damage hasn't much to do with my definition of left-wing solidarity,' Chalmers snorted.

'I know, Keith. I was teasing. But, no, not funny in the circumstances.'

'Thing is, this really means the other side have won. We've had two incidents now. First, that bloody bottle – and, yes, that was something and nothing but it could easily have turned out differently. And now this stuff with the car. And of course that guy Pallance has played it for all he's worth. Appearing on the local news claiming how shocked and disturbed he was. How it's not the actual damage to the car he's concerned about – although by the way it's going to cost umpteen thousand pounds to put it right – but what it says about the people he's having to deal with. If they're capable of doing this, who knows what they might be capable of? He can't feel safe in his bed. And so on and so on.' He took a mouthful of his beer. 'Really laid it on with a trowel, though he seems to have quietened down since. Especially after the news of Michelle Wentworth's son came out. I wonder whether he was told to can it.'

'It's possible,' Sheena agreed. 'Michelle Wentworth's always keen to get her name in the papers but, as I understand it, only on her terms. She's usually fiercely private about her domestic life. I don't imagine she'd have been keen to have that kind of speculation being bandied about.'

'No, and from what I hear one or two of the papers are already thinking of dropping hints in that direction. I don't think even they really believe there's any kind of link, but it's all grist to the anti-union mill.'

So that was why Chalmers had wanted to talk to her, Sheena thought. He probably wanted to pick her brains about how the police investigation was going. If so, he'd be disappointed. Even if Sheena had known more than she did, she wouldn't have shared it with Chalmers or anyone else. 'The papers will claim anything,' she said.

He immediately confirmed her guess. 'There's no chance of you giving me an inside track on the police investigation, is there? Just so I'm forewarned.'

'Spot on, Keith. No chance at all.'

'No, well, if you don't ask, you don't get.'

'And, in this case, even if you do ask, you still don't get. Just so we're crystal clear. No offence, Keith.'

'None taken. I wasn't seriously expecting you to tell me anything, and I've no desire to put you in a difficult position. I'm just trying to do everything I can to make sure my backside is covered on this one. I still have a suspicion there's something dodgy about what the company's up to.'

'You said that before. That you thought you were being set up. Are you serious about that?'

'I'm serious that I think it's a possibility, yes. Michelle Wentworth's never been one to pull her punches, and she's not averse to the odd underhand trick.'

'So what are you saying? That Pallance trashed his own car?'

Chalmers shook his head. 'Funnily enough, I'm pretty certain that's not the case. I gave Pallance a call as soon as the car story broke. I wanted to let him know that we were as shocked as he was by what had happened, and that we'd cooperate fully with the police and all that. I thought he might not take my call, or that he'd just use it as an opportunity to grandstand. But he wasn't like that. Maybe he's just a good actor. But it felt like he was genuinely shocked himself. Sure, he was angry and he was clearly intending to milk the story for all it's worth. But I didn't get any sense of play-acting. If anything, I got a feeling he was out of his depth. He's basically just a middle manager, after all, and he's been treating all this as a bit of a game. Trying to provoke a reaction. He might even have been set up to do that. But now it's suddenly started to turn real. I could see even the bottle thing had shaken him.'

'So if you're being set up, he's not part of it?'

'Like I say, maybe he's just a good actor. Or I'm more gullible than I think I am. But that might also be how Michelle Wentworth would play it. From my limited dealings with her, she keeps her cards very close to her chest. If this was being set up in some way, she'd want Pallance's reaction to be genuine.'

'All sounds a bit far-fetched, Keith. Would she really go to these lengths?'

'I don't know. She might. There are plenty of stories about her. It wouldn't be the first time we've had to deal with underhand tricks in this business. It's not always people like Wentworth, either. Sometimes it's the really big companies or even some of the public sector bodies who behave worst.' He swallowed the last of his beer.

'You want another?' Sheena said. Chalmers had insisted on buying the first drinks.

Chalmers shook his head. 'Pains me to say it, but best not. I need to be somewhere else later.'

'Next time then,' Sheena said. 'You're probably right. I've still got work to do tonight. Ought to keep a clear head.' Sheena wanted to catch up with some constituency work, but wasn't in any rush. Just before she'd come out to meet Chalmers, Annie had phoned her to say she'd be late home, which was par for the course at this stage in a major investigation.

Chalmers was gazing wistfully into his empty glass. 'No, you're right. I'll leave it at that. What I was going to say, though, is that I hear Michelle Wentworth's at a bit of a crossroads, business-wise.'

'What sort of a crossroads?'

'She's looking to move more into the big league. Up to now, she's built up the business relatively slowly. Started off with the transport and courier stuff. Then she took on transport contracts for bigger firms and generally proved she could manage them – well, she'd say more efficiently, I'd say more cheaply than before. Mainly by finding ways of screwing down the pay and other conditions of the staff, which is why they've tended to run up against opposition when they've taken on unionised environments.'

Sheena wasn't sure where this was going, but she had a feeling they were finally getting to the subject that Chalmers really wanted to talk about. Maybe she should have accepted that second drink after all. 'Go on.'

'The point is she's realised that as a business their real skill lies simply in running things cheaply. They started out in some specific sectors because that was what they knew, but what they do can be extended to almost any type of service, whether it's public or private sector.'

'I'm not sure I'm following.'

'What they're good at is running services cheaply. They don't necessarily run them well or even in the best long-term interests of their clients. And they certainly don't run them in the best interests of their employees. But they save their clients significant money, which is all most CEOs care about in the short term. It doesn't really matter if it's transport or maintenance or even back office processes like IT or finance. It gets outsourced, they take over the contract, they cut out the "fat", as they'd describe it, and run it on the cheap.'

'Do they have the expertise to operate across all those different fields? I mean, call me picky but wouldn't you need IT expertise to run an IT team or finance expertise to run a finance team?'

'You'd think so, wouldn't you? And of course to some extent you do. But that functional expertise will either already be there in the team you take over or if it isn't – or if the knowledgeable individuals move on because they're not prepared to try to run the service for peanuts – you just buy it in. That's not really the point. The point is that you cut staffing, you reduce pay, you make the contracts more flexible, and you cut costs. Yes, the service may well be crap, the staff may be exploited, but the company bosses are happy because they increase their profits. And Michelle Wentworth's happy because she rakes in the loot. Even if the service all goes pear-shaped, she's usually got the client over a barrel because she's taken over all the expertise and it's too late to take it back in-house, so they end up giving her more money to put things right.'

'You're painting a pretty depressing picture.'

'It's modern business. She's not the only one doing it. There are plenty of big supposedly reputable firms doing more respectable versions of the same thing. Wentworth's a bit different because she's basically an old-fashioned wheeler-dealer. A spiv, if you like. She's ruthless and she'll use any trick in the book to get what she wants. I thought at first she might flounder because she's not part of the old boys' club. But the old boys don't know what's hit them. They're not used to dealing with someone who doesn't give a flying one about the business niceties. That's why she's been so successful.'

'So what's the crossroads?'

'This is really just hearsay, you understand. But I keep my ear close to the ground with this kind of stuff, as do my colleagues. We like to have an idea what's going on before it hits our members, not that that's always easy in Wentworth's case. My understanding is that she's pitching for even more sizeable contracts than ever before. She's looking to expand various parts of the business – security, transport, back office stuff, you name it. That carries two risks.'

There was a touch of the theatricals about Keith Chalmers, Sheena thought. Probably one of the qualities that made him effective as a public speaker. He wasn't a rabble-rouser, but he knew how to tell a story, how to play an audience. 'Go on.'

'The first is that by trying to muscle in on this territory she treads on the wrong toes. She's going to come up against some big players. She's far from a pushover, but neither are her competition. They're more genteel and she's probably had them on the back foot, but if it comes to it I reckon they're likely to be as ruthless as she is, if not more.'

Sheena was silent for a moment. 'Ruthless enough to kill her son?'

Chalmers held up his hands. 'I've no idea. I mean, that's not the kind of behaviour I've ever come across in the business world. And I've dealt with some undoubted bastards. But maybe I don't deal with the kinds of people Wentworth does.'

'What sort of people?'

'You tell me. But that brings me to the second risk. To do what she's doing, she needs money. Potentially big money. She can go to the banks, and they'd support her up to a point, but I suspect they'd be reluctant to stump up the kind of funding she'd be looking for without some substantial security. She could look at floating the company, but I reckon that would be the last resort for her. The whole thing's very much her baby, and she doesn't want to relinquish any control. So I'm asking myself where the money's coming from.'

'And?'

'And I don't really have an answer. But the rumour is that there could be fair bit of it sloshing about, and its provenance is – well, let's say uncertain.'

'Why are you telling me this, Keith?'

'I'm not even sure myself, Sheena. Maybe just to get it off my chest. If I go talking to my union colleagues they'll just think it's old Keith chasing shadows again. I'm the old guard now, you know. The younger kids are all graduates with their laptops and iPads.'

'You're not that much older than I am, Keith. You can't get away with the grandad stuff just yet. You've a reason for raising this with me, haven't you?'

'The whole thing's making me feel uncomfortable. I was expecting Michelle Wentworth to try to screw us over. That's the way she works. Not fun, but at least I have an idea of how to deal with her. It's just that I'm getting a sense she's maybe less in control of things than she thinks.'

'I still don't understand why you're sharing this with me, Keith. And don't give me that getting-it-off-your-chest guff. You're not the type to start writing to agony aunts.'

'I just wanted to share. Get it out there. I'm becoming the nervous type in my old age.'

She gazed at him for a moment. He looked more troubled than she'd ever seen him. 'Nervous about what?'

'Nervous about being collateral damage in whatever battle Michelle Wentworth's involved in.' He looked at his watch. 'I'd best be off. All the best to Annie.'

Before she could offer any response, he had risen and was on his way out of the bar. She watched him with a mix of concern and mild amusement. So that was it, she thought. That was what this had all been about. It wasn't that Chalmers had been trying to pick her brains about what was going in the Wentworth investigation – though no doubt he'd have been only too happy to accept any crumbs of information she might have offered him. Instead, it looked as if Chalmers, in his usual slightly oblique manner, was giving her some intelligence he clearly thought might be of use to Annie.

Well, fair enough. In her experience, Chalmers usually talked sense, even if it was occasionally a struggle to understand quite what he was getting at. If he thought there was something in this, there probably was. Annie was no doubt pursuing these kinds of leads already, but it wouldn't do any harm to share what Chalmers had said.

She pushed herself to her feet and picked up the empty glasses to take them back to the bar. Trev was busy polishing glasses and nodded to her as she approached.

'Thanks, Trev.'

'No worries. Always good to have the local MP in here. Raises the tone.'

'Blimey.' Sheena grinned. 'How low is it normally?'

'Well, you've got me behind the bar for a start.' Trev gestured towards the door. 'Your mate there. All right, was he?'

'Think so. Why'd you ask?'

'Dunno.' Trev gave the glass he was working on a final burnish. 'Just thought he looked a bit worried. Was watching him through the window and he scurried across the car park like he had a rocket up his arse. Pardon my French.'

'Maybe just in a hurry,' Sheena said.

'Aye, no doubt.'

She stepped back out into the waning daylight. The shadows of the surrounding trees were lengthening. It was only a short walk back home, but suddenly it felt like a very long way.

Chapter Fifteen

Annie glanced at the car display screen to see who was calling, assuming it would be either Zoe calling to update her or Stuart Jennings wanting his usual evening catch-up. He'd been tied up in a meeting when she'd been called out, so she hadn't had a chance to speak with him before leaving headquarters.

Instead, the name on the display was the last one she wanted to see. She contemplated ignoring the call, but knew that would only be deferring the moment. At least this way, she could make good use of her drive over to Michelle Wentworth's rather than interrupting her evening later. She pressed the button on the steering wheel and took the call on hands-free.

'Evening, Mum. How are you doing?'

'If you called me more often you'd know how I was doing.'

'I've been busy, Mum. You remember that experience?'

'You don't know what busy means. If you ever make it into a really senior job, you'll know how it really feels.'

Touché, Mum, Annie thought. An effective double put-down. Annie's mother, Margaret, had been an Assistant Chief in the force until her retirement a few years earlier. She had strong views on most subjects, but in particular could offer unlimited insights into how and why policing had been much tougher in her day. 'What can I do for you, Mum?'

'Are you in the car?'

'Yes, I'm in the car. Not finished work yet.'

'You need to learn to work smarter rather than harder.' Margaret spoke as if offering some invaluable wisdom.

'I'll remember that.'

'I thought you'd want to know that I've done an interview for one of the national newspapers today.'

Annie's hands tightened on the steering wheel. Since her retirement, Margaret Delamere had developed a reputation for herself as a media pundit. A gob on a stick, as Sheena called her. It had initially happened accidentally, with the local media seeking her views as a former senior officer on criminal justice issues. The journalists and reporters who consulted her had quickly realised that her outspoken views were popular with readers and viewers, who saw her as a breath of fresh air compared with the usual cautious police spokesperson. For her part, Margaret had soon twigged that it didn't much matter what she said, as long as she said it in a forthright, no-nonsense manner. She was rarely asked to give evidence for any of her more controversial assertions, and she expressed them with absolute confidence.

'That's great, Mum,' Annie said wearily. 'What were you talking about this time? How policing's now a pushover compared to your day? Why the force is full of dead wood that just needs cutting out? Why police officers are overpaid? Am I getting close?'

'You think you're so funny, Annie Delamere. No, I was talking about all this trade union thuggery.'

Annie felt her heart sink even further. 'What trade union thuggery?'

'Look, Annie, I know you have a sentimental view of these left-wing groups, but even you can't excuse criminal damage. Serious criminal damage like that.'

'Like what?' Annie knew exactly what her mother was talking about, but she wanted to hear her actually say the absurd words.

'That place near Matlock. Smashing up a car. They're just taking the law into their own hands. They think they can get away with doing whatever they like.'

'We don't even know who did it yet, Mum.'

'Those union thugs. Who else?'

'We don't know that, Mum. Not yet. And whoever it was, you'll be astonished to learn that it wasn't officially sanctioned by the union. This was just some nasty piece of work deciding to smash up a car.'

Margaret offered a derisive snort in return. 'Of course it wasn't *officially* sanctioned by the union. That doesn't mean they weren't behind it. It's nod and a wink stuff, isn't it? That's how it works.'

'Is this how you approached investigations?' That was arguably a slightly low blow. Margaret had spent most of her career in operational roles and had transferred to CID only for a relatively brief period. Margaret had never explicitly said so, but Annie suspected her mother hadn't enjoyed detective work and probably hadn't been particularly good at it, which is why she'd moved on as soon as she had the relevant experience under her belt. Whatever her other talents, Margaret had always been very skilled at looking after her own career prospects.

'It doesn't sound as if the police made much progress with this one,' Margaret parried. 'If you still don't know who did it.'

'It's not my case, Mum, so I can't comment. Is that all you called me about? Just to let me know that you're the toast of Fleet Street?'

'You can laugh all you like. But my opinions are listened to.'

More's the pity, Annie thought. Margaret was entitled to her opinions, but she'd learned to play to the crowd. Her populist views went down all too well with a certain kind of voter – small 'c' conservatives who longed for some imaginary past when there were always bobbies on the beat, crime was non-existent, and the country hadn't gone to the dogs. Margaret did genuinely sympathise with some of those views, but she was an experienced enough copper to know it was mostly nonsense. The world had changed and the world of crime and policing had changed with it. The police were, by and large, doing a decent job in dealing with often unprecedented challenges with ever more limited resources. It was bad enough listening to ill-informed politicians and commentators banging on about the force's supposed failings. It was another thing to hear those views endorsed by someone who really knew better.

'You do realise this isn't going to make my life any easier, Mum?'

'I don't see how this affects you.' Margaret's tone implied that Annie's well-being was, in any case, no concern of hers.

'Because the company in question happens to be owned by Michelle Wentworth. And I'm running the investigation into her son's death.'

There was a moment's silence, suggesting that for once Margaret had been taken by surprise. 'If you phoned me more often, I'd have known that.'

Well recovered, Annie thought. Out loud, she said, 'It's a high-profile enough case as it is. If people realise my own mother is shooting her mouth off about it in the tabloids, what do you think's going to happen?'

'I was hardly shooting my mouth off.' For once, Margaret sounded almost defensive. 'I was giving them the benefit of my experience and expertise.'

Which is bugger all in relation to a case like this, Annie thought.

'Anyway,' Margaret went on, 'it wasn't one of the tabloids. It was one of the so-called broadsheets. Though most of them are tabloids too these days, I suppose.' She made it sound as if even this was somehow Annie's fault.

Annie supposed that was some small consolation. At least her mother's contribution wasn't going to be plastered luridly on the front page of some red-top. But she imagined it would still be given unwarranted prominence, wherever it appeared. She could already envisage the conversation she'd be having with Stuart Jennings the next morning.

'Stuart will probably take me off the case because of this.' Annie was conscious her tone sounded more self-pitying than she'd intended. It never paid to show any weakness in her mother's presence.

'I don't see why he'd do that. Assuming you're up the job in the first place, that is.' The implication was unmistakeable.

Annie took a breath. 'That's not the point, Mum, as you well know. Stuart can't afford any suggestion of a conflict of interest. So with me and Sheena—'

She realised straight away she'd made a tactical error. 'Oh, yes, of course,' Margaret interrupted. 'I'd forgotten about *Sheena*.'

'I just meant—'

'I know exactly what you meant. She's obviously going to be in the pocket of the trade unions, isn't she? So there must be a suspicion you'd soft-pedal any accusations against them. However unjustified.' The last two words were thrown in apparently as an afterthought.

Annie could feel her anger rising. She was never sure if her mother behaved like this on purpose or if she just couldn't help herself. Either way, their conversations too often ended up with Annie losing her temper. 'I've got to go now, Mum,' she said, biting back the response she really wanted to give. 'I've just reached my destination. Speak soon.' She ended the call before her mother could reply.

That wasn't quite true. She was still a mile or so from Michelle Wentworth's house. She wasn't even sure whether she really ought to be here. Perhaps it would have been better to have left this to Zoe. She wanted to give Zoe as much opportunity as possible to build up a relationship with Wentworth.

But Zoe had told her that Wentworth had seemed genuinely shaken by what had happened, and Annie knew that, given the increasing sensitivity of the case, Stuart Jennings would want her to front this up personally. In the end, she'd decided to detour via Wentworth's house on her way home.

She turned off the main road and followed the winding B-road to Wentworth's house. It was a glorious setting on an evening like this, the rolling hills rich with shadows in the thickening twilight, but she was conscious of how remote it was. She'd experienced the sense of isolation in her own home when Sheena had been in danger some months before, but this place was far more cut off. It was several miles even from the nearest village, set in grounds of several acres. If there really was a threat to Michelle Wentworth, this was not the ideal place to be living, whatever its other charms.

She turned off the road into the entrance to the house. This time, the external gates had been left closed but, as she drew up in front of them, they opened slowly before her car. Annie glanced up and saw the CCTV camera pointing down. Clearly Zoe had forewarned Wentworth that she was coming.

At least the security here was generally strong, Annie thought. Not that that had done much to help Justin Wentworth. The team had now checked out all the CCTV footage from the day of his death and although there were a number of cameras around the site, including the one on the gate, they'd found nothing relevant to the killing. That might mean the killer had checked out the site prior to the killing, so they were now painstakingly working through the footage from the preceding days in the hope of finding some indication of an earlier intruder.

Zoe's car was standing in front of the house. Annie pulled up behind it and climbed out into the warm evening air. Although the grapevine on the side of Wentworth's house was just beginning to turn crimson, autumn still felt far away. That could change overnight if the weather broke, but for the moment it still felt like high summer. She walked over to the large front door and pressed the bell.

After a few moments, the door opened and Peter Hardy peered out at her, the door still held in place by a secure-looking chain. She'd already noted that there was a spyhole in the door, in addition to the CCTV cameras. Clearly, Hardy at least was taking the risk seriously. 'DI

Delamere,' he said, as though confirming her identity to himself. He closed the door and then reopened it fully. 'Please come in.'

She followed him through into the living room, where Michelle Wentworth and Zoe were sitting together on the sofa. Hardy squeezed himself on to the sofa too, next to Wentworth, and put what was presumably intended to be a comforting arm around her. Annie detected a momentary look of irritation on Wentworth's face, as if Hardy had presumed too much. She sat herself down on an armchair opposite. 'I'm very sorry to hear about the call. It must have been a shock.'

'I'm just glad it was Peter who answered the phone. I don't know how I'd have coped. Not after...'

'Of course. You say it was an automated message?' Annie said. She'd agreed with Zoe that it would be better for Annie to focus on the investigative issues, leaving Zoe to provide any emotional support that might be needed. That might help Zoe to get her feet a little further under the table here.

'Yes,' Peter Hardy said. 'I've sometimes had that kind of message when someone's accidentally sent a text to my landline. I don't know if it was that or someone who'd used some device to digitise their voice.'

'Can you remember what they said?'

'Not perfectly. It was very unexpected, so I wasn't fully taking it in. But I had a go at writing down roughly what was said. To be honest, I didn't want Michelle to have to hear it.' He pointed to a notepad on the coffee table between them. 'It's in there.'

Annie opened the notepad. It was unused apart from Hardy's neat handwriting on the first page. She skimmed through what he'd written and looked up. 'I see what you mean. Very detailed and very accurate.'

'Nasty stuff, isn't it? Especially the stuff about Justin.'

'Very.'

'The question is how could they have known so much about his death,' Wentworth said. 'DS Everett said you'd only released a short media statement.'

Interestingly, she didn't sound unduly fazed either by the fact or the content of the call, Annie thought. Zoe had felt Wentworth had seemed genuinely shaken earlier, so either she had managed to regain some kind of emotional equilibrium in the meantime or she was just trying to maintain her usual impassive front. 'That's right. Just the very basic facts. No details of the killing itself.'

'So if whoever called had those details...'

Annie nodded. Wentworth wasn't stupid. There was no point in trying to sugar-coat any of this. 'Either the information was leaked to them in some way, or they had direct knowledge of the murder.'

'Is a leak possible?' Hardy asked.

'I'd like to say no,' Annie said. 'But I'm afraid it's always possible. I take it that neither of you have given the details to anyone. I'm sorry – I have to ask.'

Wentworth shook her head. 'Why would we? We've spoken to various relatives and friends about his death, but not in any detail.'

'I don't think I've spoken to anyone, except in a couple of cases when Michelle asked me to,' Hardy said. 'And again not in any detail.' He gestured towards the notepad. 'Certainly not in that kind of detail. But you're saying it could have leaked from your side?'

She was prepared for a belligerent response from them, but there was no point in denying it. 'As I say, it's not

123

impossible. It shouldn't happen, of course, and the consequences would be severe for anyone found doing it. But I can't pretend we don't have leaks. You can imagine – we have a large team involved in the investigation. Not just police officers but all kinds of roles. We've occasionally had instances of people deliberately selling information to the media. But more commonly, it's just someone who shoots their mouth off inappropriately to their family or their friends. We'll look into that, of course.'

'But why would anyone make a call like that?' Hardy said. 'As some sort of joke?'

'Again, it happens, I'm afraid. There are some sick people out there. People who get their kicks from trying to frighten people in this kind of situation. Or, yes, someone's warped idea of a black joke. Any of that is possible. But my advice is that, until we know differently, we take it seriously.'

'You think they mean it?' Wentworth said. 'Those threats?'

'We have to assume they might. We have to work on the assumption that the message is meant to be taken seriously, not just some kind of hoax.' Annie wondered whether Wentworth had already worked out the implications of what she was saying. 'If that's the case, then it does suggest that Justin's death was aimed at you, Mrs Wentworth.'

'I think we'd come to that conclusion already,' Wentworth said.

'We still have to keep an open mind,' Annie said. 'Murders are committed sometimes for the most unlikely of motives. But it does seem probable that you're the target here. I'm sorry if that sounds a little brutal, but we have to face the reality. What's not clear to me is what the threat's actually about. It's couched as a warning, but there's nothing about what they actually want.' She turned to Hardy. 'You're sure that's all they said?'

Hardy seemed to hesitate. 'I don't pretend I got it down verbatim. I wrote that after the event. At the time, I was just taken aback by it, so I might not have taken in everything. But I don't think I missed anything important. I see what you mean, though. It's very explicit, but it's also a bit – I don't know, enigmatic, I suppose. As if we're supposed to know what they're talking about.'

'And you don't?'

'Not a clue,' Hardy said. 'I can't even guess. I presume it's likely to be connected with the business in some way, but it could be anything.'

'Can you trace the call?' Wentworth asked.

'We should be able to through the phone company, but it'll take time. And if it was sent from a mobile, unless we're dealing with someone really amateur, it'll most likely just be an anonymous pay-as-you-go phone. We can put a trace on future calls but I wouldn't be optimistic of achieving much.'

'So what precisely are you doing?' Hardy said in an exasperated manner. 'About Justin's killing, I mean.'

Annie had been half-expecting some belligerence from Hardy. She still had the feeling that, for whatever reasons, he and Wentworth were keen to deflect and confuse the investigation, and their suggestions of potential suspects had so far proved unproductive. She wouldn't be entirely surprised if their next tactic was to attack her and the supposed lack of progress in the investigation. With that in mind, she'd already agreed that Zoe should use this visit as an opportunity to provide Wentworth with a detailed update based on their team debrief earlier in the afternoon.

Annie still thought it unlikely that Michelle Wentworth had killed her own son, and forensics had so far produced no evidence to indicate otherwise. But Hardy might be a different matter, if his apparent arrival just before the police's had been stage-managed. It was even possible that tonight's call had been faked. They had only Hardy's word on the details of the call.

'It's still early days,' she said. 'Zoe will give you a more detailed update. But we're pursuing numerous lines of enquiry. We're interviewing potential suspects systematically. We're in the process of identifying any potential witnesses who were in the vicinity at the relevant time. We're reviewing the forensics and all the pertinent CCTV and traffic camera footage. We're looking at burglaries and housebreakings in the area around the relevant dates, and talking to some of our usual suspects.' She was conscious that this sounded thin, even to her own ears. The truth was that, in the absence of an obvious suspect, this stage of a major inquiry was often little more than the painstaking accumulation of data.

Slightly to her surprise, Hardy seemed satisfied by her response. 'I'm assuming you're working through the lists of names we gave you?'

'We are, of course.' As well as a list of her competitors, Wentworth had also provided them with a list of supposedly disaffected employees. Annie suspected that the list comprised only a tiny subset of those who'd been adversely affected by Wentworth's business tactics, focusing on those who'd actually taken her to employment tribunals or actively protested against what she'd done. There was another small group who already had police records because they'd pushed their protests too far – usually by sending threatening communications or engaging in some form of mild vandalism. The team was slowly working through this list, but again so far had identified no credible suspects. Most appeared to have moved on with their lives. 'We're interviewing all of them, yes.' She paused. 'On that topic, can I ask you about the recent incidents at your operation near Matlock?'

Wentworth looked up, clearly surprised by the question. 'What incidents?'

'I understand your business has been involved in some industrial action, and that there was some issue of criminal damage.'

Annie noted that Wentworth exchanged a glance with Hardy, though she couldn't read its significance. It was Hardy who responded. 'Oh, that. Something and nothing, really. It's a contract we've recently taken over, and there's been an ongoing dispute about the way the employees have been affected. It's the usual story. We've every sympathy for the individuals involved but at the end of the day you have to ensure you have a viable business.'

Not to mention a large house in the country with a pool, Annie thought. 'I understand there was a car damaged.'

Hardy nodded. 'Company car belonging to the manager. Appalling. But it's a young workforce there. We think it's probably just some young hothead who went too far. The dispute's very unfortunate. We normally try our hardest to avoid that kind of thing, but we also like to delegate those kinds of matters to the local management. In this case, it appears to have got out of hand, but we're dealing with it now. If you think it might be connected to

Justin, then I'd suggest you talk to your colleagues working on the case.'

'Yes, of course. I only became aware of the incident this afternoon from the piece in the *Evening Telegraph*, so just thought I'd ask while I was here.'

'Yes, I saw that piece,' Hardy said. 'Very unfortunate. Not really the publicity we'd have wanted. Especially at a time like this.'

An interesting comment, Annie thought, given that the news story had seemed largely to be based on a lengthy interview with the manager of the site. Hardy seemed keen to bury the story, no doubt leaving the local manager to carry the can for everything that had happened. Her impression from her background research into Wentworth was that, in general, she was only too happy to parade her ruthless approach to business and employment relations, so it was odd they seemed so keen to downplay this one.

'It may well be another lead for us to follow up, at least,' Annie said. 'Meanwhile, I'll see what I can do about increasing police protection for you. It's always challenging because resources are so tight, but I'll do my best. We'll look at getting the phone company to put a trace on your phone, just in case it throws up something useful. We'll need to get your permission for that, but I'll sort the details. If you do get more calls, note the times and give us as much information as you can. I don't know if it'll get us very far, but it's all worth trying.' She looked around. 'From what I've seen of this place, the security's pretty tight, but I'll get one of our experts to have a look round and see if they can advise anything additional.

'I'll leave Zoe to talk you through in more detail where we're up to with the investigation to date, and the various lines of enquiry we're pursuing. If there's anything more you think we could or should be doing, or if there's anything else you need from us, just let Zoe know. I'll leave you to it if that's okay. I can find my own way out, I'm sure.' She had already risen to her feet, not wanting to give them a chance to object. 'Just be reassured, Mrs Wentworth, that we're putting everything we can into this. We'll find whoever killed your son.'

Chapter Sixteen

Annie's short drive home was punctuated by telephone calls. First, as she'd been expecting, she had a call from Stuart Jennings wanting, in his words, 'a quick catch-up'. 'I've just had yet another call from the Chief,' he said. 'Just to make sure we're on top of things, you know. I take it we are?'

'We're doing everything we can, Stuart.'

'So what's the story with Wentworth's threatening call?'

'It was a fairly nasty one.' She updated him on her meeting with Wentworth and Hardy. 'So three possibilities. One is that this really was the killer. The second is that it was just some sick hoaxer who'd managed somehow to get hold of the details of the killing—'

'Which would imply a leak at our end. Shit.'

'Quite. And the third is that Hardy either made the whole thing up or engineered the call himself.'

'Which would imply what? That he's covering something up? Trying to distract us from other lines of enquiry?'

'Or that he's trying to protect Wentworth, if we accept her as a potential suspect.'

'And your guess would be?'

'I don't know. Something smells wrong about the whole thing. I don't fully trust them, but I'm not sure what game they're playing.' She was silent for a moment as she negotiated the traffic roundabout that brought her back onto the main road heading south. 'Even the transcript of the call felt odd. It was very explicitly threatening but then strangely vague about the aim of the threat. Assuming the call was genuine, I wonder if Hardy deliberately omitted something.'

'Always worth listening to your instincts on something like that. If that's what you're feeling, I'd stick with it.'

'I'm just keeping an open mind.'

'Speaking of open minds,' Jennings went on, 'I hear your mother's been shooting her mouth off again.'

The grapevine had clearly operated even more quickly than Annie had expected. 'So I understand.'

'Pity you didn't let me know in advance.'

'You think she gives me any notice? I only found out myself just before I arrived at Wentworth's. I understand she's been going on about the trade unions.'

'Yeah. I just had a call from Gerry on the Comms team to give me the heads-up. The article is going in tomorrow's paper and on the website tonight, so they sent it to us for comment. In fairness, it's at least not one of the tabloids, and it's initially pitched as a general interview. But it's clear the interviewer's really just winding her up to talk about her usual hobby horses. It's presented as if she's the one who raises the Matlock case just so she can pontificate about the unions, but I wonder if she was deliberately led down that route. Your mother doesn't make the link herself but the article goes on to mention Wentworth and her son's death, mainly just to increase the outrage quotient. It doesn't imply any direct connection between the two, but that might just be because they're treading cautiously round the libel laws.'

This sounded faintly paranoid to Annie, but she could understand why Jennings was concerned. 'No mention of me, I'm assuming.'

'No, thank Christ. That really would be the icing on the cake. But we could do without this, Annie.'

'Tell me about it. If you can suggest any ways of controlling my mother, I'm all ears.'

'I know it's not your fault, but between your mother and Sheena…'

'I'm the one who's between my mother and Sheena. I don't need to be told about it.'

'Okay. But I meant what I said. If we get to the point where it looks like you risk becoming the story, I'm going to have to take you off the Wentworth inquiry.'

'I understand that, Stuart. I've no desire to be the centre of attention on this.'

'So we need some progress. Soon.'

'Understood.' She started to say something more but then realised that, in his familiar manner, Jennings had already ended the call. If nothing else, she supposed, it usually meant that he had the last word.

She was turning off the main road on to the single-track road that provided a shortcut home when the phone rang again. At first she thought that Jennings must have thought of something else to chastise her about, but then she realised it was Zoe calling.

'Hi, Zo. How'd it go?'

'Bit weird, actually. That's why I'm calling.'

'Go on.'

'I ran through the update like we'd agreed, gave them a bit more detail on the lines of enquiry, all that stuff. That was fine as far as it went. But the odd thing about it was that they didn't seem too interested. They made all the right noises, but neither of them seemed really to be engaged with it. Michelle in particular seemed to be thinking about something else, as if her mind was elsewhere.'

'Maybe she just hasn't engaged with it yet and is just still in denial about it.'

'I wondered that. But it wasn't like any other response I've encountered. Usually, it's the opposite – people who obsess over the detail of the inquiry, or who keep telling you what you're doing wrong or that you're not doing enough. There was none of that. Hardy asked a few questions but it felt as if he was just going through the motions. It wasn't just that, though. I had a general sense they were uncomfortable about me being there. Hardy in particular. Once I'd finished the update, he seemed to be almost on the point of actually getting my coat for me. I tried to spin it out a bit, have a bit of a more general conversation with Michelle, but he wasn't having it. He was very polite, but I wasn't left in much doubt he wanted me out and pronto.'

'You think they've got something to hide?'

'That was the way it felt. But why report the call at all if that's the case?'

'I don't know. Perhaps as a way of taking the focus off Wentworth herself,' Annie suggested. 'We may have to look at them again as potential suspects. But my gut's still telling me it's something else they're concealing. Which might or might not be connected with Justin's killing.'

'I don't know how much I'm likely to succeed in building up any kind of rapport with Michelle. But I did have the sense she might welcome someone she could talk to.'

'Which might be why Hardy's so intent on keeping you at arm's length,' Annie said. 'Maybe he thinks there's a danger of her saying too much.'

'All the more reason for me to keep trying to spend time with her. I'll have to try to find a period when Hardy's not around. Maybe in the daytime.'

'Worth a try,' Annie agreed. 'We definitely need to know more about both of them. I've got someone checking out their backgrounds, business dealings and suchlike, but we may need to dial that up a bit.'

'I wish I had something more concrete. I hope we're not wasting our time.'

'It's worth it, one way or another. That's why I wanted you in there. The more insights we can get into those two, the better. Like Stuart says, it's always best to trust your instincts.'

'Stuart said that? It doesn't sound like him.'

'No, took me by surprise as well.' Annie laughed. 'I thought at first he was taking the piss. And maybe he was. But you and me, we can take him at his word, can't we?'

Chapter Seventeen

'I'd like to say I've been cooking up a storm waiting for your return,' Sheena said. 'But I haven't. Though I did get as far as turning the oven on.'

'Oh, and there I was expecting a gourmet feast ready and waiting for me. Thought it was the least I deserved after taking calls from both Stuart Jennings and my mother in the past hour.'

'Blimey. I don't know which of those two is harder work,' Sheena said. 'No, I do. It's your mother. What did she want?'

'The usual. First, to remonstrate with me for not calling her more often. Second, to remind me of all the reasons why I don't call her more often.' Annie was hovering in the doorway of the living room, preparing to head upstairs to exchange her work clothes for something more comfortable. Sheena was sitting on the sofa with her laptop, working through her usual backlog of correspondence.

'That must have been nice.'

'A joy, as ever. And she's got some interview in one of tomorrow's nationals.'

'Oh, great. Why do they give her airspace?'

'Because she's good copy. Says what people want to hear.'

'Populist crap, you mean.' Sheena shook her head. 'Sorry. I shouldn't bad-mouth your mother like that.'

'Bad-mouth away. Like her, you're only saying what people want to hear. What I want to hear, anyway. You'll be interested in this one, because she's attacking those thuggish trade unions. The vandals and hooligans on the picket line.'

'Oh, Christ. Is that about that thing in Matlock?'

'In part. That sort of thing plays right into her hands.'

'Tell me about it. One of the reasons I was late back was that I went for a drink with that union guy, Keith Chalmers. He's furious about it. He spends years cultivating an image of moderation and good sense, and then some idiot goes and does something like this. Actually, he told me one or two things that might be of interest to you. You go and get changed, and I'll stick in a frozen pizza to make up for my lack of kitchen-storminess. Then I can share with you the wisdom of Comrade Keith.'

Fifteen minutes later, they were both back in the living room, Annie now in jeans and T-shirt, with a sliced pizza and two glasses of red wine on the coffee table between them. 'It's not much,' Sheena acknowledged. 'But it is pizza and wine.'

'Which is pretty much exactly what I needed. So what did Chalmers have to say?'

'He seems to be in a slightly paranoid frame of mind at the moment. First, he's got a suspicion that the union might be being set up. That there might be ringers among the local membership who are deliberately out to cause trouble.'

'Is that likely?'

'Who knows? There've always been some shady doings in industrial disputes. Look at the miners' strike. All sorts of rumours about MI5 involvement and the like.'

'And a lot of accusations levelled at the police,' Annie said. 'Some of them probably justified. There were more people like my mother at the top in those days. But there's a difference between something of that kind of national significance and some local barney, surely?'

'Oh, sure. But if there are vested interests involved, who knows what dirty tricks people might play? Let's face it, Michelle Wentworth doesn't exactly have a squeaky-clean reputation on such matters.'

'She seems to have a reputation for ruthlessness. Whether she'd go as far as that, I've no idea. She's probably got other things on her mind at the moment, anyway. When I mentioned the damage to the car to her, she pretty much just dismissed it. I didn't get the impression she was wanting to exploit it.'

'No, that's fair. But if Chalmers is right, this would all have been arranged a while ago. I imagine her priorities have probably changed now. I can imagine that winning some tawdry industrial relations battle might seem relatively unimportant if your son's just been murdered.'

Annie leaned forward to take another slice of pizza. 'So you think there might be something in what Chalmers is saying?'

'It's possible. Tempers can run high in disputes, but that kind of serious vandalism's fairly unusual. I guess we might never know.'

'I assume Chalmers has told the police about his suspicions?'

'Yes, though I don't think he's pushed it too far in case they think he's protesting too much. Last thing he wants is to be labelled as a conspiracy theorist.' She laughed. 'That's the thing about conspiracies. There must be some real ones, but we're all too afraid to say so in case people think we're cranks. Remember that obsessive guy they were trying to frame for my kidnapping?'

'Although it turned out he was probably saner than anyone else,' Annie pointed out.

'That's the point. It's how the conspirators get away with it.' She paused to take a sip of her wine. 'But that wasn't really the most interesting thing Keith said to me. He was telling me about Wentworth's business dealings. I can't vouch for the accuracy of what he said, but I've generally found him a reliable source of gossip. Anyway, I thought it might be of interest to you.'

Annie shifted uncomfortably. 'I'm not sure. I'm always wary of listening to unsubstantiated gossip, and I think we need to be careful what information we share, given Jennings' concerns.'

Sheena looked mildly offended. 'I'm only trying to help.'

Annie sighed and reached out to take Sheena's hand. 'Sorry, Shee. I'm just being oversensitive. Too much time talking to my mum and to Jennings. I do want to hear what you've got to say. Wentworth's business dealings have been troubling me.'

Sheena gazed back at her for a moment, then grinned and squeezed Annie's hand. 'Okay, apology accepted. And, yes, it is just unsubstantiated gossip. But Keith reckons they're looking to expand the business substantially. They want to pitch for large-scale contracts in a way they haven't before. The way I understand it, Wentworth's grown the company quickly but it's all been essentially organic growth. They're looking for the next step to be a huge one.'

'That fits with what I understand,' Annie said. 'I'm having one of our business analysts take a look at the company.' As she rarely talked this kind of shop with Sheena, she'd been uneasy about this conversation. But she wasn't intending to say anything that wasn't already in the public domain. If necessary, they could follow the appropriate protocols to carry out further digging into Wentworth's business affairs, but so far Annie had seen no justification for that. 'He had a look at its published accounts for the last few years. Reckoned it was impressive growth, but mostly relatively low-risk. They don't seem to be saddled with any large debt. In fact, they've always been pretty cash-rich, funding their expansion from their own profits. Whatever else she might be, Michelle Wentworth's a smart businesswoman.'

'From what Keith said, the point is that they're looking to change that business strategy to fund some really big expansion. They know they're good at what they do – even if, from Keith's perspective, what they do is mainly screw over their employees – and they want to leverage that into something much bigger.'

'Does he know what kind of things?'

'If he does, he was keeping it to himself. He said they were looking to expand various areas of their business. He mentioned transport, security, back office work…'

'Back office work?' Annie tended to switch off in the face of managerial jargon. She heard too much of it at work, especially from Stuart Jennings.

'Admin, I suppose. These companies are supposed to be able to streamline all that paperwork and processing stuff. Increased digitisation, all that guff.'

'This is why they're building the barricades in Matlock?'

'Pretty much. It's rare for Wentworth to take on a unionised workforce, although she doesn't have much choice when she takes on public sector contracts. Even when she does she's generally been canny enough to deny the unions much room for manoeuvre. I'm still not sure whether she just allowed this one to slip through the net, or whether she was deliberately looking to make an example of them. Hence Keith's concerns about dirty tricks.' She paused to take another slice of pizza. 'Keith's point was that this new business strategy carried a couple of implications. First, that it might mean that for the first time they're treading on the toes of some really big players. The second is that they're not going to be able to fund this level of expansion simply through their own profits.'

'So where are they going to get the investment?'

'That was another area where Keith was characteristically vague. He just said that there's a lot of money sloshing about and that its provenance is uncertain. I think I'm quoting more or less verbatim.'

'He's suggesting it's illegal money in some way?'

'Keith never allows himself to be too explicit. A master of deniability. But I'm guessing so.'

'That's very interesting. I probably shouldn't be telling you this, but I've had a definite sense that Wentworth's been keeping something back from us. My instinct is that it's not something directly to do with her son's death – though of course I could be wrong about that – but something else. Something like this would definitely fit the bill.'

'All I'm doing is passing on what Keith told me. I can't vouch for its accuracy, but from my limited dealings with

Keith he's not one to make these kinds of accusations lightly. I wasn't initially sure why he wanted to see me today, but my guess is that he wanted me to pass this on to you.'

'He could have called us direct.'

'That's not Keith's style. Not with something like this. In any case, what would he have said? Presumably, he's got no hard evidence for any of this. And with what's happened in Matlock it would have just sounded like another attack on Wentworth.'

'Maybe that's all it is.'

'It's possible. That wouldn't fit my experience of dealing with Keith, though. I wouldn't exactly say he always plays straight. He's too much of a canny game-player for that. But I don't think he generally just plucks stuff out of the air. There's likely to be something in this.'

'I'll get someone to have a closer look at Wentworth's business dealings. It's a tricky one because I don't want us to get deflected by something that might have nothing to do with her son's murder. On the other hand, we still don't have any clue what the motive for that might have been. If it really was linked in some way to his mother, this might be a good place to start looking. Thanks.' She smiled sheepishly. 'And sorry if I was a bit dismissive about it at first.'

Sheena leaned over and kissed Annie on the cheek. 'You're forgiven. Or you will be when you pour me another glass of wine. And don't thank me. Thank Keith. Or rather don't, because he'll probably just deny he ever said anything. That's Keith. Tosses just enough pebbles into the pond to create a few waves, then disappears back into the undergrowth.'

Annie smiled. 'Okay. Well, the next step, I suppose, is to see if I can find anything that's been washed up on the shore.'

Chapter Eighteen

It was another warm evening, only the softest of breezes drifting in off the moorland. The summer's flowers around the garden were beginning to die off, but the gardener had been skilful in creating a display that, in some form, lasted most of the year round, and there was still a rich, slightly heady scent in the air. A thin sickle moon hung in the sky ahead of her, and the first stars were starting to appear.

Michelle Wentworth knew that, if she was smart, she wouldn't be sitting here all alone. The security here was good but she knew it wasn't impregnable. If someone really wanted to break in, she imagined they probably could.

Even so, she'd felt that being here alone was still preferable to the alternative. Peter Hardy had made it more than clear that he'd have liked to stay the night, and initially she'd been tempted by the idea. She'd grown accustomed to him being here and sharing her bed when it suited her. But she didn't really want him here all the time. It wasn't entirely personal. Much of the time, she simply preferred her own company. She had little interest in Peter – or anyone else – sexually, though Peter fulfilled a physical need in that respect. And outside of their business dealings, she had only limited interest in him in any other way.

She was happier on her own. That was one reason, even though she felt a little guilty about it now, why she'd found Justin's presence so irksome. He could be irritating and he was always lazy, but that wasn't really the issue. The problem was that, even if he'd been the most perfect son imaginable, she still wouldn't have wanted him here all the time.

She wasn't even sure whether she actually liked herself or her own company. But she understood herself. She knew what she wanted and needed, and she could trust herself. She wasn't going to let her herself down. She wasn't going to screw herself over. She wasn't going to try to take advantage of herself.

She wasn't sure she could say those things about anyone else.

Not even about Peter Hardy. Especially not about Peter, just at the moment.

She had taken Peter on board and allowed him much further into her life than anyone else, because she'd come to trust him. She'd trusted his expertise. She'd trusted his judgement. And she'd trusted – well, if not exactly his integrity, at least his loyalty to her. It had taken her a long time to build up that trust. He'd been working with her for ten years or more, gradually rising in her estimation from being just another lawyer to someone with a stake in the business and her most trusted advisor.

She told herself that none of that had changed. She still had no strong reason to doubt his ability, his judgement and perhaps not even his loyalty. Since Justin's death, he hadn't always told her what she wanted to hear, but he'd generally told her what was in her best interests. Her immediate instinct after Justin's death had been to call Peter and she'd had no cause to regret that decision. Peter had calmed her down, planned out what they were going to say to the police, made sure everything was done by the book, and directed the police towards areas other than their own current business dealings. She couldn't fault him on any of that.

But the doubts had been there for a while, one way or another. And they were gradually growing. She didn't trust him as much as she had.

She wasn't sure she was even thinking clearly. Perhaps she was still just in shock at Justin's death. She knew she hadn't fully processed what had happened. She'd simply found a way to deal with the event and its implications, and, as always, that had involved throwing herself back into her work, just pressing on with everything. She couldn't afford not to, after all. If Peter was to be believed – and, for her, that was becoming an increasingly big if – they were facing one of the biggest opportunities they'd ever had. If that were true, she couldn't afford to take her eye off the ball.

At the same time, faced with the shocking fact of Justin's death and what it might mean, she was closing in on herself, falling back on her own resources. Perhaps her faith in Peter had suffered some further collateral damage as a result of that. She had to be that bit more cautious, less willing to rely on others. Whatever the reasons, all she knew was that, at least for the moment, she was feeling uneasy in Peter's presence and she didn't want him here.

Instead she was sitting here all alone, staring into the darkness. She had turned out all the garden lights, telling herself it was because she wanted to be able to appreciate the night better, see the scattered lights out across the moors, the thickening pattern of stars above her, enjoy the heady scents of the night without being bothered by the moths and other insects drawn by the lights. All of that was no doubt true. But it was also true that in the darkness she felt less exposed, less of a target.

Was she really under threat? She couldn't discount what had happened to Justin, but she still harboured doubts about the real significance of that. She knew what Justin's life had been like away from here. She knew because of all the times it had been thrust in her face and all the times she'd had to drag him out of the shit. She knew so much, and she'd never wanted to know any more. All she knew was that it was more complicated than she'd indicated to the police. As far as she was concerned, that had been his business. She wondered whether she should have said more to the police, but she couldn't really see what good it would do to wash all that filthy linen in public. She'd never shared the truth even with Peter Hardy, and it was a can of worms she had no desire to open now. If the motive for Justin's death really did lie there somewhere, she could only hope that was the end of it.

But then there was tonight's call. It occurred to her now that that might have been what had prompted her growing unease about Peter. There'd been something about his manner when she'd first found him holding the phone in the kitchen. She hadn't fully recognised it at the time but she now felt convinced he wasn't being entirely straight with her.

That might mean anything, of course. He was the only one who'd heard the threat, and she and the police had taken his word about what had been said. Perhaps the wording of the threat had been even more brutal than he'd indicated and he'd been looking to shield her. Or, conversely and more likely, it could be that he'd exaggerated what had been said for his own ends.

She'd recognised for a long time now that Peter was keen to inveigle his way further into her life. That was unsurprising, and in some ways she couldn't really blame him. She'd allowed him to get closer to her than anyone since she'd split up with Ronnie all those years ago. If she hadn't exactly led Peter on, she certainly hadn't discouraged him. There'd even been brief moments when she'd almost begun to think she might actually want a deeper, more lasting relationship with him.

Particularly in the days since Justin's death, he'd clearly been angling to spend more time here. Again, that had partly been her own fault. In the first couple of days, when she was still feeling shaken by what had happened, she'd been only too happy to have him around. He'd been a reassuring presence, physically and emotionally, and she'd encouraged him to stay.

Had he exaggerated tonight's threat in the hope of giving himself a reason to spend even more time in her company? It was quite possible. Whatever else Peter might be up to and even if her other doubts were unjustified, she had no doubt he could be a devious bugger when it suited him. She'd seen it often enough in the way he'd behaved on business matters. He'd discouraged her from going into the office since Justin's death, pointing out that she could work just as effectively from here without subjecting herself to further unnecessary stress. She wondered now whether that was another way for Peter to try to increase his influence over her and the business.

Maybe tonight's call had simply been some attention-seeking idiot who'd got hold of her phone number to make a generic threat and it had been Peter who'd added all the detail about Justin's death? Or perhaps there hadn't been a threat at all, and the whole thing had just been some elaborate charade.

The darkness had deepened around her while she'd been sitting here, and the sky was heavy with stars, the pale streak of the Milky Way visible despite the faint haze of light from Sheffield over the north-eastern horizon. The hills and moors ahead were dotted with lights from the villages across the landscape, and the night remained eerily silent.

She knew she was in danger of slipping into increasing paranoia, and she told herself to get a grip. But the reality was that she couldn't trust anyone. She could trust only her own instincts. If Peter was right and these opportunities proved to be as big as he was claiming, then she'd know where she stood with him. If not – well, then she'd still know. Either way, she was taking a calculated risk in making this next step.

Peter had made all the running. He was the one with the contacts, and at the start she'd been happy to keep it that way. If this went belly-up, she wanted to be able just to walk away. Even so, that would only work up to a point. At some stage, she did want to see the whites of their eyes.

At the start, Peter had insisted the investment was there if they wanted to take advantage of it. But his contacts had made it clear it wouldn't be there for ever. Sure, they rated her and wanted to do business with her. But if she didn't make a decision, they'd cut their losses and move on. Find some other partner who'd be prepared to play ball.

So in the end she'd closed her eyes and taken that first step into the water. Agreed to accept the first chunk of the money and take the risk. If this was everything Peter claimed, she knew they'd be operating at a different level, and that the competition here would be more intense. She could be ruthless, but these people were real professionals who she suspected would stop at nothing.

If it all worked out as Peter was promising, she'd have no choice but to place even greater trust in the team she'd built around herself, so she had to proceed with care. She'd already eased out a couple of senior managers who'd given her cause for concern in terms of both their competence and their loyalty. The core team, headed by Peter, was growing smaller and more select, but its contribution would be critical. But she needed to be wary. In the end, the only person she could really trust was herself.

Sitting there in the dark, she realised that for a few moments now she'd been half-conscious of some change in the feel of the night. She couldn't immediately pinpoint what it might be. It was almost as if there'd been a shift in the quality of the silence. Since the sun had set, the evening had grown increasingly quiet, the last of the day's birdsong fading, the breeze dropping almost to complete stillness, the trees and bushes silent and motionless.

The night remained virtually silent, but she was aware now of something at the very limits of her hearing. It took her a few more seconds of straining her ears to work out what it was. The very distant sound of a car.

The question was how distant? One of the benefits of this location was that it was almost impossible to hear any passing traffic. There were a couple of single-track roads that passed within a mile or so of the grounds, but some quirk of the surrounding topography deflected any significant traffic noise even from those roads. It was unusual to hear anything at all unless a car was directly approaching the house from the front.

The sound was growing louder. Uneasy now, she re-entered the house and continued down the hallway to the front door.

This was not the smartest move, she kept telling herself. If she was genuinely worried, it was time to call the police. If she wasn't, she should stay at the rear of the house and ignore the approaching car. What she shouldn't do, in either case, was leave the relative safety of the building.

But she couldn't help herself. Her unease was matched only by her curiosity. If there was anything to concern her, she'd lock herself back inside and call the police. She reached the front door and peered out through the spyhole. She could see and hear nothing in the darkness.

Screwing up her courage, she opened the door, still on the heavy chain, and looked out into the darkness. Even in the few minutes since she'd left the garden, the car had grown significantly louder, and she had no doubt now that it was on the narrow road leading down to the main gates. The gates themselves were still firmly shut and locked, and there was no immediate risk of the vehicle entering unless she allowed it. She could check the identity of the car and its occupants on the CCTV screen positioned in the alcove by the front door.

She wasn't even sure why she was concerned. Most likely, it was just one of the police patrols that she'd been told would periodically check out the front of the house. She hadn't really been sure what the point of this was, but it seemed to be the maximum additional protection the police had been able to offer.

After another moment, she saw the flash of headlights as the car rounded the final bend before reaching the gates. It pulled into the short driveway beyond the gates and she heard the engine stop.

She half-expected then that the driver would either press the intercom button on the gates or, if it was someone who knew her, call her mobile. But nothing happened. She closed the door and moved to check out the CCTV screen. The live feed was slightly grainy and the car headlights had been positioned to point directly towards it, so it was difficult to make out what was happening.

The car had been positioned so that she was unable to make out its registration or any detail about the car itself. She could see that there was some movement around the vehicle, with at least two people moving around in the glare of the security cameras. They appeared to be engaged in some activity rather than trying to gain access, but it was impossible to see what they were doing.

After another couple of minutes, the two figures climbed back into the car and it reversed away from the gates. She stared at the screen, trying to make out the car registration, but failed to catch it before the car turned to pull away. If necessary, she told herself, it might be possible to capture the registration later from the recorded footage.

The rear lights receded out of camera shot and the image returned to its usual stillness. She cautiously reopened the front door, hearing the sound of the car engine speeding away from the house. What the hell had that all been about? If it had been the police, surely they would just have approached the gates, perhaps stopped for a moment, and then turned round. There would have been no reason for them to leave the car.

The smart thing to do now, she told herself, would be to call the police and get them to come and check out the front gates. Perhaps the car's occupants had committed some act of vandalism or left some graffiti daubed on the surrounding walls. Perhaps some idiot had decided to follow up what had been done to the car in Matlock.

It was more than possible. She'd never deluded herself that she'd win any kind of popularity competition among those who'd been affected by some of her business activities. Even so, she felt an additional sense of unease about what had just happened. It had felt too quick, too pre-planned, too professional, just to be some hot-headed ex-employees seeking revenge.

Whatever it was, she needed to see the results before she called the police out. It was always possible that something had been done or left that was intended to cause her embarrassment. Even though she knew she was being reckless, she opened the front door and stepped out into the night.

As she made her way cautiously up the driveway, the security lights on the front of the house came on, startling her and silhouetting her figure in a way that she knew would provide a perfect target. At almost the same moment, the security lights on the gates, which had been triggered by the arrival of the car, were extinguished, so that she could see nothing beyond the cars but darkness.

By the time she reached the gates, her heart was pounding. Once or twice, she'd almost turned round and returned to the house, but had forced herself to continue, still not quite knowing why she was doing so. The sound of the car had long disappeared into the distance and the night had returned to its former warm stillness.

The house security lights were behind her now, and the area beyond the gates was lost in shadow. Stupidly, she hadn't thought to bring a proper torch, but at least she had her phone. She switched on its feeble torch and shone it through the bars of the gates.

Afterwards she was left with a sense that she'd known all along what she was going to find. That was impossible, of course. It had been the last thing on her mind as she'd made her way nervously up the driveway. Otherwise, she surely would have obeyed the instinct telling her to return to the house.

But it was true that, somehow, it didn't come as a surprise.

She played the torch beam across it, half-hoping that her eyes might somehow be playing tricks. Even so, she knew exactly what she was seeing.

A human body, lying face up on the gravel outside the gates. She forced herself to hold the torch beam steady, wanting to see whether she recognised him.

It was a white male, middle-aged, lying face down, his head twisted towards her. She moved cautiously forward, already suspecting she knew the identity of the man lying outside the gates. For a moment, as she struggled to hold the torch steady, she remained unsure. One side of the man's head had been crushed by a heavy blow to the temple, and blood was already thickly congealed across his face, half-concealing his features. Whoever he was, there was no doubt he was dead.

Then, as she took another step forward, she no longer had any doubt. She knew who was lying in front of her. And she realised now that he had been killed in exactly the same manner as Justin.

Chapter Nineteen

'Shit,' Sheena said. 'You're kidding.'

'Sheena, how long have you known me? Do you think I'm the type to make that kind of joke at this time of night?' Annie was pulling on her clothes and searching round for the various items – phone, keys, warrant card – she needed to take with her.

It was always the way, she thought. For once, she and Sheena had both been feeling tired and had decided to resist the temptation to work late. They'd been in bed for approximately ten minutes when Annie's phone had buzzed on the bedside table.

'They're sure it's him?'

'He's not been formally identified, obviously, but one of the officers who was first on the scene checked in his pockets for ID. Poor lad will probably get a bollocking from the CSIs for disturbing the body.'

'Poor bloody Keith Chalmers. It's only a few hours since I was with him,' Sheena said. 'Why the hell would anyone want to hurt him?'

'It seems like an extreme response to an industrial dispute. But these days who knows?'

'It's not even as if Keith was the provocative type. It didn't pay to underestimate him, but he always made a point of being the voice of reason.'

'Just goes to show where that gets you,' Annie said. She came to sit on the bed for a moment and placed a hand on Sheena's cheek. 'Christ, it must be a shock for you too. You must have been the last person to see him alive.'

Sheena offered a grimace in the dimly lit room. 'Apart from whoever killed him, you mean? Unless you're putting me in the frame for that. If you are, Trev in the pub will give me an alibi. Keith was definitely still alive when he left me.'

Annie was conscious they were both adopting this facetious tone as a mechanism for coping with the shock of the news. She didn't know Chalmers at all, and as far as she was aware Sheena had known him only as a professional contact. Nevertheless, it had been one of those moments that brought the reality of Annie's work a little too close to home. It was also beginning to occur to her that this would be setting off yet more alarm bells for Stuart Jennings. 'Okay, if Trev gives you an alibi that's good enough for me. I've never met a dishonest publican.'

Sheena pulled herself upright in bed as Annie stood and continued gathering her things. 'Actually, that's a point. Trev, I mean. There was something he said to me just before I left the pub. It was just the usual banter with Trev, you know. But he asked me whether Keith had been all right.'

'How do you mean?'

'Whether there'd been some issue with him, I suppose. Because he reckoned Keith had seemed worried and looked in a hurry to get to his car. "Like he had a rocket up his arse," in Trev's immortal words.'

'How'd he seemed to you?'

'I'm not sure, to be honest. At the time he didn't strike me as being much different from usual. He was always the slightly neurotic type. I was focusing more on why he was so keen to meet up with me. I thought at first he might be trying to tap me up for inside information about Michelle Wentworth. Then I realised he was looking for me to pass on the information about Wentworth's business.'

'Interesting that he was so keen to pass that on,' Annie said.

'Maybe. But that was Keith. Always playing all the angles. He might have just thought it was worth putting pressure on Wentworth from another direction. That makes him sound callous, given what had happened to her son. But if he really thought there was something dodgy about Wentworth's business, he'd probably seen that as a legitimate weapon to wield on their behalf. I'm just trying to think about his manner. Maybe this is just with the benefit of hindsight, but I suppose he did seem more intense than usual. As if he was keen to ensure he got his message across.' She paused. 'I might just be imagining that. It's amazing how the memory plays tricks even just after a few hours.'

'You should try interviewing witnesses,' Annie said. 'It's so easy to end up remembering what feel you ought to remember.'

'He definitely seemed in a hurry, though. He even turned down the offer of a second drink, which wasn't like Keith. He said he had to be somewhere else later.'

'He didn't say where?'

'I'm pretty sure that's all he said. He left fairly abruptly, though. Again, not typical of Keith.'

'All useful stuff. I'll have to get someone to take a formal witness statement from you. Assuming Stuart doesn't throw me off the case after this.'

'Is that likely?'

'All too probable, I'd say. He's already getting jittery about it.'

'That's ridiculous.'

Annie was hovering by the door, ready to leave now. 'He has a point, I suppose. I mean, there's no real conflict of interest that I can see. But once the media pick up on the links between Chalmers, you and me, then there's a risk that I start to become the story. It all just becomes a lot messier.'

'And I thought party politics was convoluted.'

'There you go. Right, I'd best be off. Don't know when I'll be back, but I'll keep you posted as best I can.'

–

As Annie turned the final corner on the road leading down to Michelle Wentworth's house, her headlights swept across the walls and gateway, illuminating the eerie tableau before the gates. There was the usual pulse of blue lights from the patrol car that had been first on the scene, the shapes of the officers caught between her lights and those from the gate, and the dark shadow on the ground before them, all set in front of the tall arch of the gateway as if part of some unearthly tableau.

She pulled up at the side of the road and climbed out into the mild night air. It seemed that, apart from the initial two uniforms, she was the first on the scene. Annie had called to update Zoe on her way over. Zoe had insisted on coming out and would be here in due course, though Annie was unsure what either of them could really do until the CSIs had examined the scene and the body, other than talking to Michelle Wentworth.

The two officers had done a decent job of sealing off the scene, and they'd also placed warning signs further back up the road on the off-chance that some other vehicle might come down here at this time of the night. As far as Annie was aware, the road led nowhere beyond Wentworth's house except to a stretch of open moorland with parking for walkers, so the likelihood of any accidental visitors at this time of night seemed low.

The two PCs were unknown to her, so she waved her warrant card in their direction. 'Evening. DI Annie Delamere.'

One of the two stepped forward to greet her. 'Evening. Glad to have someone else turn up. Jason here's scared of the dark and he was beginning to freak me out.'

'Ignore him,' the other one said. 'Pleased to meet you. Jason Vance. This is Tom Garstang. He's the one freaked out by a dead body.'

They were both young, Annie told herself, and she supposed they had to find some way of passing the time between them. 'How long have you been here?'

'About three-quarters of an hour,' Vance said. 'We were over in Bakewell when the call came in so not far away. Mind you, it took us a few minutes to find this place. Back of beyond, isn't it?' He had a fairly strong local accent, which Annie placed as being from somewhere in or around Chesterfield. For all their banter, both seemed enthusiastic enough, not obviously too fazed by forty-five minutes of standing in the dark with a corpse.

'You wouldn't stumble on the place by accident,' Garstang said. 'Why would anyone dump a body here?'

'That's the question,' Annie said. She assumed that Garstang was either unaware of Justin Wentworth's murder, or at least hadn't made the link with the location. 'One of you checked his ID?'

'That was me,' Vance said. 'Sorry. I wasn't really thinking. Shouldn't have disturbed the scene.'

'Don't imagine there's much harm done. Assume you didn't move the body?'

Vance shook his head perhaps a shade too vigorously. 'No, of course not. I'm not stupid.' He glared at Garstang, as if to defy him an opportunity to challenge this assertion. 'I just did a quick check of his jacket pockets and found his wallet. I've bagged that up properly now.'

'And you're sure it's Keith Chalmers?' The body's head was turned away from her so she couldn't see the face, although the clothing and the build of the body were in line with the short description Sheena had given her.

'That's what it said. Is he known to us then?'

'In a manner of speaking,' Annie said. 'He's a trade union guy. Fairly high-profile locally.'

Garstang nodded. 'I thought I recognised the name from somewhere. He was on the local news. Talking about that strike over in Matlock. The car damage thing.'

Vance frowned. 'Blimey. And he ends up like this.'

Somewhere beyond the trees above them, Annie saw a flash of what she took to be the headlights from an approaching vehicle. She turned back to Garstang and Vance. 'What happened to Michelle Wentworth?'

'The woman who lives here, you mean? Jesus, must have been a shock for her. She was still out here waiting when we arrived, just on the other side of the gates. I took her back in and checked she was okay. I'd have been having kittens but she seemed cool enough. I told her someone would go and check on her as soon as we got some backup out here.'

'Did she say how she'd come to find the body at this time of night?' The account Annie had received from the control room had been unclear, and she was intrigued by what might have lured Wentworth out to the front of the house after what had happened to Justin.

'She reckons she was in the rear garden and heard the car approaching so came to see who it was.' Vance gestured above them. 'She was watching them on the camera up here. Saw the car come down and two people get out, but couldn't work out what they were doing. She waited till they'd gone, then came out and found this.' He shrugged. 'That's what she said, anyway.'

It sounded plausible enough, Annie thought. The CCTV on the gate would show the same thing if it was the truth. You'd hear a car approaching from miles away at night in this place. The only question was how Wentworth had had the bottle to come right out here to the gate. But Annie suspected that, in one way or another, Wentworth was an even tougher character than she appeared.

In one respect, Annie supposed, Chalmers' death would be useful to Wentworth. It removed someone who'd been an effective thorn in her side on the Matlock contract and elsewhere. Chalmers would be replaced, but probably by someone with less skill and experience.

Even so, that was a pretty thin motive for murder. And, if Wentworth had been responsible for Chalmers' killing, why on earth would she have the body dumped almost literally on her own doorstep? That would constitute an audacious double-bluff, even by Michelle Wentworth's no doubt bold standards.

But why would anyone want to kill Keith Chalmers? He'd made a few enemies over the years, but it was a big step from industrial conflict to murder. And he'd presumably been dumped here for a reason. If Justin

Wentworth's killing had been intended as some kind of threat or warning, what was the purpose behind this? On the face of it, it made no sense.

She blinked as a set of headlights swept around the corner of the road. The white CSI van pulled up behind her own car, and Danny Eccles' substantial figure climbed out. He ambled his way down to her with the air of someone preparing to join a bunch of mates in the pub. 'Back here again, Annie? This is getting to be a habit.'

'The one with the habit seems to be whoever's dumping dead bodies at Michelle Wentworth's house.'

'She does seem to attract them, doesn't she?' Eccles peered over the police tape at the huddled body. 'Assume this one wasn't killed here?'

'Well, that's for you to confirm, Danny. But looks most likely that he was killed elsewhere and then dropped here. Michelle Wentworth saw the car arrive and depart on her CCTV.'

'What time was this?' Eccles asked, still staring at the body as if it might reveal its secrets even before he approached it.

'Just over an hour ago, probably,' Garstang sad. 'That was when we picked up the call, anyway. We were in Bakewell, so we were probably here in ten minutes or so.'

'I understand our man is Keith Chalmers, trade unionist of this parish?' Eccles glanced at the two uniformed officers. 'You two chancers checked his ID?'

Vance reddened and exchanged a glance with Garstang. 'Sorry, that was me. I was thinking…'

'Don't let it happen again, son,' Eccles said. 'But I won't tell anyone if Annie here doesn't. Probably doesn't matter too much, given that he's just been dumped from the back of a car.' He straightened up and stretched, as if just waking up. 'Okay, I'll get my gear out of the car and get everything set up. It's a fairly small area to control but I'd like you two lads to stick around just in case we get any unwanted visitors. You can kick your heels for a bit, Annie.'

'I'm going to take the opportunity to speak to Michelle Wentworth.' Annie tuned as yet another set of headlights swung round the corner. 'Ah, here's Zoe,' she said. 'She always did have immaculate timing.'

Chapter Twenty

Zoe stopped and looked around as they walked down the driveway. 'Beautiful spot in the daytime. Bit creepy at this time of night, I reckon.'

She wasn't wrong, Annie thought. The bulk of the converted labourers' cottages that formed the main structure of Wentworth's house stood ahead of them, its stone walls and the vast looming angles of the roof looking unexpectedly ancient in the pale moonlight. The gardens and shrubbery around them, which were ordered and picturesque by daylight, now appeared to be teeming with threatening shadows. She watched as Zoe took a look behind her and seemed to shiver. 'You okay, Zo?'

'Yeah, fine. Just slightly spooked for a second. Not sure why. Not been sleeping all that well the last few nights. It's too warm.'

'Tell me about it. It's so airless.'

'One reason I wasn't sorry to come over here tonight, to be honest. Give Gary a chance to get some sleep. He's usually out like a light if he doesn't have me there keeping him awake.'

Annie watched Zoe for a second longer, wondering whether this might be a return of whatever had been troubling her earlier in the year. But, as she'd told Stuart Jennings, all Annie could do was keep an eye on Zoe and be ready to offer support if there was any recurrence.

They reached the front door and Annie pressed the bell. There was silence for several minutes, and Annie felt her anxiety growing. There was still too much about this case they didn't understand, and she had no idea to what extent Wentworth herself might be at risk.

Finally, the door opened, still on the chain. Michelle Wentworth stared at them for a moment as if doubtful of their identities, and then finally closed and reopened the door to allow them entry. 'You'd best come through.'

Annie had the feeling that Wentworth had turned on every light in the house, as if trying to banish whatever might be lurking outside. She looked paler and more worn than she had earlier in the evening.

It occurred to Annie now that PC Vance had made no mention of Peter Hardy. Annie had assumed, if only because of Hardy's usual omnipresence during her visits, that he had been staying here to help support Wentworth over recent days, but there was no sign of him tonight.

Michelle Wentworth lowered herself on to one of the sofas and Annie and Zoe sat themselves opposite her. Annie noticed a half-finished bottle of an expensive-looking single malt on the table between them, with an empty but clearly used glass beside it.

'I think I recognised him,' Wentworth said, her voice flat. 'Keith Chalmers.'

'It looks like it,' Annie said. 'Subject to confirmation, obviously. But there's ID on the body.'

'Why would anyone want to kill Keith Chalmers?' Wentworth said.

It was a good question, but perhaps not the first one that Annie might have expected Wentworth to ask. A more pertinent question, from Wentworth's point of view, was why, having been killed, Chalmers' body had been dumped here. 'How well did you know Mr Chalmers?'

There was a slightly prolonged silence. 'Me?' Wentworth said. 'Only a little. I mean, we've sat on opposite sides of the table once or twice when we've had employee relations difficulties on some of the major contracts. But even that wasn't often because I used to delegate most of that.' She gave them a weak smile. 'Union negotiations aren't really my thing. I'm too prone to losing my temper and telling the other side exactly what I think, so my guys have to kick me under the table. I usually leave them to people with a bit more patience.'

'So do you have any idea why the body might have been placed here?' Annie asked.

'I've no idea at all. It makes no sense.'

'Have you had any dealings with Mr Chalmers recently? You directly, I mean.'

Wentworth blinked and there was another momentary pause before she responded. 'Not directly. I understand he was involved in the dispute in Matlock, but I'd largely left that to the local management there to deal with.'

'Otherwise, you didn't meet with Mr Chalmers yourself?'

'I don't really understand where you're going with these questions,' Wentworth said. 'It sounds almost as if you're trying to accuse me of killing Chalmers.'

Annie shook her head. 'I'm just trying to understand why the body might have been left here. As you say, on the face of things it makes no sense. I'm just trying to find out if there might have been some reason for it, however unlikely or far-fetched.'

'I'm not sure I can help,' Wentworth said. 'It's as baffling to me as it is to you. I've never met Chalmers except a few times in a business context, as I say. The only dealings I've had with him recently have been indirect. From the limited contact I've had with him, he seemed okay – straightforward, pretty pragmatic, easier to deal with than some union officials. Not a pushover, but generally sensible. I don't know that I can say much more than that.'

'What about the incident in Matlock?' Zoe asked. 'Do you think the union were behind that? Your site manager there seemed to imply he thought so.'

Wentworth glared at Zoe for a moment. 'I've had a word with Roger about the interview he gave to the *Evening Telegraph*. It was well intentioned and Roger was feeling irritated when he gave it, but it didn't reflect the company's position. I don't know who was responsible for damaging the car, though I'm rather hoping your people will find out. But I'm very happy to accept that that kind of action wasn't something encouraged or condoned by the trade union.' She sounded as if she was reading a prepared statement, Annie thought. Perhaps it was something she'd had ready for if the media had taken the story further. 'In fact, come to think of it, Keith Chalmers actually phoned both me and Roger to apologise on the union's behalf. That must have been the last time I spoke to him, and it was probably the first time I had in more than a year. We only talked for a few minutes. I just reassured him that we didn't hold the union responsible and that we'd put the matter in the hands of the police.'

Annie felt as if they were coming to a dead end in exploring Wentworth's links with Chalmers. 'Can you just run us through what you saw tonight? You went out the front because you'd heard an approaching car, is that right?'

'I didn't *go* out,' Wentworth corrected. 'Not after what happened to Justin. But you can always tell if there's a car coming up to the house. There's never any other traffic up here at night, so if there is a car there's only one place it's going. I couldn't imagine anyone I knew would have come up without calling first, so I was a bit unnerved.'

'Brave of you to go and look,' Annie said. 'I'm not sure I'd have had the nerve.'

'I wasn't exactly feeling brave. I had my finger poised to dial 999, but I thought I'd better check it out first. So I stayed in the house and watched the CCTV. I couldn't see much. They drove down, stopped in front of the gate and then – well, presumably they pulled the body out of the car. It could only have taken them a couple of minutes. Then they reversed and drove away at a fair lick. You can check the footage, but I'd be surprised if you got much from it. They were careful to park the car close to the gate and in a position where the camera wouldn't pick up the car reg. I couldn't even make out any details of the car or really see what they were doing.'

'We'll have some of our experts look at the footage. See if they can pick out anything else. Suggests they knew about the positioning of the camera. Do you have any feel for who might be in a position to know about the cameras? Around the house generally, I mean, as well as the gates.'

'You're thinking about where Justin was attacked as well?'

'Perhaps,' Annie said, noting that not much escaped Wentworth's attention. 'Whoever was responsible managed to select a spot that was outside the camera range, and also managed to reach the house without being detected. Suggests they knew where the cameras are.'

'The layout's not exactly public knowledge,' Wentworth said. 'But I guess it wouldn't have been that difficult to check out. The cameras are mostly visible. There are always one or two cars passing the gate at the weekends, particularly in summer. People park up at the bottom of the lane to go walking on the moors. Nothing I can do to stop that, but it does mean that in the daytime someone could have got up to the gate without me getting suspicious. The cameras on the house are trickier, but you could probably see most of them from outside my property if you used binoculars.'

'I'm conscious you must be tired,' Annie said. 'We won't take up any more of your time tonight. Are you okay to be here alone? We can stay until you get someone over, if you prefer.'

'I'm used to being on my own,' Wentworth said. 'Though admittedly not quite in these circumstances. I'm not easily spooked.'

Clearly not, Annie thought. 'If you're sure. The CSIs will be working into the night, so they'll be there with a couple of police officers.'

'Dedication,' Wentworth said.

'Striking while the crime scene's still hot, mainly. I don't know how long it'll take them. It's pretty certain that the crime occurred elsewhere, so there won't be a lot to capture here, but they're very methodical. I hope it won't disturb you.'

'I won't know they're there. Literally,' Wentworth said. 'Once you're in the house, you can't hear anything. I only heard the car earlier because I happened to be in the garden.'

'That's fine. Thanks for your time again tonight.'

'I'm only sorry I couldn't help you more. I'm as baffled by this as you are.'

She seemed more her usual self now than she had earlier in the interview. The initial hesitation had been replaced by a slicker confidence. But, as always in her dealings with Michelle Wentworth, Annie was left with the feeling that there was something held back. In this case, something about Keith Chalmers.

There was no point in pushing it for the moment. If it came to it and they really thought Wentworth was hampering the investigation, they could always haul her in for a more formal interview. 'We'll keep you posted, anyway.'

'Through your delightful colleague here. She really does seem to want to be very friendly.'

'That's partly her job,' Annie said. 'We want her to be a trusted point of contact for you.'

'Of course you do,' Wentworth said. 'Though I'm afraid she's wasting her time.'

'Wasting her time?'

'If she thinks I've anything more to tell you. Whatever you may think, I've really nothing more to say than I have already.'

It was as if Wentworth had read Annie's own mind, as well as seeing through what Zoe had been trying to do. 'Well, if anything does occur to you, please just let us know.'

'Of course.' Wentworth had risen from her seat, an unignorable indication that their time with her was over. 'I wouldn't hold any detail back, however trivial, if I felt it was pertinent to the inquiry.'

Annie gazed at her for a moment, wondering what was really going on inside Michelle Wentworth's head. Her son dead, the body of a trade unionist dumped at her gates, and here she was, still playing some unfathomable game.

'I hope that's true,' Annie said. 'And I hope you're in a position to make that judgement. Because if we're going to catch your son's killer, Mrs Wentworth, we'll need all the help and support we can get.'

Chapter Twenty-One

'You'd better head home and grab some sleep,' Annie said to Zoe as they walked back down the driveway towards the gates. 'There's not much more we can do here tonight. Not till Danny's done his work.' It was still only around eleven, but it felt later.

'I suppose, though I don't know how much I'll sleep.'

'You sure you're okay, Zoe?'

Zoe hesitated briefly. 'Like I say, it's just the heat. I like warm weather as much as anyone, but I'm beginning to wish this would break.'

Annie knew what Zoe meant. Out here, this late in the evening, the temperature was bearable enough, but several times recently Annie had woken in the night, conscious of the airlessness of her bedroom. It was made worse by the fact that, after what had happened earlier in the year, Sheena was still reluctant to leave windows open overnight. 'Try to get some rest, though. There's a long way to go on this one.'

'It's not making any sense,' Zoe said. 'I can see how the son's death might have been intended as some sort of warning or threat, but I don't see where Chalmers' death fits into that.'

'Me neither,' Annie said. 'We need to find out more about Comrade Chalmers. Sheena actually saw him this evening, would you believe?'

'There's a coincidence.'

'Maybe. Sheena thought he wanted to pass on some intelligence about Wentworth's business dealings. Using her as a conduit to pass it on to me. Presumably thought I'd take it more seriously if it had Sheena's seal of approval.'

'And did it? Have her seal of approval, I mean.'

'Well, she confirmed that in her experience anything coming from Chalmers was generally pretty reliable. If it is accurate, it sounds as if Wentworth's looking to expand her business massively. That might mean she's treading on some new toes. He also hinted that there might be funny money involved.'

'What sort of funny money?'

'That's as far as he got. All very enigmatic, but that was often Chalmers' way, according to Sheena. I assume he thought he'd get the chance to tell us more if we took the bait.'

'Interesting that he didn't, then,' Zoe said.

'That was my thinking. Sheena reckoned he was in a hurry tonight. Had to be somewhere else, but didn't say where. Like I say, enigmatic.'

They had reached the gates. Danny Eccles had erected a protective tent over the body, and was inside, fully suited, working on the body. Vance and Garstang were standing by their car, looking deeply bored.

'Evening, lads,' Annie said. 'Bet no one ever told you police work could be this exciting?'

'They missed this bit in the recruitment ads,' Garstang said. He gestured towards the house. 'She okay?'

'Mrs Wentworth? Yes, she's fine. Remarkably unfazed, you might say. I've told her you'll be here for a little while till Danny finishes his work. How's it going, Danny?' she called.

After a moment, Eccles' head peered out of the tent. He pulled away his mask to speak to them. 'Won't be too long. There's only a limited amount I can do here, given that the killing must have occurred elsewhere. He's not been dead long. Couple of hours, maybe. Cause of death most likely a major trauma to the head. Basically beaten several times with some heavy blunt object.'

'Like Justin Wentworth.'

'Pretty much. Almost as if someone was making a point, you might think.'

'You might. Anything else of interest?'

'Nothing obvious. Pathologist might find something more, particularly if there are any traces of the murder weapon in the head wound, but I can't see anything. I've bagged up the contents of his pockets, but there isn't much. Wallet. Bank card holder with various documents in it. Set of car and house keys. A few pennies in change. That's about it.'

'No mobile phone?'

'No, which I guess is interesting.'

'Potentially,' Annie said. 'Can't imagine he wouldn't have had one in a job like his. And I can't imagine he wouldn't have carried it about with him as a matter of habit. Union official's the kind of role where you need to be available. So either he lost it when he was being attacked, or it was removed deliberately. Which makes me wonder why.'

'Because it provided some link with the killer?' Zoe offered.

'Presumably. Although if it was a call or text we may be able to trace that through the mobile provider, assuming he was using his union phone.'

'He may not have been,' Zoe pointed out, 'if he was involved in something clandestine.'

'Indeed. Or maybe it was something else he had stored on his phone. An address or note, say.'

Eccles nodded. 'I'll leave you to your investigatory speculations and get finished up in here. I've called out an ambulance to get the body taken in, though God knows how long they're likely to be.'

'I'll give you your due, Danny. You certainly know how to live.'

—

Annie arrived back home to find that Sheena was up, sitting in the kitchen in her dressing gown, sipping a mug of hot chocolate. 'Couldn't get back to sleep,' she explained. 'Partly the heat. Partly just thinking about poor Keith Chalmers.'

Annie filled the kettle to make herself a mug of tea. It was obvious they weren't going to get back to bed for a while now. She was conscious her own mind was buzzing, running and rerunning over the facts of the case. 'Tell me about him.'

'I can't claim to have known him well. Mind you, I'm not sure anyone really did.'

'Was he married?'

'Divorced as far as I know. Lived on his own over in Eastwood somewhere, I think. He's mentioned a grown-up son, but I don't know any details. He always struck me as a private type. My assumption was always was that there wasn't much else going on his life so he'd thrown himself into the job.'

'Was he the political type? Outside his union role, I mean.'

'Not particularly. He was a party member, obviously, but not a very active one in recent years. He always told me he'd been a bit of an activist in his youth, but now he just put his energies into the job.'

'Not the sort to make enemies?' The kettle had boiled and Annie poured boiling water over the teabag in her mug. She swished it about for a few seconds with a spoon, before dredging it out and dropping it in the compost caddy.

'I wouldn't have said so,' Sheena said. 'You're bound to get up a few people's noses in that kind of role. Sometimes more on your own side than the other.'

'How'd you mean?'

'Well, these days employers either don't recognise trade unions in the first place or, if they do, they accept them as a fact of life. Just something they have to deal with. The better employers see them as a positive because they provide a structured route to consult with employees. But at worst they see them as a necessary evil. You must see that in the force.'

'I suppose. The Federation's a bit of a special case, but relations with the staff unions are generally fairly constructive.'

'Exactly. As long as the union reps are reasonable, that's usually the case. The national and regional reps, like Keith, are generally seen in an even better light because they're often the ones who keep the less experienced local reps in line. That was generally how Keith was seen. The voice of moderation. It was why he'd involved himself in the Matlock thing. He knew there was a danger of it flaring up. So if he made enemies, they tended to be on his own side.'

'Because they thought he was too moderate?'

'That sort of thing. That he'd been too emollient. That he'd not pushed the cause as hard as he should have done. That he'd capitulated too easily to management. It goes with the territory, but it can be a pain in the backside when you know you've given it everything you can.' She smiled. 'The same goes for Labour MPs sometimes.'

'I bet.'

'Internal union politics can be a vicious world.'

'Like internal Labour Party politics?'

'I'm saying nothing. But I do wish some of our lot were as committed to attacking the other side as they are to attacking each other. All I'm saying is that I think Keith suffered a bit from that over the years.'

'Enough for someone to want to murder him?'

'Not even trade union politics usually goes that far. But there might have been one or two people who'd have been happy to stitch him up, let's put it that way.'

'You don't have any names, I suppose?'

'I'm not close enough to any of it. These are nothing more than impressions I've picked up over the years. Stuff I've heard on the grapevine. I've always made a point of not getting involved. Life's too short. If you think it's an avenue worth pursuing, I'd go and talk to the union. National office is in London, but they've a team based out of Derby who basically cover the East Midlands.'

Annie sat down at the kitchen table and took a sip of her tea. 'I'll talk to Stuart in the morning about how we play this. I'm assuming he'll want to treat this as part of the Wentworth inquiry, unless of course he decides it's just coincidence that Chalmers' body ended up at her house. Whether he'll want me still to be leading it is another question.'

'Complicates things, this, doesn't it?'

'Even more than before. Although I suppose it gives a new dimension to the whole conflict of interest question. But if you were the last person to see Chalmers alive before the killer, that potentially puts me in a difficult position.'

'Surely nobody's going to see me as a suspect.'

'Not a very likely one, certainly. And Trev saw Chalmers leave the pub before you.'

'But I don't have an alibi between then and you getting home from work.'

'And even then your only alibi would be me, the investigating officer. You see the problem?'

'I suppose. It's ridiculous, though, isn't it?'

'Well, obviously. But that's not the point. The point is that the inquiry needs to be squeaky clean. We can't afford any suggestion that it's not being managed totally objectively. Anything that clouds that is a problem. On top of that, I don't imagine you want to have your name blazoned across the media about this either.'

'I see what you mean. They won't care whether there's anything in it, they'll just see it as a good story.'

'Exactly. The more I think about it, the more I'm inclined to tell Stuart I want to step aside. It's probably better if I initiate it rather than just leaving the decision to him.'

'Your decision, obviously,' Sheena said. 'And you're probably right. I just resent being coerced into something through fear of what the media might do. Especially when it's something as important as a murder inquiry.'

'There are other people who can run it as well as I can,' Annie said. 'The last thing I want is some media circus that hinders us finding whoever killed Justin Wentworth and Keith Chalmers.'

'Point taken.' Sheena swallowed the last of her hot chocolate. 'Ready for sleep?'

'I guess so,' Annie said. 'I want to be in early tomorrow. Make sure I can get my retaliation in first, as it were. Before Stuart can get his act together.'

'If you're sure it's the right thing to do.'

'To be honest,' Anne said. 'I've not sure I've much of a choice.'

Chapter Twenty-Two

Annie arrived at headquarters early but, not entirely to her surprise, Jennings was already there, sitting in his glass-panelled office, tapping busily at his computer. She dropped her bag by her desk and crossed to knock on his door. He beckoned her in.

'You're in bright and early,' he said.

'You seem to be brighter and earlier.'

'Not sure about brighter. I'm struggling to sleep in this heat. Woke up about four and couldn't get off again, so thought I might as well come in. How was last night?'

'As you'd expect,' she said. 'You've heard it was Keith Chalmers?'

'So I understand.'

She hesitated a moment before proceeding, still unsure that she really wanted to excuse herself from the inquiry. 'Look, Stuart, I've been thinking through what you were saying. I've decided you're right. I shouldn't be running this one. Especially now. You should give it to someone else.'

'That was another reason I couldn't sleep. Been trying to think it through. I mean, you're right, but it's not like I'm overwhelmed with resources here.'

'There must be someone who could take it on.'

'You'd think, wouldn't you? But I seem to be running into a brick wall.'

So he'd already been looking to replace her. That shouldn't have come as a surprise. Jennings was always keen to stay one step ahead, especially when his own backside might be on the line. So why should she care? She'd already decided to ask him to take her off the case. That was why she was here. Why should she feel concerned to discover he'd already been planning to do so? Except, of course, that was never how it worked. She was already beginning to regret her words.

'I could do a straight swap with someone. Take on whatever they're in the middle of.'

'I've been through all that. You'd be amazed how many people are just at a critical stage with some case and they really can't afford to be taken off it just now.'

'Just tell them, then. Or get someone more senior to tell them, if that's what it takes.'

Jennings frowned at her. 'I'm quite capable of fighting my own battles, you know.'

She suppressed a sigh. 'Yes, of course. I didn't mean that. It's just that I know some people won't jump unless they've a Chief Super breathing down their neck.'

'To be honest, the real problem is that they all see it as a poisoned chalice. They've seen Michelle Wentworth on the telly and they know what she's capable of. No one wants to take on this one and fail.'

'I didn't know we had the choice.'

'We don't, officially. But people can dig their heels in when they want to.'

'What if I dig my heels in?'

'Someone needs to run the case.'

'You take it on, then? You be CIO.'

He was too slow to conceal his look of distaste entirely. 'I've got enough on my plate as it is, Annie. I couldn't do the job justice.'

She paused, considering the options. 'Delegate it downwards, then. Why not let Zoe take it? It would be good experience for her.'

'You wouldn't want to risk throwing Zoe to the wolves, would you? I mean, Zoe's good but she doesn't have the experience for this. Not yet. And if it went wrong...'

'Okay. But I don't see how I can carry on with the role. Apart from anything else, it looks as if Sheena might have been the last person to see Chalmers alive, other than the killer. I'm too close to it.'

Jennings was clearly surprised by this new piece of information. 'When did she see him?'

'Yesterday evening. In our local pub. He wanted to talk to her about Michelle Wentworth, interestingly enough.'

'What did he have to say?'

'It was all about Wentworth's latest business dealings. He reckoned she was trying to take on some new and much bigger contracts. Also that there might be some dodgy money behind some of the proposed growth. Both factors that he thought would be worth our consideration. Sheena was certain he'd wanted her to pass the info on to me.'

'So much easier than just picking up the phone and calling us.'

'That wasn't really Chalmers' way, accordingly to Sheena. He preferred a more oblique approach. He presumably thought we'd be more inclined to take it seriously if it came with Sheena's endorsement.'

'I take it you're looking at all that, then?'

'Of course.' She paused, recognising that she'd just implicitly acknowledged her own continuing leadership of the investigation. She steeled herself for one more attempt on Jennings' conscience. 'But my point is that I'm too close to it. I can't oversee an interview with Sheena, even if only as a witness.'

'I realise that, but there's nothing else I can do.' He hesitated and she could see he was thinking. 'Okay, what about this? I can take on the SIO role officially, but I want you to carry on running it all. I can do the media conferences and all the stuff like that, as long as...'

'As long as I do the grunt stuff. That's clear enough. Seriously, I don't mind that. I hate the media stuff anyway. You're much better at all that. But do you think that'll work? It still only needs one reporter to join the dots between me and Sheena.'

'I'll do my utmost to keep you out of the glare of publicity.'

So you can hog it all to yourself, Annie thought. But she was being unfair. Jennings was right. This was a high-profile case with every potential to go pear-shaped. If it did, Jennings might still find a way to fade away into the background and ensure she was the one left carrying the can. Even so, he'd be taking a risk by tying himself so visibly to the investigation.

'Or is it that you don't think you're up to this one?' Jennings added.

Now that, Annie thought, was more typical Jennings. He'd never been averse to a bit of emotional blackmail. 'No, Stuart, that's not what I think. I'm only too keen to continue. You were the one who raised the concerns about my involvement in the first place.'

'I know. And I'll add a note to the file to that effect summarising this conversation. So it's clear we're aware of the issues and we've thought carefully about how to address them. But that we've come to the conclusion your expertise and experience are needed on such a major case. After all, your star's in the ascendant after your success in the Robin Kennedy case. Our focus has to be on public safety and getting a result, not what's just in our own personal best interests.' He smiled, his face a picture of innocence.

She had to give Jennings his due. He could be quite shameless at times. Somehow he'd succeeded in retaining the moral high ground, while taking every step to ensure his own backside was well covered. That was the stuff Chief Officers were made of. No doubt he'd go far.

She felt wrong-footed by the outcome of this exchange. As a police officer and a detective, all her instincts were to stay involved, to bring the case to a satisfactory conclusion. That was what she wanted. But at Jennings' prompting she'd persuaded herself it would be in everyone's interest if she stepped aside, and she'd geared himself up overnight to do just that. Now she'd found herself talked, if not actively coerced, into staying put, simply because everyone else saw the job as a hospital pass and Jennings had been left with no other choice. It didn't exactly feel like a vote of confidence. 'If you say so, Stuart. Doesn't sound like I've much option.'

He shrugged, clearly not prepared to engage in further debate. 'So, now we've sorted that, what's your theory on Chalmers?'

'I'm not sure I have one,' Annie said. 'It makes no sense on the face of it. I can't imagine why anyone would want to kill Chalmers, let alone dump his body at Wentworth's.'

'And we're aware of no strong link between Chalmers and Wentworth?'

'Only that Chalmers is the regional rep for the union involved in the Matlock dispute. She reckoned she'd had a few professional run-ins with him over the years, particularly in some of their public sector contracts. But nothing much more than occasionally sitting on opposite sides of a negotiating table. He apparently called her to assure her that the union hadn't been involved in the damage to the car in Matlock. That was the last time she spoke to him.'

'This would be a hell of a way to resolve an industrial dispute.'

'I'm going to do some digging into Chalmers' background, but on the face of it he seems an unlikely candidate for this kind of murder.'

'It's always the quiet ones,' Jennings said. 'I assume there's no doubt in your mind that the two murders are linked?'

'There's always *doubt*. Maybe it was just coincidence. Maybe whoever killed Chalmers had just read about Wentworth losing her son and thought that leaving her with another dead body would be a laugh. Anything's possible. But it doesn't seem likely.'

'What have we got otherwise? Anything new?'

'Not particularly.' In the light of their preceding exchange, Annie felt little need to sugar-coat the state of the investigation. There was plenty going on, but little sign yet of anything substantive emerging. 'We've found nothing suspicious in any of the camera footage we've obtained from the surrounding area at the time of Justin Wentworth's death, but we're still following up on the various vehicles that have been identified during the relevant timeframe. We're interviewing all of

Michelle Wentworth's business associates and competitors over recent years, including those on the list she gave us. There's a fair amount of bad blood for a variety of reasons but we've found no one who'd seem to have sufficient motive to do something like this. I know murder doesn't always require much of a motive, but none of them seems like a likely candidate. There are a few we'll be looking at further, but I'm not hopeful that that's where the answer lies.' She was ticking off the various lines of enquiry on her fingers as she spoke. 'We're in the process of tracking down as many as we can of the past employees who've had a significant grievance about the way they were treated by Wentworth's companies. It seems to be quite a list, so for the moment we're focusing on those who've tried to take her to employment tribunal or been involved in significant industrial action. We've obtained data from Wentworth's people about cases where they've settled out of court, or cases that were dropped, for whatever reason, before they went to tribunal. Again, there's a lot of ill-will out there. My gut feeling is that feels like more fertile ground than the business types.'

'Really? I'd have expected some of the business types to be pretty ruthless.'

'I'm sure some of them are, but they also tend to be pragmatic. Their attitude generally seems to be that you win some and you lose some. If they get screwed over, they put it behind them and make sure that next time they're the ones doing the screwing. As it were.'

'Very graphically expressed.'

'That's not to say there might not be some exceptions. But I think they're generally a different breed from some of the ex-employees. Not least because they can afford to be. If they lose a business deal, it's not usually the end of the world. Whereas some of the ex-employees we've spoken to really do seem to have had their lives destroyed by Wentworth's business practices. People who've lost jobs and not been able to find employment since. People who've only been able to find precarious gig economy stuff. Couples who split up because of financial troubles. People who developed serious mental health problems. You name it.'

'Sounds grim.'

'I imagine Michelle Wentworth would say they're just collateral damage. The price that has to be paid in the name of efficiency and so on.' Annie shrugged. 'I don't feel qualified to comment. I'm not a businesswoman. And, unlike Sheena, I'm not a politician. I'm just looking at it as a detective. And it's not difficult to imagine some of these people being desperate enough to want to commit a murder.'

'What about the people involved in this dispute in Matlock? That seems to have become pretty heated. And there's the Chalmers link.'

'I'm liaising with Jack Connell on that.' DI Jack Connell was the officer in charge of the investigation into the damaging of the car. The case would normally have been relatively low-key but its status had been raised because of Roger Pallance's interview in the *Evening Telegraph* and the potential link with the Wentworth case. Connell was just a few years off retirement and was seen as a safe, if uninspiring, pair of hands. In Annie's experience, he enjoyed playing the part of the cynical old-school cop, but she'd always found him easy enough to work with. 'I've been talking to him anyway about identifying who the various players are on the picket line, but that's probably increased in priority after Chalmers' death.'

'Definitely,' Jennings said. 'I was even half-considering rolling that investigation into yours, but we've still no strong reason to believe the two cases are directly linked.'

Annie wondered whether, in considering merging the two cases, Jennings had toyed with the possibility of putting Connell in overall charge. Probably not, she thought. Connell was generally respected, but the general view was that he was winding down to his retirement. He wouldn't have been keen to take on a large-scale inquiry, particularly one that might risk ending his career on a sour note. Equally, she couldn't imagine Jennings would have wanted someone with Connell's air of world-weary cynicism fronting up this inquiry. 'Jack's pretty easy-going,' she said. 'I'll make sure we're in close contact over this.'

She could tell that, as always, Jennings' mind was already moving on to his next meeting. 'Right, Stuart, I'd better get on. You joining the morning briefing today?'

'I'll try and make it for the end. Promised I'd give the ACC a quick brief on where we're up to with the case. With as positive spin as I can manage.'

The last sentence sounded like an implied rebuke. 'We'll get there, Stuart. It's the same as ever. We just need one breakthrough.'

'You'd better get one, then. Keep me posted.'

He was already picking up the phone. The signal of dismissal was unmistakeable. Annie gathered her papers and made her way back to her own desk, trying as ever to control her irritation at Jennings' inability to follow the usual rules of civilised human interaction.

Zoe was already at her desk, working her way through some case files. She looked up as Annie returned. 'How did it go?'

'It was Jennings. How do you think?'

'Are you still on the case?'

'It seems so, for all his reservations. Apparently, we've given full consideration to the possible risk of a conflict of interest, but it's felt that on reflection a case of this importance requires leadership of a type that only someone with my experience can supply.'

'Is that really what he said?'

'It's what he's going to say if he's challenged. The reality is that everyone else seems to see this case as a sure-fire route to career self-destruction. No one else wanted to take it on, so I'm afraid you're still stuck with me.'

'I'm fine with that. I was dreading some of the names that he might have brought over.'

'Glad to hear I'm not the worst, anyway. What's new?'

'Couple of things. First is that we've had a preliminary report back from the pathologist on Justin Wentworth. Most of it's as we expected. No surprises on cause of death and so on. It seems that the first blow to his temple was delivered from the front, so Wentworth must have been facing the killer. There were more blows, apparently delivered more randomly, but the conclusion is that Wentworth was probably on the floor by then.'

'The killer carried on hitting him after he'd fallen? I suppose that's not a surprise, but it's a shock to hear it. Suggests they wanted to make sure he was dead.'

'Quite possibly because if the first blow came from the front the killer knew he could be identified.'

'Yes, that's interesting in itself,' Annie said. 'Suggests Wentworth could have been talking to the killer, and was taken by surprise. Though that raises the question of how you conceal a hefty blunt weapon.'

'Not too difficult, I suppose, particularly if the killing is premeditated. Report suggests it was something metallic and heavy, but not particularly large. The nature of the wound suggests something probably only two or three centimetres wide, like a hammer or a steel spanner. You could wrap it in something or put it in some kind of bag. Or even just conceal it behind you, for a few minutes, at least.'

'Which then leads to the question of why Wentworth went out there, and what he was doing with the killer. Was he confronting him? Was he talking to him? Did he know the killer?'

'We've no reason to think he was expecting to see anyone,' Annie pointed out. 'He only went into the house because his mother sent him to refill their drinks. But you're right. Something took him out there. Even if he'd answered the front door bell, something must then have taken him out of the house.'

'The second point the pathologist raised,' Zoe said, 'is that they found traces of various Class A drugs, including heroin and cocaine, in Wentworth's body.'

Annie gave a low whistle. 'Well, that certainly seems to contradict his mother's suggestion that he was a quiet innocent clean-living young man who barely left his room.'

'She might not have known. Parents often don't. Know things about their children, I mean.'

'Or she knew but didn't want us to know. Or she suspected, but was happy to leave it to us to find out for ourselves. Strikes me that it might be worth finding out a bit more about young Justin's private life. We've already got someone looking into his university life, but this suggests we should move that up the priority list. He was at Nottingham, wasn't he?'

'One of the Nottingham unis, yes. Can't remember which off the top of my head.'

'Can you take on that one, Zo? Try and talk to his Director of Studies, tutor or whoever else is likely to be able to give us some insights into his life there. See if we can get names of any friends or others who might be able to tell us something useful.'

'I'll see what I can do. The other thing was that Jack Connell was on the phone.'

'Talk of the devil. What was he after?'

'He'd just been informed about Chalmers' death. Said he wanted an urgent chat.'

'Fair enough. I was just about to ring him to ask for the same thing.' Annie glanced at her watch. 'Okay, let's do a quick morning briefing with the team, or at least as many of them as aren't already out doing something useful. Then we can get on with the real stuff.'

Chapter Twenty-Three

'Jack.'

Connell was reading a copy of the *Daily Mail*, which he smoothly folded up and dropped into a drawer as Annie entered his office. She wasn't sure whether Connell's office was one of the privileges of long service, or whether Connell had simply always been in here and no one had had the heart or the will to remove him. Either way, he occupied a small, self-contained individual office tucked away in a corner of the oldest part of the site. She wondered whether people sometimes simply forgot Connell was there, enabling him to get on with reading his newspaper without interruption. 'Oh, aye, come in, lass. Welcome to my parlour. Sit yourself down and make yourself at home.' He gestured towards a kettle and mugs on a side table. 'You want a brew?'

She wasn't sure if he was inviting her to make it. 'Just had one, Jack. But help yourself.'

He held up his half-full mug. 'Ahead of the game. Never knowingly under-caffeinated.' He took a sip, as if to demonstrate the concept. 'I hear poor Keith Chalmers has popped his clogs.'

'Had his clogs popped for him, more to the point.' Annie sat herself next to Connell's desk. The office was chaotic, with various piles of paperwork and files scattered around. She wondered what passed for a filing system in here. 'Did you know him?'

'Ah, well. Now there's a story, which I'll come back to in a minute. But I'd spoken to him just a day or two ago about the Matlock thing.'

'How did he seem?'

'Pretty much as you'd expect. A bit wary. Concerned about the impact on the union's reputation, not to mention their ability to continue the industrial action. Absolutely adamant that the stuff with the car was nothing to do with the union. Which, in fairness, I don't imagine it was.'

'Did he have any idea who might have done it?'

'He reckoned not. There were one or two younger ones on the picket line who'd been more vociferous, but he didn't think they were likely to have done anything as serious as that.' He shrugged. 'I think he might have been underestimating his own members' stupidity.'

'You've got names for the people on the picket line?'

'Most of them. We've been interviewing the more promising ones so far. It's what you'd expect, though. Nobody admits to any knowledge of it. Some of them have conspiracy theories. That it was done by the company to discredit the strike, or by some third party for the same reason. It's possible, I guess. Even Chalmers seemed to worry they'd been infiltrated. I don't know. I'm always inclined to go for the more straightforward explanation until there's evidence otherwise.'

'So one of the strikers?'

'Or someone acting on their behalf, maybe. I suspect we may have difficulty getting to the bottom of it, to be honest. There's no useful forensic evidence. No witnesses. No CCTV. As long as everyone continues to deny all knowledge, we may not make progress.' He sounded as if this prospect didn't trouble him unduly.

'What about Chalmers' death?' Annie said. 'What do you make of that?'

'Not usually a dangerous occupation, trade union rep. Not dangerous in that way, anyhow. But Chalmers did have an interesting reputation.'

'I thought he was Mr Moderate. That was how he always came across on TV.'

'That was the image he cultivated. The king of the middle ground.' Annie had heard that, in his younger days, Connell had been a troublesome and loud-mouthed Federation rep, though he seemed to have left that far behind.

'And wasn't he?' Annie asked.

'He was in dealing with employers. To the point where some of his colleagues thought he was a bit of a class traitor, too keen to sell them down the river for the sake of a quiet life. Chalmers wasn't a popular figure in the union. He was subject to the internal disciplinary procedures on a couple of occasions. Fairly trivial stuff about inconsistencies in expenses, and Chalmers came up with some excuse, claiming it was an error. First time, they gave him the benefit of the doubt. Second time, they accepted the explanation but gave him a formal warning for negligence or some such.' Connell was clearly leading up to his big reveal. 'But there was at least one occasion when we were called in.'

'The police?'

'Aye, in the form of yours truly, initially. They reckoned Chalmers was receiving bribes.'

'Bribes?'

'From employers for soft-pedalling on industrial action or accepting suboptimal conditions for the members, that sort of stuff.'

'Anything in it?'

Connell paused to sip his tea. 'Difficult to be sure. My gut said yes, but it was difficult to make anything stick. We'd been called in by the local office, but it was clear the union at national level didn't want us in there. If there was a problem, they wanted to brush it under the carpet. So it wasn't easy to get anywhere. Chalmers had reasonable explanations for most of his actions, and there was nothing we could easily challenge. The national office didn't exactly play ball in terms of sharing information for the relevant period, which made it harder. Chalmers claimed the whole thing had been maliciously motivated.'

'But you felt there was something in it?'

'Mainly just from the way Chalmers behaved, to be honest. I felt he had something to hide. But I was left with doubts about the whole bunch, to be honest. The culture in the regional office seemed poisonous. Chalmers might well have been right that the claims were malicious. In the end, I was happy to wash my hands of it and walk away.'

'How long ago was this?'

'Not that long. Year or so back. Don't know if anything's changed since. Like I say, I spoke to Chalmers about the Matlock stuff, but he came in here for that.'

'But you don't think any of this would be a motive for murder?'

'Who knows? Most of them struck me as armchair revolutionaries. I doubt they'd be capable of much at all. Though I have been wondering whether one of them was responsible for the damage to the car.'

'One of Chalmers' colleagues you mean?'

'It wouldn't surprise me. If they thought that Chalmers was on the point of doing some too-cosy deal with management, it might have been a way of sabotaging it. I don't mean they'd have done it themselves, but I can imagine them inciting someone from the workforce to do it. It's one of the lines I've been pursuing anyway.'

'All sounds a long way from my idea of comradeship and solidarity,' Annie said.

'Always the way, isn't it?'

'Still seems a long way from a motive for murder, though.'

'I'd have said so. Mind you, if Chalmers was involved in some kind of dodgy dealing, who knows where that might have led?'

'Strikes me I need to know more about Chalmers,' Annie said. 'Anything else useful you can tell me about him?'

'Not much. Bit of a loner. No close family, other than some son he didn't see much of. He was one of those people who don't give much away, but you're never sure if that's because they're hiding something or because they don't have much in the locker to start with.'

'I suppose the next step is for me to stick my head into the vipers' nest of the regional office.'

'If you say so,' Connell said. 'In that case, all I can offer you is thoughts and prayers. And do send them my love.'

She smiled. 'I'll do that. And let's stick close on this one, Jack. We don't want to be tripping over each other, and there's benefit in sharing resources where we can. I'm not sure if we're pursuing exactly the same thing, but I've an instinct all of this is somehow connected.'

'It certainly all seems to be part of the same awful bloody mess. Anyway, you had me at sharing resources.

If you're offering some extra resources from your vastly bloated team into my one-man-and-a-dog outfit to help conduct more interviews, I'm all for it.'

'I wouldn't have put it quite like that, Jack. But, yes, since you've asked so nicely, I'll see what I can do.'

Chapter Twenty-Four

'DS Everett?'

Zoe rose to greet the tall man heading in her direction. He was probably in his early forties, with neatly swept back greying hair and a pair of wire-rimmed spectacles over which he peered at the world with undisguised curiosity. The overall effect was that of a Hollywood depiction of an academic. Zoe couldn't decide whether or not the image had been consciously cultivated. 'Dr Pascoe?'

'Ian, please. Now, I was wondering whether we should go and grab a drink in our coffee shop. It's more salubrious than my office and, given we're still a few weeks away from the chaos of the new academic year, it should be fairly quiet. If we find a corner, we should be able to talk confidentially, if we need to.' His manner of speaking matched his appearance.

'Fine by me,' Zoe said.

She followed him out of the reception and along a short corridor to a space laid out to resemble a high-street coffee shop. 'If you sit over there in the corner, I'll get us some drinks,' he said. 'What are you having?'

'Just an Americano for me. No milk or sugar.'

'Very ascetic. Is that because you're on duty?'

Zoe smiled. 'It's mainly that I get intimidated by the range of choice in these places so I tend to default to the simplest.'

'Fair enough. I tend to do the opposite, so I'll probably end up with a chai latte with a shot of lavender syrup or something equally stupid.'

He returned a few moments later with her coffee and what appeared to be a straightforward cappuccino. He slid her drink across the table to her and said, 'So what can I do for you? You said it was about Justin Wentworth. Terrible business. I only heard the other day. I understand the Vice-Chancellor's written to his mother. I was wondering whether to contact her myself, but I wasn't sure what I'd be able to add.'

'You were Justin's Director of Studies?'

'That's right. I taught him in a couple of classes too.'

'What was he like? As a student, I mean.'

There was a long pause. Finally Pascoe said, 'Do you want me to be brutally honest?'

'I'm a police officer, Dr Pascoe. Not his mother. I'd much rather you were honest.'

'Yes, of course. Well, the truth is Justin wasn't much of a student. He wasn't the brightest, but that's all relative. He'd have been quite capable if he put his mind to it, but he never seemed fully engaged. Or even partially engaged, to be honest. I genuinely don't like speaking ill of the dead, but he was basically bone-idle. My impression was that he'd managed to get half-decent A-level grades because he'd gone to an expensive school, been tutored to within an inch of his life, and been nagged by his mother to the point where it was slightly less effort for him to succeed than it would have been to fail. As soon as he got here and it was all down to him, it all went to pot. Literally.'

'Literally?'

'Well, drugs generally. I imagine pot was the least of it.'

'You know this for sure? That he was taking drugs?'

'My suspicion is that he was *dealing* drugs. Look, if I was talking in other circumstances I'd be a lot more equivocal. I've no proof he was taking drugs. But I saw the way he behaved and I heard the rumours, and I don't have much doubt it was true.'

'It can't be that unusual among students, surely?' Zoe could even recall the odd mild experiment from her own university days, and she'd largely been a model undergraduate.

'Depends what you mean. Yes, it happens of course and pretty commonly, particularly where the softer drugs are concerned. But it's nothing like as prevalent as the tabloids would sometimes want you to believe. Cases like Justin are few and far between, thankfully.'

'So did he get into trouble? With the authorities, I mean.'

'He was suspended at the end of last year.' Pascoe saw her expression and raised an eyebrow. 'You didn't know that?'

'His mother doesn't seem to have been aware of it,' Zoe said. 'Or if she was, she didn't think to tell us.'

'His mother knew full well. She was the only reason he hadn't been thrown out.'

'How do you mean?'

Pascoe leaned back and took a sip of coffee, with the air of a storyteller about to embark on a lengthy narrative. But then he paused. 'I don't know if I should be talking to you about this.'

'Dr Pascoe, I'm a police officer engaged in a murder inquiry. If you have potentially relevant information about the victim, you have an obligation to share it.'

'Yes, of course. But I don't know if it is relevant, and my involvement was on a confidential basis. I'm wondering if I should set up a meeting with the Vice Chancellor or...'

Zoe could already envisage herself getting mired in a sea of bureaucracy. 'As I say, Dr Pascoe, this is a murder inquiry and time is critical. If you have information about Justin, I'd urge you to share it with me now. If I think it's not likely to be pertinent to our inquiry, I'm happy to treat our conversation as confidential. If I think it may be, then we can go through the appropriate channels as necessary before we release anything publicly. But that will at least mean we can begin working on the information immediately.'

'Okay. The fact is that there'd been a number of complaints about Justin during his first year here. Complaints about his behaviour.'

'What sort of complaints?'

'Some were just complaints about generally boorish behaviour. We don't get many Hooray Henry types here, but there's always a handful. People from wealthy back-grounds who've been to the posher type of public school. It's not fair to stereotype them, but there are usually one or two who think that their privileged background entitles them to treat others with contempt. Justin was one of those.'

Zoe looked surprised. 'That's not the impression of him we've gained from his mother.'

'Mothers tend to see the best in their offspring, don't they? In fact, when I met his mother and realised who she was, Justin's behaviour made a lot more sense. I don't want to play the amateur psychologist, but my guess is that Justin had felt a bit of an impostor at his school and probably embarrassed by his mother. For all her money, I suspect Justin was treated as an oik by his schoolmates. When he got here, he saw an opportunity to reinvent himself as the person he'd liked to have been at school. One of the upper-class lads. He found a couple of like-minded mates, and they went around being generally obnoxious.'

'In what kind of way?'

'I don't think they actually set fire to banknotes in front of homeless people, but they'd have been quite capable of it. Most of it was trivial stuff. Being rude to the staff here. Acts of mild vandalism that they'd then pay to put right, just to prove they could. Some borderline racist and misogynist stuff. They were generally smart enough to know how far to push it. Enough to provoke people, but not so far that they couldn't find a way of laughing it off. Usually just by claiming that whatever they had said or done was a joke, combined where necessary with some sort of apologetic gift or pay-off to smooth the waters.'

'But you said Justin had been suspended?'

'Justin was always the one who pushed it too far. That may have been, again, because he was the one with the biggest chip on his shoulder. But he was also probably the least bright of them, and certainly the one most under the influence of whatever they were taking. The others were only too happy to drop him like a stone if he started being a liability. I understand there were a few occasions when Justin got carried away and the others left him standing there to carry the can.'

'They sound a delightful bunch,' Zoe said.

'Give them a few years and they'll all be politicians and captains of industry and High Court judges complaining about declining standards among young people. I've been around long enough to see the pattern.'

'So why was Justin suspended?'

'I told you there was sometimes a racist or misogynist element to their behaviour. Justin was the worst of them for the latter. We had complaints about inappropriate behaviour. Initially just offensive comments. He claimed he'd been drunk, apologised profusely to the person he'd spoken to, and got off with a warning. But then we had a complaint about a possible sexual assault.'

'Assault?'

'One of the female students claimed that he'd tried – well, to grope her, for want of a better word. It had supposedly happened in the bar here, late in the evening.'

'When you say "supposedly"…?'

Pascoe held up his hand. 'Don't get me wrong. I'm not defending it or making light of it. I'm just recounting the incident as it ultimately panned out. The female student made the accusation. Justin, predictably, denied it. Because it had been a very crowded bar and everyone had had one too many, the victim was unable to produce any witnesses. Justin's mates swore blind it had never happened. There wasn't much we could do beyond give him a woolly reminder to consider how his actions might be interpreted. But, if I'm honest, we all believed it had happened.'

'Do you think he'd have been treated differently if he'd been less well-off?'

'To be fair, I don't think so. We went out of our way to ensure it was all handled by the book. We accepted what the victim – and I'm calling her that quite deliberately because I know what I believe – was telling us. We provided every support to her in making sure her account was clearly presented and was listened to. We tried to help her find someone who might have been able to act as a witness on her behalf. A couple of her friends who'd been present were desperate to help her, but both had to admit that they hadn't actually seen the incident. But Justin was very plausible, and his friends claimed they'd been with him at the time and had witnessed nothing. He smartly stopped short of calling the woman a liar, but claimed that either someone else had been responsible or she must have misunderstood or misinterpreted some accidental contact. In the end, we didn't have a lot of choice.'

Zoe gave him a thin smile. 'Welcome to our world. It's so often like that. So that incident didn't lead to Justin's suspension.'

'No. On the contrary. I wondered afterwards if the outcome had maybe led to Justin feeling invulnerable. After all, his experience to date had been that he'd succeeded in getting away with whatever he'd done. But we then had a much more serious complaint. Another female student accused Justin of a serious sexual assault. Attempted rape, in fact.'

Pascoe had been speaking very quietly to avoid any risk of their conversation being overheard, and that somehow made this revelation even more shocking.

'I won't go into the detail,' Pascoe went on, 'but the claim was that, after yet another heavy night in the bar, Justin had followed the woman back to her room in one of the halls of residence. He'd forced his way in there, dragged her on to the bed and – well, I don't need to spell it out. The woman started screaming and people came out from various neighbouring rooms to see what was going on. She continued to scream, people started banging on her door, and fortunately Justin was stopped before anything worse happened. He came blundering out, half-cut or worse, babbling that, yet again, it had all been a misunderstanding, that she'd invited him back, blah blah blah. No one believed him. To be honest, given the strength of feeling about these issues among the students, he was probably lucky someone didn't take the law into their own hands.'

'What happened next?'

'The woman in question made a formal complaint. My impression was that she'd been reluctant initially but had been persuaded to by her friends.'

'Again, all too familiar,' Zoe said. 'She was afraid of how it would be handled?'

'I guess so. Again, I hope we did it scrupulously by the book. We've become very sensitive about the handling of these kinds of cases, quite rightly, and I think we were all acutely conscious of the needs of the complainant. We went rigorously through the process. My own view, which I think was shared by all those involved, was that it was an open-and-shut case. The woman was able to produce witnesses who confirmed that she'd left the bar on her own, telling her friends she was tired. There was no evidence either that she knew Justin or even that he'd spoken to her in the course of the evening, so the idea that she'd invited him back to her room seemed implausible. She claimed that Justin must have followed her, although she'd been unaware of him as she'd walked across to the hall. She said she'd been conscious of someone behind her in the corridor, but hadn't thought much about it. She'd unlocked her door, stepped into the room just as Justin had appeared behind her, forcing the door open before she'd had chance to shut it. The next thing she knew, this unknown man had forced her back into the room, shut the door behind them and thrown her on to the bed. That was when she started screaming.'

'Did Justin stick by his story that she'd invited him back?'

'He didn't really have much choice, unless he was going to admit the truth. He tried to bluff it out, but even he could tell it wasn't cutting much ice. I don't think anyone questioned that he ought to be slung out. The only question really was whether the woman in question wanted to take it further and make a criminal complaint.'

'And did she?'

'The university authorities felt it wasn't their position to advise her either way, but I hope we made it clear that, if she did, she'd be given all possible support. As I say, it was a more clear-cut case than these things often are.'

'Yet at the time of his death Justin was still only suspended?'

'That's where things get murky. Justin's mother had, predictably enough, intervened right from the start. She insisted he was innocent, that he wasn't capable of doing something like that. I don't think she really even believed it herself. Maybe I'm too cynical, but her behaviour felt to me more like the actions of someone who believes they can always buy their way out of trouble. She said that if we insisted on going through the formal process, she'd get the best legal support she could get to support Justin, and that she wouldn't hesitate to drag both the university and the complainant's names through the mud in the process. Even though the internal process is supposed to be confidential.' He shrugged. 'I'm sure most of it was just bluff, but she's a formidable woman.'

'The university presumably didn't let that stop them proceeding?'

'God, no. The authorities here have their faults, but they don't take kindly to anyone trying to blackmail them. It was made very clear that the disciplinary process would go ahead, and that Justin was welcome to take whatever action he wanted in line with the defined procedures.' He paused, as if for dramatic effect. 'But it didn't happen.'

'Why not?'

'Like I say, it's murky. Out of the blue, the woman in question decided not to proceed with her complaint. She claimed that she was worried on the impact on her own reputation, about what she'd have to go through if the case proceeded.'

'All too familiar,' Zoe said.

'Except that it hadn't been her tone before. She'd clearly seen it very much as an issue of principle. She wasn't doing it just for herself, but to make the point that people like Justin Wentworth couldn't get away with this kind of behaviour. I was impressed by her.'

'Principles sometimes come up against reality. Maybe the reality was scarier than she expected. And, with respect, she had no obligation to impress you.'

Pascoe smiled. 'Touché. Of course you're right. But I don't think that was it. I don't suppose we'll ever prove it, but I think she had an approach from Justin's mother or someone acting on her behalf. I don't know if she just received the same threats that the mother had already made to us or something worse. I also have a suspicion there might have been some kind of pay-off, probably a fairly substantial one. We didn't feel able to press her as to whether that was true, but there were rumours to that effect.'

'So was the intention to reinstate Justin?'

'He was suspended and sent home when the complaint was first made, pending the outcome of the process. That was all a bit academic, to be honest, because term was nearly over anyway and Justin had completed his exams, for what that was worth in his case, so the only impact was that he went home a week or so early. The whole thing has dragged out over the summer holidays, partly because of the difficulties of getting everyone together. When the complaint was withdrawn, we didn't really have any option but to reinstate Justin.'

'So he was expected to come back this coming year?'

'Except that then we ran into a different problem. The Student Union had got wind of the fact that Justin was likely to be returning. They told us that students wouldn't be prepared to work alongside Justin, that any lectures or tutorials involving him would be boycotted, and that they'd be organising protests. We told them we'd prefer them not to take that kind of action, not least because we felt we had a duty to protect the identity and interests of the woman who'd made the initial complaint. They reckoned it was out of their hands, and that all they were doing was reacting to student opinion. Which, in fairness, may well be true.'

'What was going to happen?'

'We were still dithering. Some people had hoped Justin's academic results might be enough in themselves to prevent him continuing. As it turned out, they weren't good but they weren't quite that bad. So we were left with a dilemma. We'd spoken to Justin, tried to persuade him it wasn't going to be in his interests to return next year. Suggested he take a year out, and return when things had calmed down a little.' He held up his hands. 'I'm not exactly proud of the convolutions the university was involved in. It was almost as if we ended up trying to negotiate with him.'

'Which is presumably exactly what his mother wanted.'

'I've read more about her since this all blew up. That does seem to be her forte, doesn't it? Getting a deal.'

'That's her reputation,' Zoe agreed.

'From what I saw, she seems to get what she wants,' Pascoe said. 'One way or another. We were amateurs dealing with a professional. I don't know what would have happened if Justin had lived. I suspect he'd have come back, and we'd have spent too much of our time and money protecting him from the protests. He'd have loved being the centre of attention, and would have received more personalised supervision. We'd no doubt have been painted as shameful reactionaries for sheltering him, as if what we were doing implied approval of his behaviour. And most likely the only person not returning next year would have been the woman he assaulted.'

Zoe shook her head. 'You can imagine how often we have to deal with this kind of issue. That's so often the way it pans out. There's no justice in cases like that.'

'That's not what I'd have expected a police officer to say.'

'We do our best. Quite often, it's simply not enough.'

'We've learned a few lessons from it, anyway,' Pascoe said. 'Though I don't know what we could have done differently, really.'

'And you're saying his mother was involved in this all the way through.'

'She was on the phone to the Vice-Chancellor as soon as Justin had been informed about the complaint against him. Why?'

'We've interviewed her at some length about Justin's background, and this is the first we've heard of any of this. She gave us quite a different impression about Justin's character and university life.'

'I'm sorry. We should have been in touch with you as soon as we heard about Justin's death.'

'Not your fault. We should have treated Justin's background as a higher priority. We were too willing to accept his mother's depiction of him. We made some allowance for maternal prejudice, but I hadn't envisaged that her description would be so at odds with reality. Partly as she wasn't averse to criticising him in other respects.'

'It's one thing to criticise your son,' Pascoe said. 'It's another to acknowledge that he was guilty of attempted rape.' He paused, clearly thinking about the implications of what Zoe had been saying. 'Do you think Justin's killing might have been linked to this?'

'It's another avenue for us to follow up,' Zoe said. She wasn't in a position to mention the murder of Keith Chalmers and its implications for the investigation.

'I can't imagine that the original complainant could be responsible for anything like that. She was furious with Justin Wentworth, and rightly so, but I can't envisage her as the murderous type.'

'All kinds of people commit murder,' Zoe said. 'And it's possible someone else might have decided to take action on her behalf.'

'So this is a line of enquiry you'll be pursuing?'

'I don't think we have a choice, at least until we know more. It potentially provides a motive for murder. Why do you ask?'

'You're right, of course. But it won't be straightforward.'

'Why not?'

'For a start, we've guaranteed confidentiality to the complainant. I assume you'll be wanting to talk to her?'

'We'll need to, yes. We'll handle it as sensitively as possible. But we won't necessarily be able to guarantee anonymity. It depends how the inquiry proceeds.' She shrugged. 'It's a murder investigation.'

'I appreciate that. I'm just glad none of this is my problem. There are times when I'm grateful I don't have to wrestle with anything more difficult than interpreting English literature and persuading students it's okay to use their intellects rather than waiting for me to give them the answers. All I can do is put you in contact with the Director of Student Services and let her take it from there. The whole thing's a really nasty business.'

'I'm very grateful to you,' Zoe said. 'You've given me some valuable information.'

'It's good you haven't had a wasted trip. I'm just surprised that Justin's mother didn't tell you any of this. She must have known you'd find out eventually.'

'That's something for us to look into,' Zoe said. 'I suppose parents like to think the best of their children. But I'm still surprised she withheld information that might be pertinent to her son's murder. We'll have to talk to her again.'

'Good luck with that,' Pascoe said. 'I've only met her a couple of times, but she scares the hell out of me.'

'You and me both,' Zoe said. 'But in my line of work that tends to be an occupational hazard.'

Chapter Twenty-Five

Annie hadn't been sure what to expect, but her expectations hadn't extended to anyone quite like Erica Adamsson. Her experience of trade union officials had been largely limited to men like Keith Chalmers – and they generally were men, middle-aged, besuited, overweight and balding with years of experience in working on or around the shop-floor.

Adamsson was something else. For a start, she looked young, probably no more than early twenties. She was tall, slim and blond, and Annie suspected that in an alternative life she could easily have been a fashion model. But there was also something intimidating about her, even to Annie, who had long made a professional point of not being intimidated by anyone. It was something to do with the intensity of Adamsson's gaze, the way she stared at Annie through black-rimmed spectacles as if about to challenge her right even to exist. Adamsson spoke impeccable English, although Annie could detect a trace of some kind of Scandinavian accent.

'I was sorry to hear about Keith,' Adamsson said. 'It was a shock to all of us here.' She sounded as if she'd learned the words of sympathy by rote without ever quite understanding what they meant.

Annie nodded. 'At this stage, we're really just trying to gather some background on Mr Chalmers. We've informed Mr Chalmers' son, who's the next of kin, so we're expecting he'll be able to tell us about Mr Chalmers' private life. I was hoping you might be able to give us some insights into his work.'

'Insights?' Adamsson repeated. Her tone implied she was considering a critique of Annie's use of English. 'I suppose. We were working colleagues for the last two years or so.'

'What's the set-up here?' Annie immediately regretted her choice of words, suspecting that Adamsson would view it as inappropriately informal.

'It is a small office,' Adamsson said. 'Six of us. I am office director. We have four representatives, who cover the various sectors we represent. Keith was one of those. And we have an administrator.'

'And you cover the East Midlands?'

'Yes, as we define it. That stretches across to East Anglia, and down to Northamptonshire. It's quite a large area.'

'So the representatives spend a lot of time on the road?'

'Inevitably.' Adamsson spoke as if the question was hardly worth answering. 'Most of them come in here once or twice a week. Keith less so, unfortunately.'

'Why unfortunately?'

'It made my job harder. I need to know what cases they're involved in. Any emerging issues or problems. I don't want to find I've been caught out because I've not been kept up to speed with events.'

'And was that a problem with Mr Chalmers?'

'It could be. Keith was not an easy man to work with. He was not a team player.'

'I suppose the representatives have to be very self-sufficient?' Annie wasn't sure why she felt any urge to defend Chalmers, but that was how Adamsson's manner was affecting her.

'Perhaps.' Adamsson sounded as if she'd never given the matter much thought. 'But Keith was more challenging than some of the others. He came in only rarely. Usually because I had insisted he should be present at a meeting.'

'Did he get on with his colleagues?' Annie asked.

'I suppose so. In so far as he needed to.'

Annie was beginning to feel as if she was talking a different language from Adamsson. 'What about with you? Did he get on with you?'

'With me?' There was a prolonged silence. 'Not really. We were very different people.'

'In what way?'

Another pause. 'I have certain standards. I believe in discipline. It's the only way to run an office like this, especially if staff are working remotely. Keith was not good at those disciplines. His manner was – casual.' The condemnation sounded damning, the most severe criticism that Adamsson could envisage.

'How did that manifest itself?' Annie felt she was in danger of inadvertently mimicking Adamsson's verbal style.

'He didn't follow procedures. He was a great believer in what he called "flexibility".' The quotes around the word were almost visible. 'He told me that was the secret to effective negotiation. The willingness to bend the rules to achieve the desired outcome.'

'You didn't agree with that?'

'I accept that intransigence is likely to be a barrier to success. But that is different from Keith's notion of "flexibility". In my view, his approach was at times tantamount to anarchy.'

'That seems a rather strong description.'

'But correct, I think. I have established procedures here, for example, which are designed to make everyone's life easier. Protocols about how we report, how we create files, how we record information, and so on. Keith often disregarded or even flouted those procedures. That makes everyone's life harder.'

'I understand that the disciplinary procedures were invoked against Mr Chalmers on a number of occasions?'

There was another extended silence. 'That is an internal matter.'

'I'm afraid not, Ms Adamsson. I'm engaged in a murder inquiry. If you have information that may be pertinent to our investigation, you have a legal obligation to share it with the police.'

'It is not pertinent.'

'With respect, we have to be the judge of that. In any case, I understand that, on at least one of those occasions, the police were involved.'

'We decided not to proceed with the matter.'

It was notable that, since they'd moved on to this topic, Adamsson's responses had become increasingly terse. 'I understand it was the police who decided not to progress with the investigation on the basis that there was little likelihood of being able to evidence any wrong-doing.'

'Nevertheless, the point is that the inquiry was discontinued.'

'Did you believe that Mr Chalmers had committed any wrong-doing?'

'My opinion is of no importance. We have procedures to follow. In that case, we were unable to continue.'

Annie sighed. She suspected Adamsson would be able to continue politely blocking her questions for as long as she wanted. 'Can I ask you about the nature of the accusations?'

Adamsson's expression remained blank, but it was clear to Annie that she was weighing up how to respond to the question. Finally she said, 'There were accusations that Keith was accepting payments from some of the employers we deal with. That he was being bribed to act against his members' interests. There were also accusations that he had used union funds inappropriately.'

'How did you feel about that? About the accusation, I mean.'

'If it was true, it would of course have been wholly unacceptable. Our role is to represent our members, and there can be conflict of interest. It is simple.'

'Did you believe it to be true? Did you believe that Mr Chalmers had behaved inappropriately?'

For a moment, Annie thought Adamsson would make another attempt to dodge the question. Finally, though, she said, 'I thought it was likely, yes.'

'But there was insufficient evidence to proceed with the investigation?'

Adamsson shrugged. 'Opinions differed, let us say. Keith had a better reputation with the national office than he had here. They discouraged the investigation.'

'Why was that? Why did he have a better reputation at national level, I mean?'

'You would have to ask them.' Adamsson hesitated for a moment, as if recognising that this response was insufficient. 'Much of it comes down to political divisions. The national office tends to be more old-fashioned. You might say more right-wing. They think of us as dangerous radicals.' Adamsson smiled, but Annie wasn't sure to what extent she was joking. 'They saw Keith as one of their own. He'd worked in London for a while, and was very old-school. We saw him as something of a spy in the camp.'

'I believe there was some suggestion that the accusations were maliciously motivated?'

Adamsson's smile was unwavering. 'There were some tensions in the office, but my view is that the accusations were sincerely motivated. It is academic now, though.'

Annie raised an eyebrow. 'Except that someone was responsible for Mr Chalmers' death.'

'You're not suggesting anyone here was responsible?'

'I'm suggesting nothing. But I am interested in the nature of Mr Chalmers' working relationships with his colleagues. Particularly if there were tensions.'

'It was just office politics. Nothing more. In this kind of work, people have strong feelings about what they do and how they do it.'

'Of course. But we will need to talk to everyone here. I trust that won't be a problem?'

'Not at all. I quite understand. But I'm afraid you won't find the explanation of Keith's tragic death here.'

Annie gazed back at the other woman for a moment, keeping her own expression neutral. She had little doubt that Adamsson wasn't telling the whole truth, but she suspected Adamsson was the kind of person who rarely told the whole truth. Whether it was significant in this case, Annie had no idea. But she was increasingly realising that Keith Chalmers' life was much more complicated than she'd imagined. Every step in this case seemed only to open up new questions. 'Thank you for your time, anyway. I'll organise for my team to talk to the other members of the office.'

'That won't be a problem,' Adamsson said.

'I'm glad to hear it,' Annie said, offering her sweetest smile. 'I'd hate to be a nuisance.'

Chapter Twenty-Six

Stepping back outside into the warmth of late morning felt almost comforting. The trade union offices had been air-conditioned, but Annie suspected that was not the only cause of the chill that seemed to pervade the place. As far as she'd seen, the only other current occupant of the offices had been a miserable-looking young woman who was presumably the administrator. Annie wondered whether Keith Chalmers had been the only one of the representatives who made a point of being out on the road as much as possible. She could see now why Jack Connell had referred to the office culture as poisonous. Annie had felt the same herself, even in the short time she'd been in there.

Nevertheless, she resisted making the leap from that to any connection with Chalmers' death. There were plenty of toxic workplaces, but that rarely led to murder. But it was another avenue they couldn't rule out. She'd get someone in there to talk to the rest of the team to see what emerged.

Annie had considered delegating the interview with Erica Adamsson to one of the team, particularly given Jennings' continuing anxiety about any possible conflict of interest. She had more than enough on her own plate as it was, and she knew there were risks in spending too much time away from the office. On the other hand, she'd wanted to get a feel for Chalmers' work background, and she wasn't sorry now that she'd experienced Adamsson's personality and unique management style at first hand. Even if there was no direct link to his murder, Annie felt she understood something more about what might have influenced Chalmers' attitudes and behaviour.

In the end, she'd justified her morning out of the office, at least to her own satisfaction, by organising a meeting with Chalmers' son, Andrew. It felt appropriate that she should meet Andrew Chalmers personally at this point, if only to reassure him the case was being given appropriate priority. She was beginning to build a picture of Chalmers' life and personality that seemed at odds with the person that Sheena had described to her.

She'd had a couple of local officers break the news to Andrew Chalmers at the earliest opportunity and also to seek his permission to enter his father's house. Andrew Chalmers had a set of keys to the house, which he'd used to keep an eye on the place when his father was travelling, and had offered to provide access. She'd arranged with a couple of the team to carry out the initial visit, in case Chalmers' murder had actually occurred at his home and there was a need to protect the scene. While she'd been talking to Erica Adamsson she'd received a message to confirm there'd been no sign that the killing or any other disturbance had occurred at the house, and that the two officers were, with the son's permission, conducting an initial search for anything that might be pertinent to the case. Andrew Chalmers had agreed to wait for her at the house.

Eastwood itself was just over the border into Nottinghamshire. The creation of the cross-force East Midlands Special Operations Unit a few years before had caused its fair share of headaches for everyone involved, but it had reduced the need for liaison with other forces when operating outside the county. Annie's experience was that, because of the proximity of Derby and Nottingham, both located in the south of the respective adjacent counties, the county boundary was often irrelevant to people's living and working lives. Eastwood, as it happened, lay almost equidistant between the two cities.

Her own knowledge of the town was limited to a vague awareness of its links with D. H. Lawrence and its history as a former mining town. She'd visited it a few times for work purposes and found it an unexpectedly thriving place. It seemed for the most part to have shed any signs of its mining heritage, other than the rows of terraced mining cottages that included Lawrence's birthplace.

She imagined it was now largely a commuter town, convenient for the M1 motorway and for people who worked in Nottingham or Derby, as well as in the nearby retail park with its large Swedish furniture store. Chalmers' house was to the west of the main town centre, out in the more rural Moorgreen area. Following the satnav direction, Annie found the house easily enough. She turned into the driveway and gave a low whistle.

In fairness, she had no idea what trade union officials earned – though she'd now make a point of finding out what Chalmers was paid – or of Chalmers' other financial circumstances. Maybe he'd inherited money from somewhere. It was also the case that, for some reason, property in this area remained relatively cheap.

Even so, the place was more impressive than she'd expected. Not exactly a match for Michelle Wentworth's place, but with a similar feel to it. The core of the building looked as if it was probably eighteenth or early nineteenth century, perhaps a workman's cottage of some kind. It had been tastefully extended, and the overall effect was entirely harmonious. The driveway led into a courtyard, and Annie could see a lengthy lawned garden to the rear of the house, with open country beyond.

There were two other cars parked at the front of the house, one of which was a police pool car. She assumed that the other belonged to Andrew Chalmers. The location of Keith Chalmers' own car remained a mystery for the moment.

As she approached the house, the front door opened and a young man emerged to greet her. He was probably in his late twenties, she thought, and good-looking in a slightly nondescript way. She couldn't detect any obvious resemblance to the photographs she'd seen of his father.

'DI Delamere?'

'Annie Delamere, yes. I'm very sorry that we've had to be the bearers of such awful news.'

He led her into the house, then through into a living room. The house was nicely decorated, she thought. Tastefully painted, with various items of furniture that, to her inexpert eye, looked expensive. But there was something anonymous about the place, as if Keith Chalmers had paid for an interior designer to decorate the place for him without making any personal contribution to the choice of decor. As she looked round, she could detect no strong signs of Chalmers' own personality. There didn't even seem to be any personal photographs. 'Your people are upstairs,' Andrew Chalmers said. 'I just told them to get on with it. As far as I'm aware, Dad had nothing to hide and if they can find anything that might help you catch whoever did this…' He trailed off, as if unsure how to finish the sentence. 'It's all been a bit of a shock.'

'Of course,' she said. 'If you'd prefer to wait before talking to me—'

'No, I'm happy to.' He smiled. 'It might even be therapeutic.' He gestured towards the kitchen. 'Would you like a coffee? I wouldn't mind one.'

'That sounds a good idea. I'll come and help you.' She had the feeling he'd benefit from taking a few minutes to grow accustomed to her presence before they began talking. She was also curious to see more of the house.

She followed him into the kitchen, and helped him track down the coffee, mugs and milk from the fridge. It struck her that, for all his apparent closeness to his father, he seemed unfamiliar with the kitchen. It had been a long while since Annie had lived with her own mother – and she had been only too glad to get away – but she still knew pretty much exactly where her mother kept everything.

'It just struck me,' Andrew Chalmers said, 'that this is all stuff my dad would have been expecting to use. I mean, he must have bought this milk expecting he'd be able to drink it.' He shrugged, awkwardly. 'I know that's obvious. But it seems oddly poignant now.'

'I understand what you mean,' Annie said. 'It's always the little things that get you. Were you close to your father?'

'It depends what you mean by close. He and my mum were divorced years ago. She moved away and I spent most of my time living with her, down near Loughborough. Dad had access and I used to see him some weekends, but he was always working, always busy. So we weren't particularly close when I was a child. It was only when Mum died a couple of years back that we properly got back in touch. I've seen a lot more of him over the last year or two.'

'I'm sorry,' Annie said. 'That must make it even more of a loss.'

'That's the thing. I did feel I'd finally begun to establish some proper connection with him and now, well, this.' He finished making the coffee and they carried their mugs back into the living room. Annie took a seat in an armchair and Andrew sat on the sofa opposite. 'Can I ask what happened, exactly? The officers who came to see me were a bit vague.'

'I'm afraid we can't provide too much detail at this stage, not till we've had the pathology report and other information. But we believe it was an unlawful killing.'

'Murder?'

'Potentially. Obviously until we know the full circumstances, it's difficult to be sure.'

'But that's crazy. Who'd want to kill Dad?'

'That's what we need to find out. You're not aware of any reason why someone might want to harm him?'

'Dad? I can't imagine it. I mean, he wasn't always the easiest character to deal with. That's what made him good at his job, or one of the things. But I can't imagine why anyone would want to harm him.'

'Tell me about him,' Annie said. 'What sort of a man was he?'

'Like I say, I only really got to know him properly in the last year or so. That sounds weird, but I don't have any strong memories of him from my childhood. We'd drifted even further apart as I'd grown older. I'd no great desire to see him and he made no effort to see me. I think now he was actually a bit embarrassed. He knew he'd let me down when I was a kid. He'd always been too involved in his work to devote time to me, and Mum reckoned he'd been the same when they were married. He just felt too awkward to admit that, or to make the first approach to me. He recognised I owed him nothing, and he didn't want to seem to be imposing on me.'

Annie wondered whether this was an overgenerous interpretation of how Keith Chalmers had behaved, but she could see why it was an idea that his son might prefer to cling on to. 'But you did get back in contact,' she prompted him.

'When Mum died, I met him at the funeral. We got on okay. Better than I'd expected. We had some things in common. Afterwards, I decided it was just stupid for us to stay – what's the word? Estranged? So I phoned him up and we got together, and we took it from there. We met up every couple of weeks, sometimes just for a beer or a chat, sometimes for a meal. We'd begun to enjoy each other's company...'

'I'm very sorry,' Annie said. 'What are your own circumstances?'

'I'm married,' Andrew said. 'Diane and I live over the other side of Nottingham now. We'd sometimes invite Dad over for dinner or Diane would join me when I met him. They got on okay. But she recognised I needed time alone with him. Time to recapture all those lost hours.' He smiled. 'Sorry, I'm beginning to sound really maudlin.'

'That's understandable.'

'You asked what sort of a man he was. I've just been trying to think how to answer that. As a child, I always felt he was hard-working, a little driven. Though that's probably because it was what Mum always said about him. Among other less polite things.' He gave a rueful laugh. 'She reckoned that if he'd been prepared to devote half the time to his marriage that he devoted to his job the two of them might still have been together. But he was a workaholic, and she said he'd do almost anything to get what he wanted.'

Annie considered that for a moment, wondering about its implications. 'Almost anything?'

'Maybe I'm exaggerating. She described him as a wheeler-dealer. Someone with good intentions, but who believed the end justified the means.'

'That doesn't sound entirely positive.' She wondered whether she was pushing this too far, but he seemed keen to talk honestly.

'My mum's view of him wasn't exactly entirely positive. She thought he was basically a good man with generally decent intentions, but that he was – I'm not exactly sure how to put it, but she felt he was unreliable, untrustworthy. Maybe a little weak. What he saw as pragmatism, she saw as a lack of principle.'

'How did he seem more recently? When you met him again as an adult, I mean.'

Andrew was silent for a moment. 'I'm not sure, exactly. I recognised some of what Mum had said about him. But the drive wasn't there any more. He seemed different. Disillusioned, almost. He was still doing his bit, as he called it, but he felt he'd been betrayed. He reckoned he'd been shafted – that was his word – by the people he worked with. There'd always been a lot of factionalism in the union. He reckoned it went with the territory. I work in the charitable sector now doing fundraising stuff, and I can see some of the same tendencies there. People who sometimes get so caught up in the cause that they lose sight of basic human decency. Anyway, Dad reckoned that there was a new breed of trade unionist who were more interested in furthering their own careers than in protecting the interests of their members.'

Annie thought back to her meeting with Erica Adamsson. Even if Keith Chalmers' depiction of the union was inevitably partial, Annie could see that his views might well have seemed incompatible with those of some of his colleagues.

'Dad was the old guard, really,' Andrew Chalmers went on. 'It might just have been that he didn't fit in any more. He had his own ways of doing things and I know some people thought he was a soft touch, too ready to do a deal with management.'

'You said you thought he was disillusioned. How did that manifest itself?'

'He was just going through the motions in his work. He felt he was criticised whatever the outcome. He'd get flak from his own side for being in the boss's pocket. He'd get criticised by the members for failing to protect their interests adequately. He'd see his colleagues showboating, as he saw it, to raise their own profiles. And he'd say what's the point? Why should he bust a gut trying to do the right thing by the members if nobody even recognised or cared what he was doing? I know he was looking at the possibility of retirement, but he was still a year or two off it.'

'Were you aware he'd been subject to the union's disciplinary procedures? That various… accusations had been made against him?'

'Dad alluded to it, but he never wanted to discuss the detail. Again, he reckoned he'd been set up.' He paused, clearly thinking. 'I'm sure he was right. But I also wouldn't be surprised if he'd given them the ammunition.'

'In what way?'

'From the little he said to me, I had the impression he was a little too willing to bend the rules when it suited him. I'm sure he always did it for good reasons, or what he saw as good reasons, but it wouldn't surprise me if he went too far on occasions.'

'But they didn't proceed with the disciplinary procedures, as I understand it.'

'Dad was smart, and he could talk his way out of anything. I imagine he'd have covered his tracks pretty well, and would have an answer for everything. And he was still well regarded at national level.'

'You're being very honest with me, Mr Chalmers.' Andrew Chalmers had talked more openly about his father than she'd expected, and she wondered to what extent he was still in shock.

'There's no point in not being, is there? Especially if it helps you find whoever did this.'

'You think his death might have been linked to his work?'

'I've no idea. I'm just telling you what I know. I'm not intending to speak ill of the dead but Dad was honest about his failings, especially if he'd had a drink or two. That was part of the disillusionment. He knew he'd done things he shouldn't have, and he knew he'd not always achieved as much as he could have. But then that's probably true of most of us.'

'If you don't mind me asking, why did he and your mother split up? Was it just his overworking?'

'From what Mum said, it was mainly that. That was the chronic thing that was never going to change. But there was something more specific that prompted the actual split. Mum would never talk about it, but Dad talked to me about it recently. He had an affair.'

Annie looked up in surprise. Somehow, this hadn't been what she'd expected. She'd envisaged Keith

Chalmers as someone who was largely married to the job, with no time for anything as frivolous as a romantic life. 'And that was what caused the break-up?'

'It must have been the final straw. Mum might have been prepared to play second fiddle to his job but not to another woman.' He paused. 'I never really knew for years why they split up, and if I asked Mum gave me anodyne stuff about them having drifted apart. Then later when I pressed her she talked about him being married to the job. It was only when I was an adult that Dad admitted he'd had an affair. I think he assumed Mum had told me.'

'What did your father say about it?' Annie wasn't sure why she was even pursuing this topic. Whatever Keith Chalmers had got up to twenty years earlier, it was unlikely to be relevant to his death.

'It wasn't what I expected. I assumed that it was some passing fling, maybe with someone from work. But Dad reckoned it had been serious. He was planning to leave Mum to be with this other woman. He'd actually broken the news to her and told her he was leaving. Mum had always given me the impression that she'd been the one responsible for throwing him out. I guess it's always the way. People shape their memories to suit their own needs.'

'He didn't end up with her, though, this other woman?'

'Dad was a bit vague about that. Said it hadn't worked out quite the way he'd expected. I had the sense that he felt he'd somehow been used. I could imagine that. For all his scheming, Dad was always a bit innocent in the ways of the world. He probably wouldn't have missed a trick in a union negotiation, but he'd believe anything if a woman fluttered her eyelashes at him.' Andrew stopped. 'Sorry. That sounded sexist. But you know what I mean.'

'I can imagine. You don't know the identity of this woman, I don't suppose?' Annie wasn't even sure why she was asking, but her instincts were telling her there was something worth pursuing here.

'Not a clue, I'm afraid.' He gestured towards the ceiling, where they could hear the sounds of the two officers moving around as they checked through Keith Chalmers' possessions. 'I told your colleagues to do what they wanted with his papers, so I guess they might find the answer in there somewhere. I felt it wasn't my business, so I never pushed him to say any more than he wanted to.'

'How was he recently? Did you have any sense he was anxious about anything?'

'Not really. He always seemed paranoid about the work stuff. He was prone to seeing conspiracy theories everywhere. Wasn't comfortable trusting anyone, including those who were supposedly on his own side. But I thought that was just how he was, or just how he was in recent years anyway. I didn't imagine anybody might be really out to get him.'

'We don't know that they were. We don't know the circumstances of his death or what might have led to it. It might have been connected to his work, or it might have been something completely different. All we can do at this stage is consider every avenue. Had you noticed any change in his manner in recent weeks? Did he seem more nervous or worried?'

'Thinking about it, I think he seemed a bit more anxious over the last few months. More anxious about the future, mainly. I just thought it was because he was fed up with the job. He wanted to get out, but he wasn't keen to forgo any of his pension. He kept talking about wanting to get more cash behind him so that he could make a clean break of it, but it wasn't clear to me how he was going to do that. Just wishful thinking, I suppose.'

Annie was about to offer a response when they were interrupted by the sound of the two DCs descending the stairs in the hallway. A moment later, the first, a young member of Annie's team called Colin Palmer, appeared in the doorway of the living room. He was clearly about to speak to Chalmers, and did a visible double-take as he caught sight of Annie. 'Oh, didn't realise you were here, Annie.'

'I was planning to come and talk to you once Mr Chalmers and I were finished. How's it going?'

'Fine, though I can't say we've discovered anything particularly informative so far.' He turned to Andrew Chalmers. 'We've gathered together a boxful of documents we found that we thought might merit a more detailed look. Some of them look to be work files and suchlike, but there are also some more personal items – a few old diaries and notebooks. Are you happy for us to take those away for further examination?'

'Take whatever you like,' Andrew said.

'We'll inventory all of it and give you a proof of receipt. We should be able to let you have it back pretty quickly, unless we think any of it's worth holding on to for evidential reasons. We'd also like to take your father's laptop and tablet, if that's okay. We can let our techies have a look at them to see if they can access the data. There might conceivably be something relevant on there.'

Annie was impressed by Palmer. It was too soon to say what potential he might have, but from what she'd seen so far he seemed thorough and professional.

'I can't think what, though,' Andrew Chalmers said. 'Dad had his flaws but I still can't imagine why anyone would want to kill him.'

'It's always hard to imagine,' Annie said. 'Murder seems such an extreme act that we always assume it must have been prompted by extreme motives, but it's not always the case. Sometimes it can result from the most trivial of actions or feelings – jealousy, a passing anger, wounded pride. At the moment, we just don't know.' And yet, inside, Annie suspected that she did know – or, at least, she had an inkling. Somehow Chalmers felt like a secondary figure, even in his own life. He didn't seem like someone who would have been targeted because of anything he'd actually done or said. And if he hadn't been targeted, that suggested his death might have been nothing more than tragic collateral damage.

Chapter Twenty-Seven

'Chalmers?' Peter Hardy said. 'You mean Chalmers the union guy?'

'That's the one,' Michelle Wentworth said. They were sitting at the kitchen table. The weather was as hot as ever, although the thickness of the old stone walls provided some protection from the extremes outside.

'And they dumped the body outside your gates?'

She nodded wearily. She'd already told Peter all of this over the phone, but he seemed intent on repeating back the edited highlights to her. 'Last night. After you'd gone. I had the police here, and they were out there most of the night.'

'But why the hell didn't you call me?'

She took a breath. 'Why do you think, Peter? First, because I had those two detectives round again, that Delamere and the other one who's supposed to be the Family Liaison Officer.' She gave a mocking intonation to the last three words. 'They were asking enough questions. They both strike me as pretty bloody smart and I don't want to give them any more opportunity to dig around.'

'All the more reason why I should have been here.'

'I can look after myself, Peter. I did it very successfully for years before you were on the scene. You've a lot of skills I lack, but fending off nosy fucking police isn't one of them. I just didn't want to give them any reason to wonder why you were here, what the nature of our relationship might be, or anything else.' She paused. 'I wouldn't be surprised if they're already suspicious of that list of potential suspects we gave them.'

'Why would they be?'

'Well, I wonder why. Could it be that they might think we gave them a list of largely random names from my past to distract them from looking more closely into my present?'

'You've had run-ins with all of those people over the years. Any one of them could be a suspect in Justin's murder.'

Wentworth rolled her eyes. 'Most of them probably don't even have a bloody clue that Justin exists. Some of them probably don't even remember *me*. I've not even had contact with a few of them for years. It's not much more than a scattergun list of everyone I've ever met in a business context.'

Hardy shrugged. 'That's what they asked for. They just asked us to produce a list of anyone who might have reason to want to harm you.'

'I'm just saying we need to be careful not to underestimate them.'

'You can fend them off easily enough, surely.'

'I can as long as we manage not to give them anything more to sniff at.'

Hardy held up his hands. 'Okay. I get the message. Tread carefully. That's what I always do, Mickey.'

She wanted to tell him to stop calling her Mickey. It was what she allowed her few remaining family members and one or two close friends to call her. Peter had learned about it and adopted the diminutive almost immediately. It was no doubt all part of his plan to slip unobtrusively into

233

her inner circle. She hadn't really cared at first, but now she wanted to keep him at a greater distance and somehow the use of the nickname no longer seemed appropriate. 'I know, Peter, and you're very good at it. But I'm perfectly capable of dealing with the long arm of the law.'

'I wouldn't be so sure of that, Mickey.' It sounded almost like a threat. Hardy was silent for a moment and then went on, 'But why Chalmers? We hardly knew him.'

'I've known him for ages. Years.'

'But only as someone to sit facing over a negotiating table. You didn't *know* him. He wasn't part of your business circle.'

'Neither was Justin.'

'No, but…' Hardy clearly realised he was running into a dead end. 'But if these really are intended as some kind of threat or warning, why would they target your son and some nondescript trade union rep?'

'I don't know,' Wentworth said. 'It feels as if they're just trying to attack me from different directions.'

'I can understand Justin. That's obviously hitting you where it's likely to hurt you most. Or at least it would be if you were like any other mother—'

'Don't push it, Peter.' Wentworth's voice was quiet, but carried an unmistakeable note of anger.

'No, I'm sorry. I shouldn't have said that. I just meant that people don't appreciate how resilient you are. Anyway, the point is that I don't understand why Chalmers. Why would you even care about him? If anything, it makes our work slightly easier. One more potential thorn in the side removed.'

'I don't know, Peter,' she said, more patiently. 'If I knew who exactly was behind this or how their bloody minds worked, I'd tell you. But I don't and I don't, so I can't help you.'

'But we think this is connected with our new project?'

'It must be, mustn't it? We've never had to deal with anything like this before. The odd protest, petty vandalism—'

'A trashed BMW. But I take your point.'

'Chalmers thought we were behind that, apparently.'

'Trashing our own car?'

'Roger Pallance said so when we spoke the other day. But Chalmers was adamant that no one among his membership would have done it.'

'Maybe he needs to get to know his membership better. Oh, sorry, too late now.'

'For God's sake, Peter.'

'It's just that these holier-than-thou lefties make me sick. Always leaping on the moral high ground. You're really trying to tell me that none of those yobs on the picket lines would have been capable of doing something like that?'

'I don't know. But even that was something bigger than we've ever faced before. Maybe Chalmers had a point.'

'I think I'd have known if we'd asked someone to trash one of our own cars.'

'We wouldn't. But maybe someone did, and maybe that someone wasn't from the trade union.'

'You mean the same person who's responsible for the killings?' Hardy said. 'Why would they do that?'

'It's a different level from murder, but it's still more cost and inconvenience to us. And it raised the temperature in the dispute. From what Pallance tells me, behind the scenes Chalmers wasn't far from capitulating. He knew they couldn't stay out on strike for long, and he knew we were planning to rejig things to make further action virtually impossible. Chalmers was trying to finalise some kind of face-saving outcome that would let the strikers think they'd not been completely wasting their time. But the car thing raised the stakes again. I was talking to Pallance about it. He thought that if we agreed something now, it would look as if we were surrendering to violence and intimidation. So it had kiboshed any immediate chance of a settlement.'

'All for the best as far as I'm concerned. We should just tell the unions where to stick their deals.'

'And that's why I've never let you anywhere near our union negotiations. Yes, they're a pain in the arse and I'd far rather we didn't have to go through the charade. But, at least for the moment, we do, particularly with our public sector contracts. And we've done it systematically so we weaken their hand with every deal we sign.' She sighed. 'You know all that, Peter. You just like playing the hard man. But it's not the point, anyway. The point is that the trashing of the car, although it was only small beer, was yet another thing that made us look bad. Made us look as though we weren't fully in control.'

'So you think this is all connected?'

'I really don't know. I just know that we seem to be facing a bigger threat than we've ever faced before in the business. I've made a good few enemies over the years but I've always made sure I'm well and truly in control. Now I'm beginning to feel as if things are slipping away from me and I don't like it.'

Hardy was nervously drumming his fingers on the table. 'I think we're in too deep to pull back now, Mickey. I don't think our partners would appreciate it.'

'That's another thing I don't like. I don't like the fact that the only contact I've got with our so-called partners is through you. That's another reason I don't feel on top of any of this.'

'We've talked about this. It's partly to protect you. If this should go pear-shaped for any reason – not that it's going to – you're not too deeply embroiled. You can deny all knowledge of the funding.'

'And I went along with that. But I'm beginning to think it's bollocks. If this does go tits-up and that funding turns out to be as dodgy as I suspect it is, then I'm as deep in the shit as you are. Nobody's going to believe I didn't know the full story. And the fact is that I do know the story, or at least enough of it. So don't give me any crap about protecting me. It's just that I have to depend on you to act as the conduit.'

'And, as you know, that's also partly because they insisted on it. I've worked with some of these people for years. They know me and they trust me. That's why they were prepared to deal with me in the first place.'

'Has it ever occurred to you that maybe they're dealing with you because no one else is prepared to deal with *them*?'

'Now you're the one talking bollocks, Mickey. With respect. They could deal with anyone they wanted to. They're dealing with us because they know we're good at what we do.'

'I still don't like not being in control.' She was aware that a note of petulance was creeping into her voice. That was another thing about Peter, she thought. He had a habit of taking on a quasi-paternal role with her, which meant that she slipped, often without realising it, into a state almost of dependency. It was another way he'd insinuated himself into her life, by creating the illusion that she couldn't manage without him. It was nonsense, of course. She'd never been dependent on anyone in her life, and she had no intention of changing now.

There was no question, though, that for the moment she needed Hardy. He was right that they were now too deeply caught up in all this to withdraw. In any case, she had no idea what the consequences of withdrawing might be, although she imagined their unnamed partners would not take it with good grace. As long as they continued, she needed Hardy's knowledge and experience. There'd come a time, though, and it wouldn't be too far distant, when she'd discard him in the same way she'd discarded everyone else who'd believed they were indispensable to her. If she was going to do that, first she had to claw back full control of the business.

'It's about delegation,' Hardy went on. 'That's all. You're just delegating that aspect of the business relationship to me.'

Patronising git, she thought. Out loud, she said, 'It's not good enough, Peter. I've been thinking this through since last night. This is my business, and I'm taking a big risk with it.'

'For big rewards.'

'Potentially for big rewards, yes, or so you tell me. But none of that's guaranteed, and if this goes badly wrong we could end up very seriously exposed. At the moment, I don't really even know what the consequences of that might be.' She paused, watching his face. 'The thing is, Peter – the really important thing – at present it's showing all the signs of going badly wrong.'

'We've barely even started yet, for Christ's sake. We haven't even begun to pitch for a lot of this work. How can it be going wrong?'

'That's exactly what I'm asking myself. We've hardly even begun this and my bloody son's been murdered. Not to mention Keith Chalmers. How can that be?'

'We don't know that that's anything to do with all this.'

'So what are you suggesting? That it's all just a great big bloody coincidence?'

'No, but—'

'But what, Peter? Somebody's targeting me. I don't know who or why, but I do know this kind of thing hasn't happened to me before. Then there was that threatening call you took last night. It could be me next, Peter.'

'So what are you suggesting?'

'I want to know what I'm really getting into here. I want to take back some control of it. I'm not looking to throw my weight around, but, with the best will in the world, I can't do a decent job if I don't know what it is I'm dealing with.'

'I don't—'

'I want to meet them, Peter. I want to meet these mysterious partners of ours. I want to be sure that they're dealing in good faith.'

'You can't do that, Mickey. Anyway, why wouldn't they be dealing in good faith? They put up the money with no conditions attached. No strings.'

'Except that they expect to see a suitable return on their investments. Oh, and they've told us which sectors and which contracts to pitch for.'

Hardy shook his head, as if exasperated at her failure to understand. 'Of course they want a decent return on their investment. They're business people. They're not just going to throw money down the drain. And, yes, they've opened doors for us, introduced us to sectors and companies we couldn't have got near before.'

'But how?' Wentworth said. 'If these people are as publicity-shy as you keep telling me, Peter, how come they've got all these big business contacts?'

'That's how it works, isn't it? You're not naive, Mickey. They've got all kinds of people on the payroll. That's part of the point.'

'Including us, now.'

'If you want to put it like that.'

'There's no other way to put it. That's where we are. And that's why I want to meet them.'

'I don't know—'

'You don't know what, Peter? You don't know if they're willing to meet me? Well, let's put it this way. If they're not willing to meet me, I'm not willing to work for them. If they're not prepared to see me, I want to be taken off their bloody payroll.'

'That's not how it works, Mickey.'

She could tell he was striving for his usual paternalistic patronising tone, but this time it didn't come off. He simply sounded desperate. 'So how does it work?'

'They call the shots. That's how it works.'

'Look, Peter, I'm not looking to be difficult for no reason. I'm not being unreasonable. But if I'm going to be out there on the front line taking the risk, I want to have at least some idea who I'm working for. I'm not asking them to divulge their innermost secrets or send me three years of their company accounts. I just want reassurance that these people really do know what they're doing, and that I'm not being hung out to dry.'

'For Christ's sake, Mickey, of course they know what they're doing.'

'Fine. So all they need to do is reassure me of that. If they can't do that, the deal's off.'

'That really isn't how it works. You don't tell them what to do. You don't issue ultimatums. Not to these people.'

'Is that right? I was under the impression I'd done just that.'

'I can't go—'

'If you don't, then I'll take a lesson out of poor old Keith Chalmers' book. I'll just withdraw my labour. I'll leave the money untouched in that mysterious offshore bank account, so they can just take it back. Or they can leave it there, I don't care. And that's it. I'll go back to business as usual.'

Hardy was staring at her. She couldn't tell if he was terrified or furious. Probably some unholy combination of the two, she thought. 'You really mean it, don't you?'

'I really do. You ought to know me well enough by now to know that.'

'Shit. But what I am supposed to do?'

'That's your problem, isn't it? I'd say go and talk to them. Tell them what I've said. Tell them it's the price of getting me to carry on with them. If they aren't prepared to do it and don't want me to carry on, we'll know where we stand.'

'I already know where we stand,' Hardy said. 'Deep in the shit, if you carry on with this.'

Watching the expression on Hardy's face, she almost got cold feet. But she knew she was right. It wasn't even that she was really that concerned about meeting these people, though it was true she wanted to know more about who they were and what interests they represented. In her experience, if you went blundering about in the dark, you almost invariably ended up tripping over the wrong person's feet.

In reality, her real interest was in Hardy. She needed to reassert her authority, demonstrate her leadership. She'd conceded too much to him. If he was worried about the task she was setting him, so much the better. 'That's your considered opinion, is it, Peter?'

'All I'm saying is—'

'I don't much care what you're saying or what your considered opinion is. I just want you to do what I tell you. And I want you to do it now.'

Hardy gazed back at her, his face unreadable. 'You're not giving me a choice, are you?'

'Not so's you'd notice, Peter, no. So there's a good chap. Just get on and do it, eh? As I believe you old heroine Maggie Thatcher used to say: "I want people who bring me solutions, not problems." So bugger off and find me a solution.'

He was angry now, she thought. She couldn't be sure if that was because he really found the task she'd set him as worrying as he claimed, or simply because she'd made such an explicit point of shifting her attitude towards him. Apart from anything else, he presumably realised it was likely to be a long while before she allowed him back into her bed.

But it was the right thing to do, she had no doubt about that. Hardy had been gently leading her down the proverbial garden path. He'd built up her dependence on him to the point where she was conceding more and more power and influence. That had been a mistake, and it was fortunate she'd caught it in time.

She didn't believe for a minute that, if it came to it, their mysterious partners would really refuse to meet her. They'd probably fob her off with some relatively junior contact, but that was fine. This wasn't really about the partners. This was about taking the initiative from Peter, preventing him from acting as the gatekeeper. She should never have allowed that to happen in the first place. Peter's misery now wasn't because he was anxious about how the partners might respond. It was because he saw that, step by step, she was rendering his own role here redundant.

Well, that was how it worked. This was her business, and she had no intention of handing any of it over to the likes of Peter Hardy. He'd soon realise how dispensable he really was.

'And, Peter,' she added, as he was getting up to leave, 'please don't try to bullshit me. I really don't like people who do that.'

Chapter Twenty-Eight

Zoe Everett was leaving the centre of Nottingham, heading out over the seemingly endless sequence of traffic lights and roundabouts along the A610 towards the M1 junction, when Annie called. She took the call on the hands-free and updated Annie on the discussion with Ian Pascoe.

'Interesting,' Annie said. 'That certainly gives a whole new perspective on young Justin's university life. It's striking that his mother chose to share none of that with us.'

'Isn't it? She must have known we'd find out.'

'Maybe she thought we wouldn't. She might have thought she'd deflected us from enquiring into his life at university. Or maybe she thought that the university would close ranks and prefer not to wash its dirty linen in public. We might have got a different response if we'd gone in through formal channels first. Although I can't imagine that they would have held back everything.'

'So what do you think it was? Her reason for not telling us, I mean. Just a mother being protective of her son?'

'Maybe,' Annie said. 'Or, more cynically, a mother being protective of her business. That might have been why she was so keen to suppress the whole thing in the first place. Not just to protect Justin but also because it's not the kind of story she'd have wanted to see splashed all over the tabloids. I suppose the real question is whether there's any connection to Justin's murder?'

'It must be worth considering, surely,' Zoe said. 'If the person who Justin assaulted was denied proper justice, someone might have decided to take the law into their own hands. If not her, then some friend or relative. Or maybe it wasn't a premeditated murder. Maybe someone came to challenge Justin about it, got into an argument and…'

'It went a few steps too far? Of course it's possible. Although I don't see how that would link to Chalmers' death – assuming the two killings are connected. But I'll get on to the university formally and persuade them to give me the name of the woman in question. Whatever confidentiality assurances they've given her, at the end of the day this is a murder inquiry. We can treat it all as discreetly as possible, but we can't play games.'

'That's pretty much what I told Pascoe.'

'We'll get things moving in that direction, anyway. The main reason I was calling is that I've just been speaking to Jack Connell. He's in charge of the investigation into the Matlock thing. The damage to the car. That's suddenly seeming a lot more pertinent in the light of Keith Chalmers' killing.'

'Go on. Don't worry if I go quiet. I'm just trying to find my way round this bloody roundabout.' The roundabout in question was part of the major junction that linked the A610 to the M1 as well as to a series of local roads. In the course of Zoe's life, she'd witnessed the junction grow increasingly large and complex as the authorities had struggled to cope with the increasing weight of rush-hour traffic.

'They've been working their way through the list of union members working at the Matlock site – that is, those who were out on strike. A lot of them make pretty unlikely vandals, according to Jack, but there are a few possible contenders. Anyway, they've had an anonymous call suggesting that they talk to one of the people on the list. Young guy called Sammy Nolan. Worked in an admin role there, and was one of the people whose job had been transferred to some regional office miles away. Had only been there for a few months so was entitled to bugger all redundancy. He was already on Jack's list and they were planning to pay him a visit today, but the anonymous call has made Jack take more interest in him. Given the possible link with Chalmers, Jack wondered if one of us wanted to sit in on the interview.'

'You want me to do it?'

'Only if you can. I can always send one of the team from here, but I thought if you were out anyway. Might be a waste of time from our perspective, but who knows.'

'Yeah. Was heading out to see Michelle Wentworth later. One of our regular debriefs in my liaison role. So it's no real hassle to head to Matlock first.'

'Thanks.' Annie gave her the address. 'Connell's heading up there with one of his DCs. Said he'd meet you there.'

'I'll look forward to it.' Zoe had finally passed the M1 junction and had turned on to the dual carriageway that led back out towards the border with Derbyshire. The A610 actually took her directly to police HQ in Ripley, but she'd continue beyond that towards Matlock. Here, the countryside was largely rolling hills and fields, inter-mittently visible between what had once been mining towns. As she headed west and north, the landscape would become wilder and more hilly.

Matlock was one of those places she recalled from her childhood. Adjacent to the town itself was Matlock Bath, a former spa town that, despite or perhaps because of being located about as far from the sea as it was possible to be in the UK, had over the years taken on the style of a coastal resort, with the familiar mix of amusement arcades, fish and chip shops and cafes. The sharp cliffside, with its unexpected cable cars, dominated the road and the shining strip of the River Derwent running alongside.

Even though it was a weekday and the schools had gone back, the sunshine and heat had brought out the crowds, and the pavements were thronged with day trippers and other visitors. Zoe navigated her way carefully through the town, eventually emerging into Matlock itself. Here, the shops were a little less touristy but it was still an attractive place, set among the greenery of the surrounding hills.

The satnav took her through the town centre, then out to the east into a residential area. After another half a mile, she turned off into the street where she'd been told Sammy Nolan lived. The houses along here looked as if they'd once been social housing stock, but the 'For Sale' and 'To Let' signs indicated that at some point they'd been sold off by the local authority.

She pulled into the roadside a little way short of Nolan's house. Annie had told her Connell had suggested that he should meet her outside, and that they should avoid making their presence too obvious.

As she pulled up, Connell's squat figure emerged from the car parked in front of her. A younger man climbed out of the driver's side. Zoe left her car and walked across to meet them.

'You must be Zoe,' Connell said. 'I'm sure we've met before but I've a lousy memory for faces.'

'I've seen you about,' Zoe said. 'My trouble's with names.'

'Oh, aye. I'm crap with them as well,' Connell said. 'So young Ben here'll have to introduce himself.'

'Ben Francis,' the DC said.

'Zoe Everett.' Zoe smiled back at him. 'So what's the story with this Sammy Nolan?'

'He's known to us,' Connell said. 'Only small-time stuff and he avoided going down. Couple of shoplifting things when he was much younger. Then some minor drug use, criminal damage, the odd drunk and disorderly. He seems to have turned over a new leaf in recent years. Found himself gainful employment, most recently at the place in Matlock.'

'He was one of the strikers?'

'Apparently. He'd only been with the company for a few weeks. Some kind of junior admin role. He was in one of the functions that was outsourced, and Sammy was apparently given the choice of taking an equivalent job at some regional office some distance away or taking redundancy. Which in his case amounted to three-fifths of bugger all.'

'And you think he was behind the damage to the car?'

'I don't know, to be honest. He's been very active in protesting about the way the staff have been treated, apparently, but he doesn't seem to have been regarded as a troublemaker. He was involved in the union, got himself elected to the local committee. Obviously, we had him in the picture already because of his past record, so he was already scheduled for a visit. But, given his recent unblemished record, I hadn't seen him as a prime suspect. Then this morning we got an anonymous tip-off. Knew some of the detail, so it sounded like Sammy or someone had been shooting his mouth off about it.' Connell paused. 'Don't know if I'm wasting your time here, of course. Even if he was behind the car damage, I can't really envisage him being involved in the killings. But I did tell Annie I'd keep you involved in any developments.'

This thought had also occurred to Zoe, but, like Annie, she also recognised the importance of keeping colleagues like Connell onside. He often had his ear to the ground in a way that was more difficult for the officers in the senior crime team. Furthermore, Keith Chalmers' murder had brought the focus back on to the trade union link. It was just possible that Nolan might have some intelligence that would be useful to them. 'I was out on the road anyway,' she said. 'And you never know.'

'You never do. Okay, let's go and see young Sammy.'

Most of the houses along the street seemed well-maintained and in a decent state of repair. Sammy's was more neglected, the small front garden overgrown and the paintwork peeling. To Zoe's surprise, the front door was slightly ajar.

'Not one for tight security.' Connell stepped forward and pressed the doorbell, holding it down for several seconds. They heard the shrill tone from somewhere inside the house, but there was no other response. 'Just our luck if he's buggered off to the shops or something.'

'Assume he's not gone far if he's left the door ajar,' Francis said.

'You'd think not, wouldn't you? Mind you, you've got two brain cells to rub together.' Connell pressed the bell again.

There was still no response. Connell gingerly pushed open the door. 'Sammy! You in there?' He looked back at the other two. 'Could be in the bog, I suppose. Or the back garden. If there is a back garden.' He pressed the bell once more, this time holding it down even longer.

Zoe peered past him into the relative gloom of the hallway. She was suddenly feeling uneasy. She couldn't have pinned down exactly why. Something to do with the quality of the silence in the house. Perhaps something about the way the bell was echoing. Somehow she already had the feeling that there was no one in there to hear it.

Connell turned and peered down the street, as if expecting to see Nolan striding down the pavement towards them. 'I'm just going to have a quick look inside. In case he's out at the back or something.'

Zoe could tell from Connell's tone that, for whatever reason, he was beginning to share some of her unease. He walked a few steps down the hall, then stopped. Zoe and Ben Francis had initially hovered by the door, but now Zoe followed Connell into the house. She paused behind him, knowing now what had made Connell stop.

It was unmistakeable to any experienced police officer. The stench of blood, here mixed with the even more unpleasant scent of decomposition. Connell looked back at her and she nodded. 'Which room?'

They were standing beside what Zoe took to be the door to the living room. For all its intensity, the smell seemed too distant to be emanating from there. 'Kitchen?'

Connell fumbled in his pocket and produced a hand-kerchief, which he held over his mouth and nose. Zoe had nothing similar on her, so she followed a little behind holding her sleeve to her face. Connell pushed open the kitchen door.

The first thing that struck her, other than the smell, was the buzzing of the flies. She peered over Connell's shoulder. The body was lying spreadeagled face down across the floor of the small kitchen. It was a man, probably young, although it was difficult to be sure because of the damage inflicted to his head and face. The head itself was surrounded by a pool of congealed blood.

Zoe suspected that he hadn't been lying there for too long, perhaps only for twenty-four hours or so. But the body had fallen beside the closed patio windows, and the sun had been shining full on it for some hours. In the summer heat, the body was already beginning to decompose.

'Shit,' Connell said. 'Poor bastard.'

'You think that's Nolan?'

'I'm guessing so,' Connell said. 'Not easy to tell, is it?' He turned back towards her. 'Who the hell would want to kill a wee gobshite like Sammy Nolan?'

'I don't know,' Zoe said. 'But the MO looks very like our other killings.'

Connell stared back at her, his expression suggesting he was scarcely taking in what she was saying to him. He was an experienced cop, and he must have seen worse than this, but he looked genuinely shocked.

'Come on,' she said, trying to maintain her own calm. 'Let's call this in and get the place sealed off.'

Connell blinked at her and nodded. 'Aye, yes, you're right.' He followed her back down the hall, but then stopped and looked back. 'Poor bastard,' he said again.

Chapter Twenty-Nine

The afternoon team briefing had been a sombre affair, the team's tension and anxiety almost palpable. Annie had forced herself to remain positive, and Jennings had done his usual decent job of morale-boosting, but she couldn't ignore the growing sense that the case was slipping away from them.

Usually when that happened, it was because of a shortage of leads. That was relatively uncommon, particularly in murder cases. Murder investigations were often some of the more straightforward, with an obvious suspect and a clear-cut motive, even if the circumstances might be sordid or depressing. The trickiest ones were generally the most random, the seemingly unprovoked killings where there was no obvious link between the perpetrator and victim and no evident motive for the crime. In those cases, you could be left clutching at straws – the painstaking gathering and analysis of intelligence, the minute examination of video evidence, the hope that some friend or relative of the perpetrator would report their suspicions. Mostly, those cases came good in the end, usually through sheer hard work and persistence. Occasionally, though, they didn't. The mystery remained unsolved, and those involved in the investigation would never sleep quite so soundly again.

This didn't feel quite like that. In this case, they had no shortage of leads. If anything, they had too many. Too many possible roads to explore, pulling the team in different directions with no certainty about which if any of them might be important or relevant.

They were still working on the assumption that the murders of Justin Wentworth and Keith Chalmers were linked. The problem was coming up with a motive that convincingly accounted for both deaths. Justin Wentworth's murder could be linked to the accusations of attempted rape that had been brought against him, or possibly to his dealings with illicit substances, but what relevance would that have to Keith Chalmers? Similarly, Chalmers' death might have been linked to his trade union activities or to the disciplinary and corruption charges he'd faced. But, again, what relevance would that have to Justin Wentworth?

And now, to muddy the waters still further, they had this Sammy Nolan. Sammy Nolan who had at least a tenuous link with Keith Chalmers but, as far as they were aware, none with Justin Wentworth.

It was quite possible that Nolan's death wasn't linked to the others, that he'd been killed for some squalid reason unconnected with the wider investigation. Maybe he was in debt or had simply trodden on the wrong person's toes. That kind of thing happened, and people like Sammy Nolan were usually the victims.

But it was a hell of a coincidence that he'd been murdered just as they were going to talk to him about an incident involving one of Michelle Wentworth's companies. And it was a further coincidence that his killing was so similar to those of Justin Wentworth and Keith Chalmers. Coincidences happened. But, like all good detectives, Annie had learned never to take them at face value. Shit might happen, but it often happened because someone, somewhere had wanted it to.

She could tell that these or similar thoughts were going through the heads of every officer round the table. She remembered something she'd read about the anxiety of choice, that if we're presented with too many options, we tend to freeze and not pick any of them. This felt like that. The team was losing motivation because it simply didn't know which of the many leads to pursue.

That was her job. She'd used this afternoon's meeting to set out the priorities clearly and to make sure that each part of the team, every individual, knew precisely what they should be doing and what their objectives were. At this stage don't worry about the big picture, she'd told them, because we still don't know what the big picture looks like. Focus on completing your corner of the jigsaw. Then we can see what it's showing us.

She could tell that, for the most part, it had worked. The team had gone away with renewed energy, regained focus. But she could also tell, not least because she was feeling it herself, that they were not entirely convinced they were all working on the same puzzle.

'So what about Sammy Nolan?' she asked Stuart Jennings again after the meeting. 'You think we should treat him as part of the same investigation?'

'What do you think?'

It was his usual infuriating response to that kind of question. But he was right. She was still SIO in practice, even if Jennings had taken over the public profile stuff. 'For the moment I think we should. I can't begin to imagine how he fits in, but there's too much of a connection for us to disregard it. He had met at least one of the victims and worked for a business owned by the other's mother. But we have to keep an open mind. There could be countless other reasons why Nolan was killed. The similarity of the MO might mean nothing. It's not as if repeatedly beating someone around the head is exactly a sophisticated way of committing murder. We should treat it as a separate strand but keep it under the umbrella of this investigation.'

'Well fudged,' Jennings said. 'You'll make the senior ranks yet. But I think that's the right answer.'

'And you're still happy for me to continue?'

'With every baffling development this case seems to move further and further away from any potential conflict of interest. I need someone level-headed on this one. Feels like we're knitting fog.'

'I'll take that as a compliment.'

Jennings looked surprised. 'It was intended as one. I do make them, you know. Occasionally. When I feel they're merited.'

'Well, thank you. I'm glad you feel it's merited. I'm not sure I do at the moment.'

'It's a mess, this one.' He held up his hand. 'Not your handling of it. It's just one that seems to make no sense. It would be really easy to lose your way. But I thought you did well just now. Kept them engaged, kept them motivated, kept them focused. It's all you can do. But it's making me more and more nervous. So far, the media haven't really made the connections I thought they would. That's partly been due to the way Comms have handled it. They've released enough to keep the media happy, but held back on a lot of the critical details. They said that Chalmers' body was dumped in the heart of the Peak District, for example, but not that it was at Wentworth's house. That's not a line we can hold for long. Someone's going to tip them off, or some journalist's going to be bright enough to ask awkward questions.'

'I get the message,' Annie said. 'We need a result.'

'That's always the message. Although, just at the moment, I'd settle for at least some kind of breakthrough. Something that starts to give us some answers, rather than just raising more questions.'

'You and me both.' She pushed herself to her feet. 'Thanks for the support, Stuart. At the meeting and just now. I needed it.'

For once, he actually looked mildly embarrassed, as if he'd been caught out in some social faux pas. 'You're doing a good job.'

'Don't push it, or I'll start to think you're taking the piss.' She left the office, pleased that for once she'd managed to have the last word. Pleased also that, finally, she did seem to be building some kind of positive working relationship with Jennings.

She arrived back at her own desk to find DC Colin Palmer waiting for her. He'd sent his apologies to the meeting because he was in the middle of working through the mass of documentation they'd gathered from Keith Chalmers' house. 'Sorry for missing the meeting,' he said now. 'I had the feeling that if I stopped ploughing through Chalmers' stuff I might not summon the will to start again. He wasn't the most organised man.'

'You didn't miss much. Mainly a pep talk and a recap. Not that that absolves you from attending,' she added. 'We need to make sure we're all on the same page. But it wasn't a three-line whip this time. How are you getting on?' As she asked the question, she realised Palmer was looking pleased with himself. 'Don't tell me you've got something?'

'Maybe. I don't know how significant it is, but it's interesting.'

'Go on. Even "interesting" would cheer me up at the moment.'

'Like I say, I've been working through Chalmers' papers. There's a fair bit of stuff. Some of it's just trade union casework. Individuals he's represented in discipline and grievance cases, that sort of stuff. We'll need to check through all that systematically, but on the face of it, there's not likely to be much of interest. Then there's a lot of personal stuff. Again, most of it not likely to be particularly interesting. Just copies of old bills and household documents. But then, tucked away at the back of one of the drawers in his bedroom, we found these.' He held up an evidence bag that appeared to contain a number of used envelopes.

Annie peered at the offering. 'And?'

'They're letters addressed to Chalmers. I suppose they're what you might describe as love letters.'

'Might you?'

'Well, I'm not sure "love" is quite the right word.'

She was amused to see that Palmer was showing signs of blushing. 'Ah. Right. A bit raunchy?'

'Something like that. The letters themselves don't seem to be dated, but the postmarks suggest they're around twenty years old.'

'I'm not sure how to break this to you, Colin. But people have been doing raunchy stuff for a lot longer than that.' She smiled. 'So these – well, let's call them romantic letters were sent to Chalmers?'

'To his office address.'

'Not from his wife, then?'

Palmer grinned awkwardly. 'Definitely not from his wife. The letters are clearly responding to ones sent by Chalmers. It comes across as if they're trying to outdo each other in – well, you know…'

'Raunchiness?'

'Exactly. It feels intrusive just reading it.'

'Just doing your job, Colin. But you presumably think there's something interesting about these letters other than their smut value.'

'That's the point. It's who these letters are from.'

'I can see you're dying to tell me.'

As he told her, she sat back and gave a whistle. She'd already half-guessed and was trying to work out what, if anything, it might mean. 'Well,' she said, 'I think we'd better go and break the news to Stuart. It may not be quite the breakthrough he was hoping for. Not yet. But as you say, it's definitely very interesting.'

Chapter Thirty

After her bust-up with Peter Hardy, Michelle Went-worth had sat by the pool, her eyes half-closed, watching as the sun slowly descended over the moorland. There were clouds gathering on the horizon, she noticed, and a stronger breeze blowing in from the moors. The forecast had predicted a change in the weather this evening, and as night fell she thought she could almost taste it in the air.

She'd tried to throw herself back into work but had found that, unusually for her, she'd been unable to focus on anything. The words and numbers had swum before her eyes as if she'd lost the ability to read or to count. Tomorrow, she'd head back into the office. She wondered now about Peter's motives for advising her to work from home over the last few days. Whether or not it had been good advice, she realised now that she was beginning to go stir-crazy.

She'd made some mistakes over the past year. She was sure of that now. She'd taken her eye off the ball. She'd allowed Peter Hardy to get too close, given him too much influence and authority. She'd been seduced by him, and in more ways than one.

She had a suspicion now that he'd been bullshitting much more than she'd realised. He'd always been very plausible, but she should have had the nous to see through that. The question she was left wrestling with now was just how much substance there really was below the layers of bullshit.

There couldn't be nothing, she thought. There'd been enough evidence of it. The initial money had been there just as he'd promised, no questions asked, no strings attached. She'd allowed herself to be seduced by that, too. Who wouldn't have been? Free, apparently unconditional money to fund their business expansion. All she'd needed to do was produce the returns they'd been expecting, and she knew she had the capability to do that. At that point, it had been just as Hardy had promised. A few more years of that, she'd thought, and she'd have had the freedom she wanted.

But she'd spent her life telling people that nothing came for free. If you wanted something, you had to work for it. That was just how it was. Or, at least, that was how it was for people like her, people who weren't born to privilege. You could claw your way up the social scale, but you had to work and you had to keep working.

That was the lesson she should have taught Justin. She'd failed there. She'd felt guilty about Justin – for bringing him into the world, for depriving him of a father, for that whole mess. Above all, she'd felt guilty for not loving Justin the way she should have.

In retrospect, she'd have been better not having him. That had been an option, she supposed. But she'd thought things would change. She'd thought she would change. She'd thought that, once she was free of all the other encumbrances and it was just her and Justin, it would somehow magically be all right. It hadn't been, of course. Justin had just become another burden, another weight that meant she had to work even harder.

The only compensation she'd been able to offer him had been financial. She'd spoiled him. She bought him pretty much everything he'd ever wanted, even at a time in those early days when she hadn't really been able to afford it. She'd provided him with the best education money could buy, with the aim of ensuring that, even if he wasn't exactly the brightest, he'd still have the ability to make something of himself.

He'd made something of himself all right. An utter arsehole who was nothing but an embarrassment. Drowning in drink and drugs, and without even the ability to behave like a civilised human being. But that again had been her fault. She'd thought she'd been doing the right thing in sending him to that school, but really it was just another way she'd used her money to avoid taking any real care of him. He'd been out of his depth in every way – too common to be respected by the posh kids, too dim to be respected by those on scholarships, too unloved to feel comfortable in his own skin. He hadn't even been able to tell her any of that. She guessed now that, for years, he must have just hated every second of it. Then, when he'd managed to scrape his way into university, he'd tried to reinvent himself, tried to become the kind of person he'd been mocked for not being during his time at school. The result had been that he'd simply become a nasty, inebriated, uncaring bastard.

All that had been her fault. Now, she couldn't really even bring herself to miss him. She had an awful feeling that, if his death had occurred in other circumstances, she'd probably have felt only relief. One less burden. One less thing for her to worry about. She'd assumed at first that his murder had been somehow connected with the way he'd lived – maybe he'd owed money to the wrong people, maybe some friend or relative of that young girl had decided that money wasn't a substitute for justice, maybe it was some other mess he'd managed to get himself into.

She should have told the police that, told them what Justin's life had really been like. But she'd felt that, if she could give him nothing else, she should provide him with at least that limited protection. She didn't imagine it would take the police long to discover the truth, but at least they wouldn't have heard it from her.

Instead, at Peter's instigation, she'd sent the police on a series of what were most likely wild goose chases, getting them to focus on her previous, largely legitimate business dealings, in the hope that it would deflect them from paying too much attention to the sources of their current funding. She had no idea if Peter's strategy had worked. She imagined that, whatever Peter might say, the police weren't stupid. She could tell they'd had some suspicions from the start. That was no doubt why they employed that so-called Family Liaison Officer to get close to her.

The thought of Zoe Everett made Wentworth sit up. Shit. She'd been so caught up in her thoughts that she'd lost track of the time. Zoe was due to arrive for one of their regular debriefs.

Wentworth's first thought when Zoe had brought up the subject of meeting regularly had been to wonder quite how long they expected the inquiry to continue. But that was the great unknown, of course. The police might have a quick breakthrough, but If they didn't make progress, the investigation could continue for months. That was the last thing she wanted, but it might be unavoidable. On that basis, she'd thought that at least with a regular meeting, she could be prepared for Zoe's visit. She could make sure that nothing inappropriate was left lying around, plan what she was going to say.

Except, of course, today she'd been too tied up to do any of that. She looked at her watch. Zoe was due in a few minutes. Wentworth sighed, pushed herself to her feet and made her way back into the house. She conducted a quick check around the kitchen and living room to make sure that no documents or paperwork had been left out. Her office was more problematic as she always had files and papers spread all over the desk. The papers were mostly innocuous, and there was no reason why she should have to bring Zoe in here, so one option was simply to leave the papers out and lock up the room. But she knew only too well how sod's law could confound those kinds of assumptions. In the end, when she heard the buzzing of the intercom from the main gate, she hurriedly gathered up all the papers and dropped them into an empty drawer of her filing cabinet, then locked the cabinet and the room.

She'd just finished doing that when her mobile phone rang.

'Hi, is that Michelle? It's Zoe. I'm just at the gate. I tried the intercom but there was no response.'

'Sorry, I was in the office and lost track of the time. Hadn't realised how late it was. Hang on.' Wentworth walked through into the hallway, checked the CCTV coverage to see Zoe's car waiting outside the main gate, and then pressed the control to open the gate.

She opened the front door and watched the car head up the driveway towards her. A small, slightly battered old Fiat. Wentworth had wondered sometimes what it must be like for these people, carrying out their demanding, risky jobs for such limited reward. Even that DI probably

wasn't on a large salary, presumably. They must be suscep-
tible to bribery, she thought. Maybe that was something
to bear in mind if things ever became really sticky.

Zoe Everett climbed out of the car and beamed up at
her, with the air of an eager young social worker visiting a
particularly needy case. 'Looks like the weather's breaking
finally, doesn't it?'

Even in the brief time Wentworth had been inside, the
clouds had thickened across the sky. The air felt heavy and
humid, charged with the threat of an impending storm.
'Feels like it could rain at any moment,' she said. 'Amazing
how it can change. You'd better come in.'

She led Zoe back through the house to the kitchen.
'Can I get you a drink? I'm thinking of a glass of wine,
but I'm guessing you're not allowed that.'

'Better not. Not on duty, and not when I'm driving.
Anything cold's fine.'

Wentworth poured a glass of white wine for herself and
an orange juice for Zoe. Outside, just as she had predicted,
the first fat drops of rain were beginning to fall. 'I guess
sitting by the pool's out of the question. We'd better make
ourselves comfortable in here.' She'd been intending to
keep the meeting as short as possible, but now Zoe was
here, Wentworth felt quite glad of the company.

Zoe had placed her slim case of papers on the table
between them. 'I'll try not to keep you too long,' she said.
'This is really just an opportunity to catch up with progress
in the inquiry.'

'I take there've been no major developments? With
regard to Justin, I mean.'

'There is one thing. Not directly connected to your
son, but I just wanted to discuss it with you in case it

throws any new light on the inquiry. But I'll come back to that in a second.'

Wentworth frowned, wondering at the significance of this enigmatic statement. Perhaps it was intended in some way to wrong-foot her. 'Whatever you think best.' She paused, deciding that in the circumstances it might be better to take the lead in the discussion. 'Are you assuming that Keith Chalmers' death is linked to Justin's?'

'We're treating them as part of the same investigation, but we're keeping an open mind about any link between the two cases. Obviously, we can't disregard Chalmers' connections with you and your business, not to mention where his body was found, but otherwise the links seem rather tenuous.'

Wentworth nodded. 'That's very much my feeling. It may just be a dreadful coincidence.'

She sat back and listened as Zoe ran through her update on the investigation. It was still mostly routine stuff, although there was plenty of it. Wentworth's conclusion was that the police still had few genuinely compelling leads, and were compensating through sheer diligence and hard work. At least that was preferable to them poking about in her business. 'That's all very reassuring,' Wentworth said when Zoe had finished. 'You seem to be throwing a lot at the case.'

'We're deploying all the resource we have available, yes. But if you think there's anything we're missing or if there are other lines of enquiry we should be following up, please do tell us. You know more about Justin than we do.'

That sounded almost like a jibe, Wentworth thought. Although Zoe had talked volubly, Wentworth had had the sense she wasn't being told everything. Perhaps this was a test, she thought. Perhaps they'd discovered the truth about Justin's university life, and they wanted to see whether she would be prepared to reveal it before they did. 'I'm not at all sure that's true,' Wentworth said. 'There are times when I felt I hardly knew Justin at all. He spent years at boarding school, and then went straight off to university without really looking back.'

'But he'd been here over the summer?'

'Justin wasn't exactly the talkative sort. He didn't give much away, and I didn't feel it was my business to pry into his affairs.' Zoe's questions definitely suggested she knew more than she was saying. But if it came to it, Wentworth would claim she'd been embarrassed and ashamed about what Justin had done and that she'd simply wanted to protect his reputation. After all, that wasn't far from the truth.

'I can imagine,' Zoe said. 'I've got a young nephew who's a bit like that.'

Michelle was keen to move on. 'You said you had something else you wanted to raise with me?'

'Yes. It's not public knowledge yet, so I'd ask you to treat this as confidential. We've had another unlawful killing reported today.'

'And you think this might be connected with Justin's death?'

'There's no direct reason to believe so,' Zoe said. 'In that sense, it's a little like Mr Chalmers' death.'

'I'm not sure I entirely understand.'

'It was a young man named Sammy Nolan. Does the name mean anything to you?'

Wentworth stared at Zoe for a moment, trying to process what she was hearing. The real question was if she should simply take Zoe's question at face value, or whether the police knew more than they were revealing. But if that were the case, she told herself, it would surely be that DI Delamere sitting here, not her sidekick Family Liaison Officer.

'I don't think so,' Wentworth said, conscious she'd hesitated too long. 'Should it?'

Chapter Thirty-One

Stuart Jennings had been finishing off a meeting with the Assistant Chief, and it was some minutes before he was able to join them. Colin Palmer spent the time setting up a projector to his laptop, so they could present the material as clearly as possible. 'I bagged up the letters,' he said, 'because I thought we might want forensics to check them over, but I took pictures of some of the salient pages.'

'I'm assuming "salient" isn't just a smart way of saying "smutty"?' Jennings said as he took a seat at the table. Annie had given him a brief outline of the find over the phone, though she'd held back on the most interesting facts.

'This better be good, too,' Jennings went on. 'I've just cut short a meeting with the ACC. Told him we've had an important development in the case. So you've raised his hopes as well.' He grinned, but Annie wasn't at all clear whether he was actually joking.

'You talk us through this, Colin,' Annie said. 'You've read the whole bundle. I've only seen snippets.'

Colin Palmer stood up, looking awkward in Jennings' presence. Annie had wanted to give Colin his deserved moment in the limelight, but she hoped now that she wasn't just throwing him in the deep end.

'Well,' he said, 'what we've got here is a set of letters. There are twelve here in total, but it reads as if there are others that are missing. There seem to be some gaps in the chronology, and there are references to previous letters that aren't here.'

'So one question,' Annie added, 'is whether the others have just become lost over time. Or whether for some reason Chalmers deliberately chose to hang on to these ones, either for sentimental or some other reason.' She paused, thinking. 'Or whether he deliberately destroyed some of the others.'

'I'll come back to that point,' Colin continued. 'These are obviously responses to letters from Chalmers himself. So again we don't know what was in his letters, though obviously in some cases you can infer the content from the response.'

Jennings had closed his eyes. 'Okay, cut to the chase. I can see you're all dying to tell me. Who's this mysterious other party?'

Annie gestured for Colin to provide the answer.

'Michelle Wentworth,' he said. 'These are love letters from Michelle Wentworth.'

Jennings opened his eyes and blinked. 'Wentworth? You're sure?'

Colin looked uncomfortable for a moment, as if he'd been caught out by an unexpected question. 'Definitely. It didn't occur to me at first. The letters are all handwritten and mostly signed Mickey, which obviously didn't ring any bells, but then I found a few that were scribbled on Wentworth's headed paper.' He blushed slightly. 'I'm not quite sure how to put this, but she seems to have got something of a kick out of writing the – well, the steamier stuff on business paper. There are a couple of references to Chalmers doing the same on the trade union's notepaper.'

Jennings snorted. 'Bloody hell. One for Sigmund Freud right there, isn't there?' He paused. 'But, seriously, you're absolutely certain about this. That these were letters written by Michelle Wentworth to Keith Chalmers?'

'Have a look.' Colin pulled up the relevant image on to the screen. The notepaper was clearly headed 'Wentworth Holdings'. 'The address isn't their current one,' Colin added, 'but I've checked and it was their company address at the time. I've also looked at a couple of examples of Wentworth's handwriting on the statements she's signed for us. I'm no expert, but the style of the signature looks the same. In any case, there are several references in the letters that don't leave much doubt that the author is Wentworth. I'll come back to those, because they're interesting in themselves.'

'Okay,' Jennings said, 'let's take this step by step. Wentworth told us that her only dealings with Chalmers had been professional ones. Is that right?'

'Absolutely,' Annie said. 'She gave us the impression that she'd had a number of dealings with him over the years but didn't know him well. That basically the main contact had been over the negotiating table.'

'I'm still trying to make sense of all this,' said Jennings. 'So she told us that she hardly knew Chalmers, when in reality twenty years ago they were going at it hammer and tongs?'

'Delicately put, Stuart,' Annie said. 'But yes. She was lying to us. Which raises the question of why. It might be embarrassing but there's nothing illegal about her having had an affair with Chalmers.'

'She'd have been married at this point, presumably?' Jennings said.

'Yes, but this would have been in the dying days of her marriage to Ronnie Donahue.'

'Is this why they split up?'

'Not according to her or to Donahue. She walked out on him, accusing him of unreasonable behaviour. She later claimed he was having an affair, though he denies that. But Donahue did say that if anyone was playing away, to use his words, it was her. But she doesn't leave Donahue for Chalmers. It's clear from the last couple of letters here that she splits up with Chalmers at roughly the same time as she leaves her husband.'

'Does she say why?'

'It's not clear from the letters,' Colin said. 'The sense I get is that she just thought the relationship had reached the end of the road.'

'Donahue reckons she dumped him basically because he ceased to be of use to her,' Annie said. 'Admittedly, his probably isn't the most dispassionate view, but he felt she took what she needed from him and then tossed him aside. From what Colin's shown me, there's a similar sense here. That she's used Chalmers and then thrown him aside.'

'So how's she used Chalmers?' Jennings was still peering at the screen.

'That's one of the other interesting things in the letters,' Colin said. 'It's not particularly clear, so I may be jumping to conclusions. But the impression is that she used Chalmers to open doors for her, particularly in the public sector. The implication is that she was paying backhanders to various individuals to bend procurement rules on contracts, and also that she was paying off Chalmers to help smooth passage in terms of any dealings with the trade unions. At that time, the unions would still have held a lot of influence in some of those organisations.'

'That's what Chalmers was being accused of by some of his union colleagues,' Annie added. 'That he was basically signing sweetheart deals that weren't in the best interests of his members.'

Jennings remained intent on the screen. 'Judging from the language of these letters, sweetheart seems an under-statement. But why would she dump Chalmers if he was giving her what she wanted?' He coughed. 'As it were.'

'Maybe because it was becoming a bit too personal. A bit too intense. There's nothing to say she didn't continue paying off Chalmers. But maybe she just didn't want him in her bed any more. She seems to value her independence.'

'There's one other thing,' Colin said. 'Quite an important thing.'

'Go on,' Jennings said. It was difficult to tell from his expression whether he was depressed or exhilarated by what he was hearing.

'The letters were written sometime in the year after Justin Wentworth was born. There are various refer-ences to the challenges of balancing the business, not to mention the affair with Chalmers, with childcare.' Colin smiled. 'Though she seems to have largely solved that by outsourcing the childcare to a succession of nannies.'

'With respect, Colin,' Jennings said. 'I'm not that inter-ested in Michelle Wentworth's childcare problems twenty years ago.'

'No, sorry. That wasn't the point. The point is that, although the letters don't quite say so explicitly, it looks as if there was doubt about – well, about Justin's paternity.'

Jennings stared at Colin, his expression now one of definite excitement. 'You're kidding?'

Annie smiled. 'No, Stuart. I'm still not sure if it's the breakthrough you were looking for. But it's definitely an unexpected step forward. It turns out that our first two murder victims might well have been father and son.'

Chapter Thirty-Two

The storm had arrived almost before they'd realised. When Zoe had first arrived, the first drops of rain had begun to fall. Now, as they sat in the kitchen, they could see it coming down heavily outside, the air from the open doorway growing rich with the scent of the damp grass and the trees.

'I can't say I'm entirely sorry,' Zoe said. 'The heat was beginning to get to me.'

'I love the warmth,' Wentworth said. 'I don't even know why I stick around in Britain. I've been wondering lately if I should just sell up and go and live out the rest of my days somewhere with better weather than this.' She made her way across the kitchen and began to fill the kettle. 'Coffee to warm yourself up?'

'Not sure I need warming up,' Zoe said. 'But coffee would be good.' She'd had the sense, from the moment she'd first mentioned Sammy Nolan's name, that Wentworth had been rattled. She'd tried hard to hide it, but Zoe had had little doubt that the reference to Nolan had come as a shock to her. Zoe had expected that Wentworth might try to hurry her out of the house at the point, but instead the opposite had happened. In an apparent effort to conceal her initial reaction to Nolan's name, Wentworth had carried on talking, chattering about inconsequential nonsense as if trying to steer Zoe away from discussing any further what might have happened to Nolan.

Zoe had decided simply to go with the flow of Wentworth's conversation. There was no point in trying to interrogate her about Nolan. She would simply deny any knowledge of the young man, and Zoe would have no justification for pressing further. It was better to let Wentworth talk, in the hope that she might relax enough to let something slip.

For her own part, Zoe had largely completed her briefing. She'd run through all the work-streams that were under way, and tried to give Wentworth a sense of their progress. She was all too conscious that as yet there was still little of substance she could offer. There was a lot of work going on, but so far relatively little to show for it. Wentworth, though, seemed largely unconcerned.

That was odd in itself, Zoe thought. Even though Wentworth had come across from the start as not being one for showing emotion, Zoe would have expected her to take a greater interest in the pursuit of her son's killer.

Wentworth finished making the coffee, pouring boiling water on to ground coffee in a cafetière, and then brought it over to the table where Zoe was sitting. 'Have you ever thought about going into the business world?'

'Me?' Zoe said. 'God, no. I've got no business brains at all. I'd be a disaster.'

'I suspect you wouldn't be. It's all stuff you can learn and you'd make a lot more money.'

'Or lose a lot more.' Zoe smiled, sensing an opportunity. 'You must have a real nose for it, though. Business, I mean, not money.'

'I've got a nose for both, I suppose. I'm not sure it's anything to be proud of.'

'It's bought you a place like this.'

'And that's nice. But I sometimes wonder if there isn't more to life.'

'It's easier to wonder that if you don't have to worry about the necessities,' Zoe pointed out.

'Oh, I know that only too well. When I was a child, we could barely scrape by. That's one of the things that's always driven me. I've no desire to go back to living like that, believe me. But I do wonder whether there could have been more of a balance.'

Zoe was content to let Wentworth talk. This was the kind of conversation she'd been hoping to initiate since she'd first taken on this role. Something that would help her build up a relationship with Wentworth. Zoe knew that generally this was one of her skills. It was partly, she suspected, because she tended to be self-effacing. She contributed enough to the conversation to keep it going, without trying too hard to impose her own personality on it. People seemed almost to forget she was there, or at least that she was a living, thinking person who might have opinions and interests of her own. It meant that people tended to talk freely and openly in her presence, sometimes saying more than they'd intended. This was all something that came naturally to her – it was simply the kind of person she was – but it was also a skill she'd tried to cultivate during her time in the force. 'Would you have done things differently?' she asked Wentworth. 'Looking back, I mean.'

'I don't know.' Wentworth stopped. 'I mean, the honest answer is no. That wouldn't have been me. Making money's what I do. I don't really do it for things like this house, though I won't deny that's a bonus. I do it because I have to. It's the only thing that excites me, really. It's the only thing I want to do.' She sounded now as if she was primarily talking to herself. 'I don't know if it ever could really have been different. But I do sometimes wonder if I could at least have done it differently. Left fewer bodies in my wake, as it were.' She sounded almost as if she intended the phrase literally, Zoe thought.

Wentworth suddenly shivered. 'It's really turned cold, hasn't it?' she said. 'I might need to turn the heating on.' She rose and slammed the back door shut.

Zoe couldn't feel it herself, though there was no doubt that the change in the weather was stark. She could hear the rattling of the rain against the patio windows, the downpour hammering on the skylights above them. The drive home wasn't going to be fun, she thought. Some of the back roads in the vicinity were prone to flooding in weather like this. Even so, she felt reluctant to leave until it became clear that Wentworth no longer wanted her company.

Wentworth still seemed shaken by the news about Nolan. She looked haunted, shocked; even more than she had about the news of her own son's death. She seemed almost to be willing Zoe to stay, as if for once she was afraid of being left alone. That in itself was unexpected. Zoe's impression of Wentworth, right from their first meeting, had been one of utter self-sufficiency. Now, for the first time, she looked vulnerable, perhaps even a little lost.

Zoe decided it was time to push Wentworth a little harder. There was a risk that she might simply close down, perhaps even decide to show Zoe the door. But there was just a chance she might finally open up, give her a glimpse of what lay below that enigmatic facade. 'What do you mean?' she asked. 'About leaving bodies in your wake?'

Wentworth stared at her for a moment. 'Oh, God, dozens of them. More than I can count, probably. More than I know. A lot more than I know.' She suddenly seemed conscious of what she was saying. 'Not literally, of course. I mean people who've suffered from my business decisions. But that's life, isn't it? That's how it works. Nobody's ever given me a helping hand. Whatever I achieved in life, I've done it all myself.' She tailed off, as if lost in thought. She was still taking mouthfuls of wine along with her coffee, and it occurred to Zoe to wonder how much she had already drunk.

'Do you think that's just the nature of business?' Zoe asked. 'Not everyone can be a winner, I suppose.'

Wentworth gave a shrug. 'It's the nature of my business. Maybe it doesn't have to be. I don't know. I've always believed there's no room in this line of work for sentiment. If you're soft, you just get crushed. In the end that helps no one, does it? It's all very well whining on about a living wage and job security and all that stuff, but if the business goes under you'll never get any of that. So the first priority is always to make money.' She was sounding defensive now, as if Zoe had launched an attack on her business ethics. 'That's what I used to tell Ronnie.'

'Your ex-husband?'

'The very same. He had a good business brain. Good contacts, too. But he was soft as shit. We were never going to get anywhere as long as he was involved. Strictly small-time.' She shook her head. 'You just have to be ruthless. Do what it takes.'

Zoe was surprised to see that Wentworth's eyes were damp with tears, her expression now almost that of a woman in mourning. She seemed to be shifting emotional gears even as Zoe watched. Perhaps the shock of her son's death had finally hit her. 'Are there things you regret? About the business, I mean?'

'I've never done anything else,' Wentworth said. 'And I've never done it any other way. I wouldn't have known how. There are moments, sometimes when I wake in the night, when I wonder if I've wasted my life. But by and large I think I've got it right. Until the last few months, anyway.'

Zoe looked up, suddenly alert. 'The last few months?' she asked casually.

Wentworth took another swallow of wine. 'Maybe. I don't know. I made the mistake of trusting someone else more than I trusted my own instincts.' She laughed. 'Maybe I was a bit too soft for once. But I've put that right now. Or at least I hope I have.'

'In what way?' Zoe tried to keep her tone neutral, as if she was simply making conversation.

'I wasn't properly in control.' Wentworth waved a finger vaguely in Zoe's direction, as if offering a personal admonishment. Zoe had little doubt now that Wentworth was at least slightly drunk. She'd almost polished off the bottle of wine by herself, and Zoe had a suspicion it might not have been the first of the afternoon. 'There's a lesson there. Everybody says you ought to delegate. But you can't really. Or only the small stuff. Once you start delegating the big stuff, everything can slip away from you. You don't know who you're really dealing with.'

Zoe wasn't sure she was really following any of this. 'I can see you've got to be careful.'

'I mean, you've met him, haven't you? That bastard Hardy. Would you have trusted him?'

The direct question was unexpected. 'Hardy? I've no idea,' Zoe said. 'I only met him briefly.'

'I trusted him too much,' Wentworth said. 'I'm not sure what he's led me into, but I'm sure as hell not going to go any further. There's too much at stake, and these bastards seem to know far too much about me.' She poured the last dregs of the wine from the bottle into her glass and swallowed them in a single mouthful. She rose and took another bottle from the rack in the corner of the kitchen. She opened the screw-top and poured a glass. 'You sure you don't want any?'

'Better not,' Zoe said. She was beginning to feel the conversation itself was in danger of going too far. But she also felt that Wentworth might be on the verge of a real revelation.

'I mean, it's genuinely scary,' Wentworth continued. 'It's as if they're been picking apart my life, bit by bit. As if they know every secret.' She rose, still clutching her glass, and walked, slightly unsteadily, into the living room. Zoe followed, intent on maintaining the dialogue.

Wentworth was standing by the patio windows, staring out into the blackness. The rain was still pounding against the glass. The sun had set now and, although it was still only early evening, it felt like midnight, the garden pitch black beyond the glow from the kitchen. 'It feels like they're circling me. Growing closer. Just letting me stew until they're ready...' She seemed almost to have forgotten that Zoe was there, as if she were talking only to herself. 'Christ, look at it out there. It's unbelievable.'

Wentworth reached out and pressed a switch by the patio doors. Immediately, the patio area and the pool were flooded with light from a bank of spotlights positioned above the doors. The effect was that of a curtain being raised on a stage, and it was possible to see the seemingly endless rain crashing on to the surface of the pool and the tiles around it.

And then suddenly Wentworth screamed and, as if trying to shut out the night, she extinguished the lights, plunging the garden back into darkness.

Zoe had risen and was standing behind her. The glare of the light was still burned into her retinas and for a moment she could barely see. 'What was it?'

'He was out there. Just standing out in the rain, staring back in here. What the hell's he doing?'

'Who? Who was it?'

'I threw him out earlier. Gave him an ultimatum, but he's still there.'

'Who is?'

'Him. The person we were talking about.' Wentworth was staring at her, her face pale. 'Peter Hardy.'

Chapter Thirty-Three

'Well, that's that,' Annie said. 'Christ.'

She'd spent the last half-hour on the phone to the forensics unit. As she'd expected, they'd tried to fob her off this late in the afternoon, but she had quickly managed to persuade them of the urgency of her query. DNA tests had been done on both bodies as a matter of routine, although the purpose had been only to enable them to be excluded from any subsequent forensic analysis. For that reason, the results hadn't been entered on the national database, and it hadn't occurred to anyone to compare the two results.

'Spill the beans, then,' Jennings said. 'We're all dying to know.'

'No doubt about it. Chalmers and Justin Wentworth were indeed father and son.'

'Christ,' Jennings said. 'And Michelle Wentworth didn't think to mention that when both were murdered on her doorstep?'

'She's been hiding stuff from the start,' Annie said. 'She and Hardy always seemed more interested in concealing their business from us than in helping us catch whoever killed Justin. I'm convinced that the list of supposed suspects that Hardy gave us was just a smokescreen.'

'So what's she got to hide?'

'That's the question. I felt it was something to do with the business, rather than anything directly to do with Justin.'

'You said Chalmers suggested there was some kind of dodgy money behind their latest ventures?'

'That was what Sheena said.'

'So was Chalmers threatening to expose something?' Jennings said. 'Is that why he was taken out?'

'It's a possibility,' Colin Palmer said. 'Remember I said I'd come back to the reason why Chalmers had kept these letters and not others? If you look through the ones he kept, my guess is that they weren't retained just for sentimental value.'

'How do you mean?' Jennings asked.

'Almost all the letters that Chalmers had kept make some reference to the way in which Wentworth was bending or breaking the procurement rules to win contracts. Sometimes with Chalmers' help, but it was obviously just part and parcel of her business methods. A lot of it is fairly opaque in the letters but you can piece enough together to get the picture. And the picture's far more incriminating for Wentworth than for Chalmers.'

'So you think he was blackmailing her about that?'

'Maybe. Or maybe he'd just held these letters back as some kind of insurance policy. A way of screwing money or some other favour out of Wentworth if he needed it. Either way, I don't think it's accidental that he kept these letters and discarded others.'

'So if he was prepared to blackmail her about that, whatever she's involved in now might have created an even better opportunity to turn the screws on her,' Jennings said.

'But that doesn't make sense,' Annie pointed out. 'If Wentworth and Hardy were behind Chalmers' murder, why would they dump his body outside Wentworth's house? If that hadn't happened, we probably wouldn't have even thought to connect Chalmers' death to Wentworth.'

'Whatever the truth is, we clearly need to talk to Wentworth again urgently,' Annie said. 'Find out why she decided not to bother mentioning that she had such an intimate connection with both of the first two victims.'

'Are we still assuming that Nolan's death is connected to the others?' Colin Palmer asked. 'I can't see there's much of a connection. The link with Wentworth could easily be nothing but a coincidence.'

'I'm not keen on coincidences,' Jennings said. 'Not in investigations. They always make me nervous. That's really the only rationale for keeping the cases aligned. Mind you, I don't know if it's better to have one multiple killer or two separate killers. Maybe one of you could let me know. But in the meantime, yes, we need to talk to Michelle Wentworth now. If she's playing silly buggers, whatever the reason, we need to know.'

Annie nodded. 'Zoe should be over there already on one of her routine visits. I'll get over there straight away. I want to see the whites of her eyes when we ask her about this. She's a great one for the poker face, but she can't keep hiding things from us for ever.'

–

'You saw him too?' Michelle Wentworth's tone sounded almost accusatory.

'I didn't see anything,' Zoe said. 'I'm sorry.'

'It was definitely him. Why the hell was he out there on a night like this?' Wentworth paused. 'That's the second question. The first question was how he got back in without me knowing. Shit!' She jumped to her feet and hurried through to the hallway. Zoe followed her, and heard her muttering at the CCTV screens.

Wentworth looked up as Zoe approached. 'I've been fucking stupid,' she said. 'I've been sitting here feeling safe, snug and secure, and I left the bloody gates open when I let you in.' Her tone was accusatory, as if this had somehow been Zoe's fault.

'But whatever he's up to out there, it's still only Peter Hardy. He's nothing to be concerned about, surely,' Zoe said.

Wentworth stared at her. 'I told you, I gave him an ultimatum and effectively threw him out of the house. So let's just say that, for the moment, Peter and I are not quite the bosom buddies and business colleagues we once were. As to whether he's anything to be concerned about, I've no real idea. All I know is that, for reasons best known to himself, he's prowling around my house in the pouring rain and pitch darkness trying to scare the hell out of me.'

'We don't know that—'

'Why the hell else would he be out there?'

Zoe had no ready answer to that. 'Let me go and take a look out there. Maybe he's ill or something.'

'You don't know him, do you? He can be a ruthless, cold-hearted bastard. I don't trust him.'

Zoe took a breath. 'Okay. I can call in some backup if you really think it's needed. I don't know how long it'll take them to get here, but I can get it treated as a priority if you think there's something to be concerned about.'

'I don't know,' Wentworth said. She hesitated, and Zoe guessed she was thinking about the implications and possible consequences of summoning the police out here. Zoe was still unsure whether Wentworth really had seen Hardy, or whether this had been some further attempt at distraction, but for the moment she felt she had to take Wentworth at her word.

'Are all the doors and windows locked?' Zoe asked.

'They should be,' Wentworth said. 'The security's pretty tight here. Even the patio windows are extra-toughened glass. It would take a lot to break through them.'

'You said Hardy could be ruthless. Is he a violent man?'

Wentworth looked momentarily taken aback by the question. 'He's never been violent with me, if that's what you mean. But I don't know. He's always struck me as the type who'd do whatever it took to get what he wants. I don't know what he might do.'

'Okay, let's double-check all the ground-floor doors and windows first, at least make sure there's no risk of him effecting an entry without us knowing.' Another thought struck her. 'He doesn't have his own keys, does he?' She still wasn't sure how close Wentworth and Hardy were, or at least had been. She'd had the sense previously that they were some kind of an item.

'Christ, no,' Wentworth said. 'I don't let anyone get that close.'

Which, Zoe supposed, was at least some kind of answer to her speculations. 'So I'll call in some support. We check the doors and windows. And then we can decide what to do next.' It didn't sound much, but Zoe supposed it was some kind of a plan.

The next few minutes were spent carrying it out. Zoe phoned back to the control room and asked them to get a car round urgently. Then between them they checked all the downstairs doors and windows, with Zoe finally ending up back in the kitchen, leaving Wentworth in the living room.

Like the patio doors, the back door was constructed of toughened glass. Despite Wentworth's fears, Zoe decided to take one last look outside, conscious that it would be better to have some idea of Hardy's movements if he really was still out there. The switch for the spotlights was beside the door. She pressed it, peering out as the patio was again flooded with light, steeling herself for the possibility that Hardy might now be standing closer to the house.

He wasn't. The patio and poolside areas looked deserted, the rain pounding down as heavily as ever. She was about to extinguish the light when, peering for one last time, she saw something just at the far edge of the illuminated area.

She pressed her face to the glass and peered out into the glare of the spotlights. It was right at the edge of the light, very close to the point where Wentworth had claimed Hardy was standing. It took a few moments for Zoe's eyes to adjust to the point where she could see what it was.

It was a body, lying on the grass beyond the pool,. From this distance, she could make out nothing but a pair of feet, the body itself lying further into the darkness. It was motionless. Perhaps her earlier thought that Hardy had been ill had been correct, after all. Though that failed to explain why he was in the rear garden, or why he hadn't simply arrived at the front door if he'd come here to see Wentworth.

Zoe hesitated, unsure what to do. If it was Hardy, and he really was ill, she couldn't just leave him out there. Finally, feeling she had no choice, she unlocked the back door and opened it far enough to allow her to slip out into the night.

The first few yards were under the shelter of the house, so she was able to take a moment to close the door behind her. Then, conscious she had no real protection against the rain, she ran towards the body, keeping her head down against the downpour.

This was utterly stupid, she realised now. From inside, it hadn't been clear quite how intense the rainstorm really was. Just in the space of a few yards, she was soaked almost to the skin. But there was little point in turning back. She stepped off the tiled pool surround and approached the figure.

There was no doubt that it was Peter Hardy – and from closer up and with the aid of the spotlights, it was equally clear that he was no longer the threat that Michelle Wentworth had feared. He was lying on his back, his eyes staring blankly into the darkness. Except for his feet, his body lay largely outside the intense pool of light the spotlights cast. Even so, Zoe could see the pool of blood seeping into the grass beneath Hardy's head. She couldn't be sure from this angle, but her guess was that he'd beaten savagely about the head in the same way as the previous three victims.

She was soaked to the skin now. The only saving grace was that, although the temperature had dropped with the arrival of the rain, it was still a relatively warm evening. She crouched down by Hardy's body and took one of his wrists, searching for a pulse, although she had little doubt that he was dead.

Up to this point, she'd been acting largely on instinct and adrenaline alone, not really considering the implications of what she was dealing with. Now, presented with the undeniable fact of Hardy's death, she suddenly realised the vulnerability of her own position.

Hardy was no longer a threat, if he ever had been. But somewhere out here there was a killer. Presumably the same person who, for whatever reason, had been responsible for the deaths of Justin Wentworth, Keith Chalmers and quite possibly Sammy Nolan.

Still crouched on the ground, Zoe looked anxiously around her. In the darkness and heavy rain, she could see nothing. She rose slowly and moved back out of the light, still on the alert for any sign of movement, any sound other than the beating of rain on leaves.

She could see and hear nothing, but some instinct made her glance back towards the house. She froze, and suddenly the night felt much colder. As she watched, a figure slipped swiftly across the patio and entered through the door she'd left unlocked and slightly open. The figure was little more than a silhouette against the kitchen lights, but she could see that it was dressed in some kind of heavy waterproof coat with a large hood pulled over its head. From where she stood, it was impossible to make out whether the figure was male or female.

Her first thought was to curse her own stupidity. She should never have come out here, and she should certainly never have come out here and left the doors unlocked behind her. She'd expected to be out here only for a few moments, and she still hadn't really believed there was a serious threat from Hardy, but that didn't excuse her negligence.

She hurried back towards the house, alert for any other movement around her, conscious that the figure, whoever it was, might not have been alone. Her thin summer clothing was now completely drenched, and she was finally beginning to feel the cold. For the moment, there was no sign of the storm abating. Somewhere in the distance, she heard the low rumble of thunder.

Zoe reached the patio and, moving more cautiously now, tried the back door. As she'd expected, it had been locked again from within. She knew the rest of the house was secure because she and Wentworth had checked all the doors and windows thoroughly. Michelle Wentworth was alone in the house with this unknown visitor, and Zoe had no means of gaining entry.

She concealed herself as best she could in a sheltered corner of the patio and dug out her mobile phone. For an awful moment, as she struggled to operate it with her cold, numb fingers, she feared that the phone might have been damaged by the rain. But after a few moments, she managed to get it working.

Her first call was to the operations room to update them on developments. She was assured that a car was on its way and should only be a few minutes.

'I need more than that,' Zoe said. 'I need whatever backup we can get out here as soon as possible. I don't know how dangerous this person is but we've reason to believe they may have killed at least four people. I'll speak to DI Delamere myself.'

After a moment's hesitation, she decided to try Michelle Wentworth's mobile number first. As she'd half-expected, it simply rang out to voicemail. She left a brief message, saying simply: 'Hi, it's Zoe. I'll try again.' On the remote chance that Wentworth might find some way of accessing it, it would at least reassure her that Zoe was still safe out here. And Wentworth might have the presence of mind to find some way of giving Zoe access back into the house.

Beyond that, there was nothing else she could do until support arrived, and even then she was unsure how easily they'd be able to gain entry without this escalating into a hostage event. She dialled Annie Delamere's number.

'Annie, it's Zoe. We've a problem. A pretty serious one.' She was keeping her voice as low as possible even though she assumed there was little risk of being heard from inside the house.

It sounded as if Annie was driving and had taken the call on hands-free. 'What is it?'

'I'm still at Michelle Wentworth's. Outside it, to be more precise.'

It took her only a few seconds to update Annie on developments. 'There's backup on its way, and I've asked them to send whatever they can.'

'Okay,' Annie said. 'We may need armed police and a hostage team. I'll sort that all out with Stuart on the way. Funnily enough, I was heading in that direction anyway. We've had a few interesting developments at this end too.'

'The main gates are open. How far away are you?'

'Maybe ten minutes. I can hear some sirens too, so I suspect you may have company before too long. How are you doing?'

'Cold, soaked to the skin. Very conscious that this is partly my fault. But other than that, I'm okay.'

'Don't start blaming yourself. We know this person, whoever they are, is dangerous. If he wanted to get to Michelle Wentworth, he'd have found a way to do it. As it is, at least you're not stuck in there with her, and at least you've been able to summon help.'

'I'll bank that for the moment,' Zoe said. 'If only to keep myself going.'

'Just keep safe, Zoe. We'll be there shortly.'

Zoe was silent for a second, watching the endless downpour of rain, wondering what might be happening inside the house. 'Thanks,' she said. 'I'll do my best.'

Chapter Thirty-Four

Michelle Wentworth looked up as he entered. She'd assumed it would be Zoe Everett returning from the kitchen, but succeeded in concealing her surprise at his presence. After all, she'd been expecting his arrival. She was surprised only that he'd already managed to gain access to the house.

'Ah,' she said. 'Already.'

'I thought you'd be more shocked.'

'Hardly. It's been obvious from the start. Who else would it have been?'

'You always were the coolest of customers, but even I don't believe that. Maybe you've put some of it together now I'm here. But don't try to fool me you've got it all worked out.' He took a seat on the sofa opposite her, stretching out his legs as if to demonstrate that he was making himself at home.

'That would disappoint you, wouldn't it? If even now, you can't manage to keep one step ahead. The truth is, you were always one step behind. Always at your most hopeless when you thought you were being smart. Nearly as bad as bloody Peter Hardy. Where is he, by the way?'

'He's... outside. I've taken care of hm.'

'Ah. Okay, I'll give you that one, for what it's worth. I didn't think you'd be quite that ruthless. Or that insane.' She paused. 'No, that's not right. I didn't think you'd be that stupid. I thought you'd realise how much you needed him.'

'You didn't think he was the brains behind this? You've always underestimated me, Michelle.'

'You've always overestimated yourself. Although I suppose it does make sense if you were the brains behind this half-baked scheme.'

There was a moment's silence. 'It never changes, does it? Your attempts to belittle me. But I've got exactly what I wanted. That's what Hardy didn't realise. That what I wanted was different from what he wanted.'

'Is that right? Hardy wanted money. Specifically my money. Isn't that what you want?'

'Not any more. What would I do with it now?'

She gazed back at him, her face emotionless. 'So it is true then. What I'd heard on the grapevine. How long have they given you?'

'They reckon a couple of months. But I reckon they're perhaps being generous. I can already feel it, even with the medication.'

'I'm sorry to hear that. Genuinely. I wouldn't wish that on anyone. Not even you.'

'Gracious as ever, then.' He shrugged. 'I've come to terms with it. It's not as if I've much to live for. And this has been – what's the word? Cathartic?'

'You tell me. You were always the one who bothered with books.'

'Whereas the only books you were interested in were the company's.'

'And that's the difference between us. That's why you're where you are, and I'm here.' Her voice was defiant even now.

'No, that's not the difference. The real difference is that, while neither of us has long to live, I've finally got what I wanted. And you never will.'

Wentworth felt a flash of fear as the significance of the words registered. 'And what is it that I want, other than money? And look around you. I've plenty of that.'

'That's not really what you've ever wanted. That's just an addiction. That's like saying a junkie wants heroin or an alcoholic wants booze. It's true. But it doesn't tell you why.'

'So you've taken up amateur psychology now?'

'It doesn't take much insight to understand you, Michelle. Money's only ever been a surrogate for all the things you've never been able to have. Respect. Love. A sense of belonging. A sense of purpose.'

'Jesus,' she spat out. 'Do you have any idea how pathetic you sound? Doling out this bollocks like some evangelical fucking preacher. As if you ever had the first clue what I wanted.'

'If all you wanted was money, you've had more than enough of that for years now. And yet you've still continued to chase it, regardless of the consequences. Too much was never enough. Doesn't it strike you that there's something psychotic about that?'

'Given you're presumably responsible for – what is it now? – four deaths and counting, I'm not sure I'm the psychopath.'

'You still don't get it, do you? I didn't kill those people. They were already dead. Or they might as well have been. They were just people you'd used for your own ends. Even poor bloody Justin, who was just your way of fulfilling your social-climbing fantasies. As if he was ever going to be accepted into the elite. He was just a dumb yob with pretensions.'

'A yob I bailed out more than once.'

'Only because you were afraid it would damage your own social ambitions. You're utterly transparent, Michelle. You think you're so smart, but we can all see right through you. You use people. You suck them dry and spit them out. It's what you did with Keith Chalmers. It's what you've done with Peter Hardy. It's what you were going to do even with poor Sammy Nolan—'

For the first time, she felt a real flare of fury. 'Don't. Just don't go there. You bastard.'

'Ah. So what was it with Sammy Nolan, I wonder? What had you seen in him? Another protégé? A surrogate Justin? There've been a few over the years, haven't there?'

'You've no idea what you're talking about.'

'Oh, I think I do. I've kept an eye on you over the years. I know exactly what you've been up to. Every step of the way. I'm the only person who knows how to hurt you.'

'Is that right? And you think I'm the one that's addicted?'

'Like I say, Michelle, the difference between us is that, in the end, I've got exactly what I wanted.'

'And what would that be?'

'Just one simple thing, Michelle.' He leaned forward, smiling now. 'Revenge.'

Chapter Thirty-Five

Zoe shivered. The storm still showed no signs of lessening. The rumble of thunder had grown closer, and she had seen the occasional crackle of forked lightning through the rain-washed night.

The cold was beginning to get to her now. The night was still mild, but her soaked clothes clung to her skin, draining the warmth from her body. She had looked around the patio, hoping to find something she could wrap around herself, but found nothing.

She'd checked along the front of the house, trying to find any point that would enable her to see what might be happening inside. The blinds over the patio doors had been closed, presumably by Michelle Wentworth. The kitchen was empty. Wentworth had also lowered all the remaining blinds in the living room while they'd been double-checking that the windows were closed and locked, so it was impossible to see if anything was happening in there.

Zoe made her way around the house so she could be ready to greet either the patrol car or Annie on their arrival. She turned the corner of the building – and stopped.

Along the side wall of the house, there was an open ground-floor window.

How was that possible? Between them, she and Went-worth had checked all the doors and windows. Could the intruder have opened it for some reason? She guessed it was possible, perhaps to allow access to another person.

She moved cautiously closer. The window was that of Wentworth's office. The room was in darkness, but there was a ring of light around the door at the far end, suggesting it had been left slightly ajar. It was Wentworth herself who'd checked this room, Zoe recalled. Was it possible that she'd somehow missed the open window? It seemed unlikely.

Zoe hesitated, then dialled Annie's number. The call was answered almost immediately. 'Zo. All okay? We're about five minutes away.'

'All fine with me,' Zoe said. 'But I've just found an open downstairs window. I'm wondering whether to go in to see if I can get some idea what's going on.'

There was a moment's silence at the other end of the line. 'I'd rather you stayed safe, Zoe. We don't know what you might be heading into.'

'It's my fault that this all has happened. I shouldn't have left the door open.'

'Look, we'll be there in a few minutes. Wait till then. I'm not prepared to take any further risks until we've had a proper opportunity to see the lie of the land.'

'Yes, but—'

'This isn't a request, Zoe. I'm telling you. Wait for us.'

Before Zoe could respond, she heard the sudden sound of raised voices from within the house. Then the much louder sound of a woman's voice, a scream seemingly pitched somewhere between terror and fury. 'Something's happening in there,' she said. 'I'm going in.'

'Zoe—'

She didn't end the call, thinking it might be important for Annie to hear what was happening, but she pushed the phone back into her damp pocket. Then she scrambled, as quietly as she could, through the window into the room.

Once inside, she stopped to listen. The house seemed silent and she could detect no signs of movement. She moved to the door and peered through the gap. She could see from here across the hallway into the open door of the living room, but her vision was severely limited by the angle.

Zoe hesitated for a moment, then cautiously opened the door and stepped out into the hall. She could hear something now. Something she couldn't quite make out. A strained muttering as though someone was struggling to speak. Then, unexpectedly, an almighty crash and the sound of breaking glass.

She stepped forward and peered into the living room. Michelle Wentworth and the figure in the waterproof were struggling on the ground. The figure still had a hood pulled up, the face concealed, but there was no question now that he was male. He was larger and heavier than Wentworth and was pressing her back on to the carpet, holding one hand firmly across her mouth while his other hand fumbled in the pocket of the waterproof. Wentworth's glass-topped coffee table lay overturned on the carpet beside them, presumably knocked over in the struggle, the glass shattered into countless pieces.

Zoe rushed forward, grabbing the man by the shoulders, trying to pull him away from Wentworth. He twisted and, without removing the hand from Wentworth's mouth, struck out savagely with his other to drive Zoe away. Zoe dodged and tried again. She had no idea how she could stop him, and no other thought except to try to buy some time till Annie could get here. She looked desperately around for something she could use as a weapon.

The man gave a sudden cry of pain. Michelle Wentworth had managed to reach one of the glass shards from the table, and jabbed it hard towards his face. He swore and drew back, loosening his grip on Wentworth. She tried to slash again with the glass, but the man raised his head, easily avoiding her flailing hand. There was blood running from a gash in his cheek, but he seemed barely to notice. He reached back into the pocket of the waterproof and this time produced a large steel spanner. He raised his arm, with the clear intention of bringing the spanner down hard on Wentworth's head.

Zoe grabbed his arm, clutching tightly to prevent him completing his intended action. The man clawed at her arm, trying to free her grip, then reached down with his other hand and grabbed another piece of glass. Zoe could see the blood seeping from his palm as he gripped the jagged shard tightly in his hand, but he seemed oblivious to the pain. She pulled hard on his arm, forcing it back, trying to drag him away from Wentworth. Zoe could see that he was preparing to use the broken glass to force her to free her grip.

From the corner of her eye, she saw that Wentworth had extricated herself from beneath the man and was pulling herself backwards towards the sofa, reaching for something beneath it.

The man thrust the piece of glass towards Zoe's hands. She flinched instinctively, closing her eyes, waiting for the inevitable contact, the agony of the cut. It was only in that moment that he turned fully towards her and she finally saw his face.

Then there was an explosion, the deafening noise of gunfire in an enclosed room, and she felt the man falling away from her.

She opened her eyes, and there was blood everywhere.

Chapter Thirty-Six

'You're happy to talk now? You wouldn't like a solicitor present?'

Michelle Wentworth gave a wan smile. 'My legal advisor's lying dead in my garden. I'm not concerned about finding another one, just at the moment.'

Annie exchanged a glance with Jennings. Zoe had been taken into hospital for checks, but she'd seemed to be physically unharmed. Following her arrest, Michelle Wentworth had also been kept under observation overnight, but had not been well enough to be interviewed until now. In view of the rumours already beginning to leak to the media, Jennings had decided to involve himself directly.

'But you appreciate that you're under arrest, charged with manslaughter?' Annie had carried out the formal arrest procedure at Wentworth's house but, at the time, hadn't been clear how much Wentworth had been taking in.

'For the killing of my ex-husband, yes. I'm not an idiot.'

'We just have to be sure you're being treated appropriately in the circumstances. We appreciate yesterday's events must have been a shock.'

'At the time, yes. But as soon as I saw Ronnie standing there, it all made sense.'

'I'm glad it makes sense to you,' Jennings said. 'I'm not sure it makes much sense to us.'

'No one else could have known. No one else could have made the connections.' Wentworth shrugged. 'Frankly, no one else would even have bothered. Ronnie was obsessed.'

'You'll need to join the dots for us,' Annie said. 'We know you had an affair with Keith Chalmers at the time of your marriage to Ronnie Donahue. And we know that Justin was Chalmers' son rather than Donahue's.'

For the first time, Michelle Wentworth looked surprised. 'You know more than I do, then. We always thought it was probably the case, but I never confirmed it.' She nodded. 'But of course you have DNA results for both of them.'

'You should have told us. It would have provided us with a clear link between Justin and Keith Chalmers. That might have led us to your ex-husband more quickly.'

'It didn't occur to me that would be the link,' Wentworth said. 'I didn't imagine that Ronnie would suddenly have decided to take that sort of revenge twenty years after the event.'

'So why did he?'

'He didn't. Not on his own. The whole thing's nagged away at him all this time, but it was never really about the affair. That just added to the humiliation for him. It was the fact that, as he saw it, I'd used his experience and knowledge to establish the business and then I just dumped him. He'd probably have been happier if I had left him for Chalmers, but I didn't. He thought I was a cold-hearted bitch who just used people to get what I wanted and then moved on.'

And I'm not sure he was wrong, Annie thought. There was something about the way that Wentworth was telling this story that Annie herself found chilling. It wasn't just that she was talking so dispassionately about the deaths of people who'd supposedly once been close to her. It was that she seemed almost pleased, as if she'd achieved an outcome she'd been striving for.

'You said he wouldn't have done this alone,' Annie said. 'What did you mean?'

'Ronnie was terminally ill and had nothing to lose. But he wouldn't have had the wit or initiative to have done this by himself. He'd spent twenty years brooding on this stuff, developing a deep hatred – for me, for Justin, for Chalmers. But I don't think he'd ever have acted on it. Until Peter Hardy came along.'

'Hardy?'

'Hardy became involved in the business, initially advising us on various legal matters. He came highly recommended. An ambitious business lawyer who seemed to have good contacts in the areas we wanted to get involved in. He did a few bits of good work for us, and I eventually brought him on board in a non-exec role. He built up his credibility with us – by which I mean with me – and I began to trust him more and more. Which, in retrospect, was bloody stupid of me. About six months ago, he came to me with a business proposition. He had contacts with an overseas group looking to invest in the UK, in a business like mine. To be honest, it all seemed slightly shady and I resisted. But he gradually persuaded me that it would enable us to take the business to a new level. I'd been looking for a while to be able to expand the business to the point where it was less dependent on me, so that I could maybe begin to wind down a bit.'

Annie wasn't sure where all this was heading. 'So you went along with the proposed deal?'

'I agreed to pursue it further. Peter was playing his cards very close to his chest, which made me suspicious.'

'Suspicious of what?'

'Both about the source of the investment and about whether Peter was looking to use this to muscle his way into the business. But he could be very persuasive. He suggested I just dip a toe into the water, take a limited amount of the investment and use it to pitch for work in some of the new areas.'

'And you were looking to do what? Test out what he was up to?'

'To test the ground. I'm ambitious in business, but my instinct's always to be cautious. This sounded too good to be true. But I didn't know whether someone was pulling the wool over Peter's eyes, or whether he was trying to pull it over mine. Or whether it might actually be legitimate.'

Annie was trying to make sense of this. It was a world she didn't fully understand. 'What happened?'

'It went okay at first. We won the contracts. That didn't surprise me. We're good at what we do. But then things started to go wrong.'

'Such as?'

'Business stuff at first. Unexpected technical problems. Issues in the contracts we hadn't expected. I always make a point of checking everything we sign up to, but some of this was outside my areas of experience so I was more dependent on Peter than I would have been normally. And we started to run into industrial relations problems. Even after we split up, Keith and I had had a good working relationship, and, well, one way or another, he'd usually managed to smooth the waters for us in dealing with the workforce. But he thought he was being undermined from within, that there was some ringer stirring up trouble.' She stopped. 'Then the really serious stuff happened. The stuff that brought it really close to home. Justin. Keith himself. And then poor bloody Sammy Nolan...'

'I don't understand,' Annie said. 'What's the link with Sammy Nolan?'

Wentworth was silent for several seconds. Eventually she said, 'There've been a few Sammy Nolans over the years. Young men in the business I've taken a shine to.' She stopped and laughed ruefully. 'That sounds awful. I don't mean in a sexual way or anything like that. Just a few that I've thought had potential. I've always told myself it was a smart business move. Growing internal talent so that the business might outlive my involvement. But I'm not sure that was the sole motivation. Quite often they were kids from disadvantaged backgrounds who I thought I could do something for. Ronnie called Sammy a surrogate Justin, and he was maybe not wrong. I failed Justin from the start, and I've wanted to make up for it ever since.' She paused, as if expecting Annie to respond. 'I've not always got it right. A couple have progressed in the business, but others I've had to let go. I've always made a point of looking after them. Financially, I mean. I've treated them fairly.' She sounded defensive now. 'Sammy was the latest of those. I came across him when we first took over the contract. He seemed bright, conscientious and ambitious. This was when things were starting to go wrong, including some unexpected operational glitches. I was beginning to distrust Peter, so I wanted someone to be my eyes and ears on the shop floor. A spy in the camp. Sammy was working directly for me, though no one else knew it.' She shook her head. 'It seemed like a good idea. We concocted a story about planning to make him redundant along with other local staff, so that people would trust him. He got himself on to the local union committee but I was ultimately intending to move him to another part of the business. He'd already fed back some useful stuff to me, not least that Keith was right about there being some deliberate troublemakers in there. It was something else that increased my suspicions about Peter.' She paused again. 'The truth is, I was fond of Sammy. I thought I could help him make something of himself. I never imagined it would end like that. Poor bugger.'

'But it was your ex-husband who committed the murders?' Jennings said.

'There was never any grand conspiracy,' Wentworth said. 'Never any mysterious overseas investors. I'm sure of that now. Peter wasn't short of a bob or two, and the limited funding that appeared was just what he'd raised from his own sources. He'd concocted the whole scam with the aim of either driving me out of the business or at least making me increasingly dependent on him. He was making romantic overtures at the same time, though he should have known he stood bugger all chance in that direction. He knew he wouldn't be smart enough to beat me in business — he was a clever man but not streetwise in the way I am — so he had to resort to something more basic. And he got Ronnie to do his dirty work for him. Everything from the killings to that supposed threatening phone call. All designed to scare the hell out of me, so he could step in as my knight in shining armour. He must have inveigled his way into Ronnie's life in the same way he tried to inveigle himself into mine. Then he wound

Ronnie up into making real the revenge he'd dreamed of for twenty years.'

'But Hardy ended up dead too?' Annie said.

'Peter was never as smart as he thought he was. He understood law and numbers, but he never really understood people. He'd have thought he was using Ronnie. Probably tried to entice him with a promise of a share in the business or some sort of pay-off. I presume that's why they came here tonight. Peter had realised I was seeing through him and that he wouldn't be long for my inner circle. I assume he'd brought Ronnie here to issue some kind of threat or ultimatum to me.' She was smiling now, her tone unexpectedly calm in the circumstances. 'But Ronnie never really cared about any of that. There was something obsessive about him. When I left him, he didn't really care about the business. He cared because he thought I'd used him, sucked him dry and then cast him aside. In that sense, he saw Keith as a fellow victim rather than a rival. And in different ways he thought I'd done the same to Justin and to Peter, and that in due course I'd do the same to Sammy. I'm no psychologist, but my guess is that he thought he was putting all those people out of the same misery that he'd endured for twenty years. He was killing the drones before he finally killed the Queen Bee.'

She laughed, but Annie was finding all this deeply chilling. There was a note almost of glee in Wentworth's voice now, and it suddenly occurred to Annie to wonder how much Wentworth had engineered all this. To wonder how long she'd known what Hardy was up to, whether she'd realised that Ronnie Donahue had been responsible for the killings. If in some way she might have actively engineered last night's denouement.

Annie had spoken to Zoe earlier, and there were several points that had struck her in Zoe's account of the evening. It was Michelle Wentworth who'd claimed to have seen Hardy standing in the garden. Zoe hadn't seen him there alive. It was Wentworth who'd left the gates open, supposedly accidentally, so allowing Ronnie Donahue access. And then, after Donahue had succeeded in entering the house, someone had left the side window open, allowing Zoe to be present when Donahue was killed.

Was it possible that there was an alternative scenario to that which had apparently played out tonight? Had Hardy and Donahue really come to Wentworth's house together to issue that ultimatum? Or was it possible that Hardy had come earlier, and that Michelle Wentworth had been responsible for his death? Was it conceivable that she had engineered for her ex-husband to enter the house, even leaving the window open so that Zoe could be present at the moment he was killed?

Annie had no evidence to support that idea, and she suspected that, even if she was correct, they'd never find any. The spanner Donahue had been carrying had apparently not been used on Hardy or, as far as they could judge, in the previous killings. If a different murder weapon had been used to kill Hardy, it could have been any suitable heavy object, and might well be anywhere by now. There was little prospect of searching all the woodland in this vicinity. There might be evidence from phone calls but it was unlikely that Michelle Wentworth would have been careless enough to use her usual phone. Some burner phone could have been dumped or even destroyed anywhere, with little chance it would ever be found. Even if they found traces of Hardy's blood or DNA on Wentworth, it would be difficult to prove that those hadn't been transmitted by Donahue during their struggle.

It was an absurd idea, Annie thought, generated by nothing more than her own unease at Michelle Wentworth's unexpectedly relaxed demeanour. But Wentworth had been through a severe shock, and shock could affect people in very different ways. There was no reason to go searching for some more convoluted explanation.

'You're being charged with manslaughter,' Annie said to Wentworth. 'Clearly, you have a very strong mitigation in terms of self-defence. One of our officers was present and witnessed the events that led to your ex-husband's death. Even so, at this stage we can't offer you any guarantees as to the potential outcome. It'll be up to the Crown Prosecution Service as to whether this goes to trial. And if it does then it'll ultimately be a decision for the jury.'

Wentworth nodded. 'Of course. I've every confidence in the due process of law.'

'There are some questions we need to ask you, though. You had a loaded shotgun concealed beneath the sofa. I take it that's not usually the case.'

'Of course not. But you can check it out. I do field sports from time to time. The shotgun's fully licensed and I've complied with all the regulations. It's normally stored in a shotgun safe, unloaded. I'd just literally taken it out of the safe and loaded it while DS Everett and I were checking the downstairs of the house. It was stupid of me, I know, but I'd been genuinely rattled by seeing Peter outside. I couldn't envisage any good reason why he'd be out there. I was intending to seek DS Everett's advice on the gun when she returned. I imagine she'd have told me to put it back.'

'I imagine so,' Annie said.

'Although, as it turned out, if I hadn't had the gun, both DS Everett and I would probably now be dead.'

Annie took a moment to digest this. 'The gun was concealed under the sofa?' she prompted.

'I'd just put it down on the carpet. I thought that would be the safest place. Then I was startled to see Ronnie enter the room. I wasn't thinking very clearly. I must have just kicked it under the sofa so he wouldn't see it. To be honest, it's all a bit of a blur now.'

Annie nodded, conscious she had nowhere to take her suspicions. 'This is obviously a tremendous strain for you in the circumstances. I suggest we adjourn the interview for the moment to give you a break. I'll organise some refreshments for you.' She completed the formalities for the recording, and followed Stuart Jennings out of the interview room.

'What do you think?' Jennings said once they were out in the corridor.

Annie hesitated. 'It's a hell of a mess.'

'It could have been a lot worse, though. She's right that, if Donahue had succeeded, we'd be dealing with two more deaths. Including one of our own. At least we won't have to go through the challenges of bringing him to trial. Christ, just imagine what that would have been like.'

Annie nodded. Jennings was right. As it was, the whole case was largely tied up and completed. The only real loose end was Michelle Wentworth's arrest. Annie could already envisage the lurid terms in which the media would cover that, and she suspected the case would never come to trial. Jennings was already planning the media conference he'd be leading alongside the Chief Superintendent later than afternoon. Fair enough, Annie had thought. It wasn't something she had any desire to be involved in, and she couldn't blame either Jennings or the force for wanting to grab any positive publicity that was going. Apart from anything else, Jennings had told her he was intending to highlight Zoe's courageous role in helping to save Michelle Wentworth's life. After Jennings' doubts of recent months, that should provide a welcome boost to Zoe's morale, not to mention her career.

Whatever might or might not have happened back at Wentworth's house, there was nothing to be achieved by undermining all that simply to indulge a half-baked suspicion she'd almost certainly never be able to substantiate.

'You're looking thoughtful,' Jennings said. 'Something wrong?'

Annie glanced back into the interview room. Through the glass panel in the door, she could see Michelle Wentworth gazing apparently at nothing in particular. Annie recalled a training session she'd once attended on body language. The trainer had talked about a phenomenon called 'duper's delight', the giveaway smirk that passes across the face of a con artist who thinks they've pulled off a successful deceit. 'I was just thinking about Wentworth.'

'She's some woman, isn't she?' Jennings said. 'Though I suppose in some ways she's not had the happiest of lives. She's lost her son. She's lost this other young man. Her ex turns out literally to have been a psychopath. She's going to have to go through the hell of a possible manslaughter trial. I suppose it just goes to show that, however single-minded you might be, you still can't always get what you want.'

Annie was still gazing through the one-way glass at Wentworth. Wentworth's expression had changed now, and there was something playing across her lips that might almost have been a smile.

Annie felt a chill run down her spine. 'You know, Stuart, I sometimes wonder if that's true at all.'

CANELO CRIME

Do you love crime fiction and are always on the lookout for brilliant authors?

Canelo Crime is home to some of the most exciting novels around. Thousands of readers are already enjoying our compulsive stories. Are you ready to find your new favourite writer?

Find out more and sign up to our newsletter at canelocrime.com